MEMPHIS

MEMPHIS

A Novel

TARA M. STRINGFELLOW

JOHN MURRAY

First published in Great Britain in 2022 by John Murray (Publishers)
An Hachette UK company

1

Copyright © Tara M. Stringfellow 2022

Copyright © 1971 by Toni Morrison
Reprinted by permission of ICM Partners

A CIP catalogue record for this title is available from the British Library

Hardback ISBN 9781529339239
Waterstones Hardback ISBN 9781399804561
Trade Paperback ISBN 9781529339246
eBook ISBN 9781529339260

Printed and bound in Great Britain by Clays Ltd, Elcograf S.p.A.

John Murray policy is to use papers that are natural, renewable
and recyclable products and made from wood grown in sustainable forests.
The logging and manufacturing processes are expected to conform to the
environmental regulations of the country of origin.

John Murray (Publishers)
Carmelite House
50 Victoria Embankment
London EC4Y 0DZ

www.johnmurraypress.co.uk

To Miss Gianna Floyd—

i wrote you a black fairy tale
i understand if you not ready
to read it yet or if your mama
told you to wait a bit and that
just fine this book ain't going
nowhere this book gon be right here
whenever you want it
whenever you get finished playing
outside in that bright beautiful world
your daddy loved so much child,
it's just right to set this aside
Lord knows not a soul on this earth
gon blame you for being out in it—
running laughing breathing

For years in this country there was no one for black men to vent their rage on except black women. And for years black women accepted that rage—even regarded that acceptance as their unpleasant duty. But in doing so, they frequently kicked back, and they seem never to have become the "true slave" that white women see in their own history. True, the black woman did the housework, the drudgery; true, she reared the children, often alone, but she did all of that while occupying a place on the job market, a place her mate could not get or which his pride would not let him accept. And she had nothing to fall back on: not maleness, not whiteness, not ladyhood, not anything. And out of the profound desolation of her reality she may very well have invented herself.

—Toni Morrison, "What the Black Woman Thinks
About Women's Lib," *The New York Times*, 1971

The South got something to say.

—André 3000, Outkast, *Source* Awards, 1995

North

Hazel
b. 1921
m.1943
d. 1985

Jaxson
b. 1957
m.1978

Miriam
b. 1955
m.1978

Joan
b. 1985

Mya
b. 1988

Family Tree

Myron
b. 1922
m. 1943
d. 1955

August
b. 1963

Derek
b. 1980

Contents

Part 1

CHAPTER 1

Joan

1995

The house looked living. Mama squeezed my hand as the three of us gazed up at it, our bleary exhaustion no match for the animated brightness before us.

"Papa Myron selected and placed each stone of the house's foundation himself," she whispered to me and Mya. "With the patience and diligence of a man deep in love."

The low house was a cat napping in the shade of plum trees, not at all like the three-story Victorian fortress we had just left. This house seemed somehow large and small at once—it sat on many different split levels that spanned out in all directions in a wild, Southern maze. A long driveway traversed the length of the yard, cut in half by a folding wooden barn gate. But what made the house breathe, what gave the house its lungs, was its front porch. Wide stone steps led to a front porch covered in heavy green ivy and honeysuckle and morning glory. Above the porch, my grandfather had erected a wooden pergola. Sunlight streaked through green vines and wooden planks that turned the porch into an unkempt greenhouse. The honeysuckle drew humming-birds the size of baseballs; they fluttered atop the canopy in shades of indigo and emerald and burgundy. I could see cats on the porch—a dozen of them, maybe, an impossible number except for what a quick count told me. Some slept in heaps that looked softer than down, while others sat atop the green canopy, paws swiping at the birds. Bees as big as hands buzzed about, pollinating the morning glories, giving the yard a feeling that the green expanse itself was alive and humming and moving. The butterflies are what solidified my fascination. Small and periwinkle-blue, they danced within the canopy. The butterflies were African violets come alive. It was the finishing touch to a Southern symphony all conducted on a quarter-acre plot.

"Not now, Joan," Mama said, sighing.

I had out my pocket sketchbook, was already fumbling for the piece of charcoal somewhere in the many pockets of my Levi overalls. My larger sketchbook, my blank canvases the size of tea-cups, my brushes and inks and oils were all packed tight in the car. But my smaller sketchbook, I kept on me. At all times. Everywhere I went.

I wanted to capture the life of the front porch, imprint it in my notebook and in my memory. A quick landscape. Should've only taken a few minutes, but Mama was right. We were all dog tired. Even Wolf, who had slept most of the journey. Mya's face was drained of its usual spark, and as I slipped my sketchbook into my back pocket, slightly defeated, her hand felt hot and limp as I took it in my own.

Mya, Mama, and I walked up the wide stone front steps hand in hand. My memories of staying here felt vague and far away— I'd been only three years old, and it felt like a lifetime ago—but now I remembered sitting on the porch and pouring milk for the cats. I remembered Mama cautioning me not to spill, though I usually did anyway. Her laughter, too—the sound of it like the seashell chimes coming from inside the house while I played with the cats echoed in my mind from years ago. And the door, I remembered that. It was a massive beast. A gilded lion's head with a gold hoop in its snout was mounted on a wood door painted corn yellow. I had to paint a picture of this door, even if I had to spend months, years, finding the perfect hues. It was as magnificent as it was terrifying. By knocking, by opening the door, I knew we'd be letting out a whole host of ghosts.

Mama raised her arm, grabbed the lion's hoop, and knocked three times.

A calico kitten wove in and out of Mya's legs in a zigzag, mewing softly.

Mya let go of my hand in order to stroke the kitten's mane, coo to her gently.

We'd left Wolf in the car. Mama explained she'd have to be let in through the backyard, so she wouldn't be tempted to attack all the roaming wildlife in the front. She was in the passenger seat with the window down. She wouldn't jump out; she was too big for that. More mammoth than dog. And even though she was friendlier than a church mouse to all dogs, she mistrusted all humans not family. The curl of her lip and the baring of teeth were enough to send most grown men running to the other side of the street. As a baby, Mya called her "Horse" instead of "Wolf." Wolf would carry her, Mya tugging at her ears like reins, and Wolf never minding. Mya's chubby toddler legs all akimbo in Wolf's thick mane. Wolf grew to expect it, these pony rides. She would nudge Mya first with a face-covering, eye-closing lick, followed by a gentle nip on Mya's button nose that let us know she was ready to be ridden.

Now Wolf stuck her thick head covered in gray fur out the van window and growled, low. She sensed the front door opening before we did. Just as Mama lifted a hand to knock again, the yellow door opened to reveal Auntie August. Her hair was pinned up in big pink rollers, the kind I'd seen in old pinup-girl photos, and she wore a long, cream-colored silk kimono. Embroidered along the front panels were sunset-colored cranes taking off from a green pool. The kimono appeared like it'd been tied in a rush: A beet-purple man's necktie held the fabric haphazardly together, barely concealing the full breasts and hips aching to break from the folds. My auntie stood blinking at the bright morning light, an expression of resignation and exhaustion on her face that made her look just like Mama.

"What war y'all lost?" Auntie August asked.

My aunt looked like the taller, more regal version of Mama. Auntie August was nearly six feet tall. I had read Anansi stories. I knew that it was the women tall as trees and fiercer than God that ancient villages often sent into battle. If Mama was Helen of Troy, August was Asafo. She seemed to go on forever, seemed to be the height of the door itself. She had hips, the kind Grecian sculptors would spend months chiseling, big and bold and wide. Her skin was noticeably darker, darker than mine even, and I felt a welt of pride. I had always coveted darker-skinned women their color. There was a mystery to their beauty that I found hypnotizing, Siren-like. They were hardly ever in *Jet* or *Ebony* or *Essence*, the magazines we subscribed to, unless they themselves were famous— the mom from *The Fresh Prince of Bel Air*, Whoopi Goldberg, Jackie Joyner, Oprah. Most of the Black women the public pronounced beautiful looked like Mama. Black Barbies. Bright. Hair wavier than curly. Petite figures. So, when my Auntie August opened that door, and I saw that her skin was so dark it reflected all the other colors surrounding it—the yellow of the morning light, the yellow of the door, the peach tan of the calico cat weaving in and out of Mya's short legs—I knew that the aunt I could barely remember was, in and of herself, a small, delicious miracle.

"Got any food in the fridge?" Mama asked.

August opened the door wider, taking in the spectacle before her. "Is the pope Catholic?"

Mama shrugged.

I could hear Wolf growl again over the hum and buzz of the bees and the hummingbirds.

"My word," August said in a whisper then. "Did it get that bad?"

"I'll take my old room if I can have it," Mama said.

Auntie August fumbled into the deep silk folds of her kimono, her face momentarily scrunched in mild annoyance. Like she had an itch she couldn't quite reach. From out of her robe's pocket came the unmistakable green-and-white packaging of a pack of Kools, and the relief was visible in Auntie August's face. That pack of smokes. I felt a pang, sharp in my ribs, like one of them was missing. Daddy had smoked Kools. Would religiously pull out the green-and-white carton and smack it against his knee a few times before removing and lighting a cigarette and asking if Mya and I wanted to hear another ghost story.

In a series of deft movements, August removed a cigarette and positioned a lighter in her other hand, ready to strike. She motioned with her cigarette, first at Mya, then at me. "And them girls?" Her glance seemed to rest longer on me than on Mya.

"Together. In the quilting room," Mama said, with a sharpness to her voice that almost sounded defensive, but with something else there I couldn't place.

August, with the quickness of a serpent, reached out her hand and grasped Mama's chin in her palm, turned her face this way and that.

"The foundation don't match," she said.

Auntie August lost her swagger then. A flash of rage quickly turned to tears, and her face broke down like Mya's when she was told not to open her graham crackers directly in the grocery store. August reached for Mama, and all near six feet of August collapsed, leaned like a weary palm tree into her sister's arms.

"What hell you been through, Meer?" August asked, sobbing into Mama's hair.

"Mama, who them?"

The voice was male. Not adult, but on the crisp cusp of it, burgeoning with masculinity. It shocked us. We hadn't heard a male voice in days except for Al Green's over the radio and that white man at the gas station a half day's drive back. It was like a predator had suddenly announced its presence in our new safe haven.

A boy, almost as tall as August but with a body slender and young, stepped into the doorframe, blocking the entry.

He didn't look like us. He didn't have the high cheekbones, the slightly upturned top lip, the massive forehead everyone else related to me had. He had a copper hue to his skin that seemed slightly foreign to me, like meeting someone from an entirely different tribe.

But I recognized him. My cousin Derek. And in that split second, I also remembered what he had done to me—a memory I'd forgotten after all these years suddenly coming for me with a force I was powerless to stop.

"Derek," Auntie August said, exhaling her cigarette, "these here your cousins. That's Mya," she said, pointing with her cigarette. "Mya was a newborn last y'all was here. And that there is Joan."

"Derek, you as tall as your mama. How old are you now?" Mama asked.

"Fifteen," he said and puffed out his chest.

"A man almost," Mama said, quiet.

On the drive to Memphis, I had noticed deer grazing in the woods, right alongside the highway. While we were eating tuna sandwiches atop a park bench at a rest stop west of Knoxville, high in the Smoky Mountains, a family of deer had walked right up to our table. Mama placed a pointed finger over her mouth to signal silence. We said nothing, but I sat open-mouthed as Mya fearlessly, gracefully, extended an apple slice. A young doe had plucked it like Eve must have that apple. Without much thought at all. Simple desire. Later, in the car, Mama had explained that deer will walk right up to you if you're silent, or on horseback. They really only fear us when we're hunting them. But if you're silent among them, it's almost like you're invisible. You blend in with the nature around the deer.

Seeing Derek now, I wanted to disappear into the flora and the fauna of the front porch and yard. The cats hunting the birds, the hummingbirds competing with the bees for honeysuckle—that all made sense to me. There was a logical order to the chaos. But no one, not even God, could sit there and explain to me why that boy had held me down on the floor of his bedroom seven years before.

August leaned back from Mama, taking shaky breaths. "Well, come on in, y'all," she said, with a new warmth in her voice that their embrace had seemed to kindle in her. "We standing out here like y'all some salesmen, like we ain't kin. Come on, I'll warm something up. Made lamb chops last night. Y'all welcome to it," August said, drying her eyes on the sleeves of her kimono. Her hands trembled slightly with emotion as she finally lit her waiting cigarette.

"It's Friday," Mama said. Her voice sounded small, exhausted.

"So?" Derek asked.

August smacked Derek hard on the back of the head. "Watch who you talk to. And how. Meer, y'all going to eat meat, eat your fill today, so help me God." Derek slipped past her, into the dark room beyond the door.

I would not, could not, move.

"Joanie?" Mama asked. "You all right?"

Suddenly, I felt Mama's hands on my shoulders, and I jumped almost a foot in the air.

Auntie August paused on the threshold, one foot inside.

I couldn't seem to move my eyes from the darkness of the hallway behind her, not even to look at Mama. The blackness started to overtake my vision; I realized, vaguely, that I was holding my breath. He was in there, somewhere. From the inside, I heard a grandfather clock strike a half hour.

"The girl don't speak?" Auntie August asked.

My heart was pounding in my ears. Then—

"My God," August said, clasping one hand to her mouth. She pointed her lit cigarette at my pant leg.

The lion's snout on the door appeared to sneer at me. I felt paralyzed, as if I'd live the rest of my life standing in this spot on the front porch until I grew ivy myself and became just another vine for the bees to explore. The bees—the buzzing came from far away now. I realized, as if from a distance, that the volume of the whole world seemed to have been turned down. Except for the warning sound of my heart pounding.

"Joanie?" Mama spun me around so hard I nearly stumbled. Her big eyes had flecks of yellow in them that caught the sun streaking in between the vines, the sudden brightness assaulting my eyes. I felt warmth all down my left leg, a wet heat that was quickly going cold. It was pee, I realized, feeling vaguely surprised, as if I were observing someone else's body, someone else's life. I didn't even feel embarrassed. Mama shook me hard.

"She's just exhausted," she said, now looking into my eyes. "We had a long trip." I felt Mya's eyes on me, watchful.

"Well, y'all home now," Auntie August said, her voice slightly higher than before. It sounded almost like a question, or maybe a prayer.

"Come on now, Joanie," Mama said softly, in the same voice I remembered her using to soothe Mya when she was only a baby. "Let's get you cleaned up." In a louder voice now, as if answering a question, she said, "Mya, you go on ahead."

Auntie August held out a hand. Mya looked at me, then Mama, then me again, then took our aunt's hand and began to follow her inside.

It seemed impossible to ever move again. I thought I would die right there. I even hoped to. Except . . . Mya.

"Come on, Joanie." Mya had turned back. Mya. My baby sister. Seven years old and yet, unafraid. Something small sparked back to life within me. I might not be able to move an inch for myself, but for Mya . . . I forced myself to take one step and then another. I would not let her walk in there without me. I had to, at the very least, be a fortress for Mya.

I entered, Mama's hands still on my shoulders.

Inside, the parlor was a continuation of the front porch. There was foliage everywhere. Black wallpaper with hand-painted pink peonies covered the tall walls and mounted to a high octagonal beam in the center of the room. The windows were the kind I'd seen in old Mafia movies set in Chicago, corners lined with stained glass that was flecked with intricate emerald vines and purple violets, casting the room in a gem-studded light. After adjusting to the melody of dark and light, the contrast of the black wallpaper with the brightness of the painted peonies, the morning sunlight hitting the stained-glass windows just right, so that the ivy vines danced upon the floor in a rainbow of light—my eyes took in the furniture. The room was filled with antiques: a pearl-handled rotary phone that rested atop a small Victorian-looking maid's table; mason jars filled with stuffed yellow birds; the same blue butterflies I'd seen outside, but pinned on parchment and framed in glass; a Victrola; a piano.

"Wow," Mya let out.

A worn-in Persian rug stretched out before us toward a brick fireplace. That's where Derek stood.

Derek's gaze moved in three quick motions: at me, down to my wet pants, and then down further to the floor, where they stayed. I saw now that he had the same deerlike eyes as the rest of us. Proof that he was our kin. I hated that fact. That he belonged to us—to me. Bile crept into my belly, and I swallowed hard to hold it in.

As Derek's eyes turned toward me, I saw that he looked different and familiar at the same time. He wore his hair in a short fade that I hated to admit was becoming on him.

"Oh, look at all the old furniture!" Mya exclaimed and was gone. She ran into the dark recesses and crannies of the parlor and the adjoining hallway, off exploring. As brave as she was, she was still seven. She lived for hiding in a good cabinet.

Left to ourselves in the octagonal room, Mama stood behind me, and August stood behind her son. No one spoke for what seemed like an eon.

Silence settled into the room like a dense fog. I could feel my own hot blood burning and coursing through my veins. Felt the cold dampness of my pant leg.

"We should probably get cleaned up first," Mama said and guided me, gently, to the bathroom.

It was strange, that I'd peed myself without realizing it. But more than the pee turning cold on my leg, more than the swelling dizziness and sickening twists of my stomach, more than any shame sensed, I felt an entirely new emotion. As my mother helped undress me with a gentleness that only increased my fear, I understood then why the first sin on this earth had been a murder. Among kin.

CHAPTER 2

Miriam

1995

Blue mist clung to the mountains like a lace shawl. She'd figured they'd be gray—the Smokies. The blue of everything astounded her. She held up her right arm. The usual caramel of it was muted. All colors were unable to compete with the blue glory of these Tennessee mountains. She was home, or close to it. That morning, she thought she could smell Memphis—a waft of familiar perfume in a crowded restaurant. *We going make it,* she thought, *we going make it.* She locked the '92 Chevy Astro van with her two children and one husky bitch inside it.

"Wait here."

Four brown eyes stared back, eyes that were hungry for an answer, for home. They reminded Miriam of lost soldiers.

She walked slowly toward the Exxon filling station. Hyper-aware of her surroundings. The only Black woman for miles, she knew. A mountain ridge crested like a tsunami before her. A blue that would put any ocean to shame, she thought. *Almost home, Meer. Almost home.*

When she pushed open the door of the Exxon, a wind chime sang above her.

"Morning, little lady."

"Morning."

"What can I help you with?"

He smiled. A good sign, she thought. No malice up front. He was round, meaty but short. A second good sign. She could outrun him if need be. Keys in her back pocket. She could reach the van, her children, in a good fifteen seconds, max. Then pray the fucking van would start. Pray. Throw it into first.

He wore his long silver hair swept back in a ponytail and stroked his peppered goatee when he cheerfully announced, "You're my first customer this morning. Sure is early. Where you headed?"

"Memphis."

He let out a whistle. "You know you got another ten hours solid? You reckon you up to it?"

"I will be. See, the AC keeps flickering. In and out. In and out. Wondered if you knew anything about cars."

He let out another whistle. "Little lady, if it got four wheels, I ain't even need a steering wheel to drive the thing. If washing machines came on wheels, I'd paint mine red and name her Long Tall Sally. The *only* thing I'm good at, my missus says. What kind of car?"

Miriam smiled. She couldn't help herself. He had pronounced "washing" like there was an *r* somewhere in the middle. *Almost home,* she thought.

"A Chevy Astro. A '92. Manual."

"Little lady, you driving stick all the way to Memphis?"

She relaxed. This white man was all right. As far as white men can be all right. "Well, I prayed for wings, but the good Lord just laughed."

"Well, no one's here. Let's go take a look at this testy girl. If you want." He put his hands up, palms forward. "Can't promise anything. But I'll sure as hell try for a little lady like you."

Miriam's neck tensed, the nerves there expanding, contracting.

He eased off the stool he was perched atop, letting out small groans with every small shift of weight. He pointed a meaty index toward the door. "Ladies first."

The mountains had turned into a silvery moonstone color that made Miriam pause as she turned.

"It's a sight, ain't it? And after all these years, I can't get used to it. Mountains. How did they even come to be? Sometimes I sit in that shop all day wondering. Don't make no sense to me how a fella can question the existence of God waking up to mountains like that every morning. All the proof I need. Got any kids?" He aimed his thick finger toward a curtain in the van suddenly fluttering closed. Those pairs of brown eyes, observing all.

Miriam nodded. "Husband, too. We're meeting him in Memphis. There's a naval base there." The lie was a SweeTart in her mouth.

"Your man is military, then?"

"An officer and a gentleman." She almost laughed at herself. Then almost raised her hand to her left brow, still tender, covered in cheap Maybelline foundation not her shade because no drugstore ever carried her shade. She nodded at the hood of the white van. So big her kids called it "the White House." So irksome she'd christened it "the Reagans."

"Can you fix it?"

He was in the innards of the van now. She peered over his hulking frame. Then—

She didn't hear the gentle creaking of the passenger-side door opening, just a crack, or the tiny pitter-patter of feet. But she did hear the growl.

Wolf was three feet away, Mya right behind her. Her youngest daughter. Mya stood on legs not seven years old. Wolf, the color of snow atop the Smokies, keeled low and flashed white teeth and pink gums bespeckled with black.

The white man turned. Looked aghast.

"Wolf, get back in the car. Mya, you, too." Miriam held her brown arm straight, pointing at the passenger door.

"Woman, you got a Noah's Ark full."

"Who he, Mama? Where is Daddy?" Mya asked.

"Come on." Miriam saw Joan poke her tiny head out the side window.

"My. Wolf. Come. *Now*."

Miriam would have smiled if Mya's question hadn't sent the muscles in her neck into an entirely new level of tension. Joan's tone was sharp. Mya obeyed her older sister. Wolf backed away, never taking her eyes off the white man. Suspicious. Protective. A snarl was forming in the jowls. Mya followed, though Miriam could tell she did so reluctantly.

The white man turned back toward the van's innards. "See this here? This is the vacuum valve. See these holes? All I got to do is put some duct tape on them. Between meat and God, the only thing man needs is duct tape. Saved the crew of *Apollo Thirteen*, did you know? Your man a pilot?"

"If I could be that lucky. Have that man stationed in space instead of Memphis." The sweet sour candy taste in her mouth had dissolved. Miriam was taken aback by the truth she told.

The white man paused in his work. Folded his arms into an Indian crisscross and settled against the van. "My missus got Alzheimer's. Get so she don't even know who she is. Calling out for me in the night. *What am I? What am I?* I've loved that woman for thirty years. Not all of them good. But together. Together. I reckon if she was on Mars, I'd hot-rig that there truck to get me there." He sighed. "Come on, look here, see this? Toggle it like this if it goes out again."

Ten minutes later, Miriam was back in the driver's seat, pulling out of the station, a palm up in thanks to the stranger. Her daughters' four tiny brown palms pressed against the windows in thanks. He raised an arm, saluted.

The air conditioner on full blast. The girls could breathe again.

Wolf stopped her panting, curled up around Mya's feet and slept. The tension of the encounter behind her, Miriam found herself wiping away tears with the back of her forearm. Trying to hide her sniffles. But she knew her girls knew. Understood the impact of the fatherless journey they were taking. Her voice cracked when she said, barely audible above Al Green, "We're almost there, y'all. We're almost there."

She thought about where they might stop to get lunch. Hopefully, there'd be a place in an hour or two where they could get something to go. She'd rather stop in somewhere and eat there, but Joan had been refusing to eat inside most restaurants. The mustard. She wouldn't go near the thing. And she refused to say more or go inside. Would just sit in the car with Wolf and wait.

Miriam let her mind drift back to the day before. The yard had been full. Armoires and chests and jade elephants, a vast assortment of Japanese geisha woodblocks, and a cast-iron slave stove any Southern woman would be proud to make biscuits in covered the green.

The neighbors. Miriam remembered the shock and awe in their eyes, their open mouths, their hands cupped to hide their dismay. Everything she owned out on display. A butter churner with a pearl handle was going for twenty. As if Miriam herself lay splayed out in the yard in an open kimono, bare-breasted and utterly spent.

The neighbors—especially the women, Miriam recalled—shook their heads. She knew they were thinking about the ball the night before. Who wouldn't have remembered when Miriam showed up wearing a gold sequined dress with bloodred high-heeled shoes? She was certain they thought it was all because Jax had made major.

The neighbors' necks crooked this way and that, and like hungry pigeons, they searched for the major. But he was nowhere in sight. Just his children. The girls. Mya, tiny, smaller than Wolf, hollering on top of a vanity that they'd let go for only ten.

And then there was the Shelby. Resting like some black beast at the very foot of the yard. The entire base, from general to private first class, knew Jax loved that black panther as much as, if not more than, the Corps. More than the china or the furniture or Jax's absence, it was the sign in the window of the '69 Mustang that proclaimed that Miriam and Jax's storm of a marriage was finally over. In bold block letters the same shade as Miriam's blush rose lipstick, the sign simply read, FREE.

The van's AC broke again just outside Sugar Tree, Tennessee. Miriam parked the Chevy in a lonely rest stop shaded by an ancient hickory. Thrust her arms deep into the entrails of the van and fixed it herself, the hickory over her head heavy in green bloom.

CHAPTER 3

Miriam

1978

Miriam did not look up from her novel when the bell above the record store door announced a new customer's entrance. It was all she could do not to roll her eyes. She took a bite of the peach she held, buried her head farther in her Brontë. Miriam did not like working at the record store; she did not much like working. She preferred to be studying. Chemistry. Physics. Anatomy. This was a summer job—a gig to make some money in between her college graduation and the start of nursing school that fall.

The record store was decadent and dusty, walls lined in vinyl covers: smiling Bessie Smith, a forlorn Roberta Flack, and the Beatles' *Sgt. Pepper*. Overflowing stacks lined three sides of the store, and a high reception desk the fourth. Afternoon light streaked in through the tall windows, creating long diagonals of floating dust motes.

Miriam wore her hair in a large, curly Afro that rivaled Diana

Ross's. Her halo of tight-coiled curls shook at the slightest turn of her head. Except for her hair, she was the spitting image of her mother. Her breasts had grown, not much, but enough to attract attention. The beauty of her shape rested in her hips—as wide and welcoming as a front porch. And yet, Miriam knew, men usually found her the opposite of welcoming. She was indifferent to their catcalls, invitations, and their hanging around by her house. She'd shrug her shoulders at their compliments or cock her head, bemused, and walk back in the house, muttering to herself that men were strange things.

"Got any EJ?"

Miriam did not want to take her eyes off the page of her book. Heathcliff had returned, victorious and furious. Catherine, pregnant, had fallen ill. "Lord, if his woman dies . . ." she said.

"You know—EJ! EJ? Elton John." Miriam recognized Jax's sharp accent when he belted out the first few lines of Elton John's 'Bennie and the Jets'.

She rolled her eyes. Miriam did not rightly care if this nigga was asking for Elton John or for the pope. She cocked her head to the right, her eyes attached, deep to her book. "Over. There," she announced the words slowly, separately, making sure her irritation was known.

"Engrossed in your book, huh? I understand. Hell of a one. I'm convinced Heathcliff was Black."

Miriam lifted her dark brown eyes from her novel and fixed them on the stranger in front of her. Miriam—who had only ever regarded men as inevitable oddities and annoyances, nothing more than mosquito bites in the summer, moths that made their way into chests in the winter months, the dust that settled atop books— Miriam, ever indifferent to the wiles of men, fell in utter, marrow-boiling love the moment her doe eyes locked with those of the young man in front of her.

She had never seen anyone that dark. He was the color of a lonely street in the middle of the night. Almost indigo. He had a wide nose that became a bulb at the end, and large lips that curved to a fine point at the top. It was all Miriam could do not to kiss them. And his hair—Miriam stopped herself from running a hand through it. She could tell his hair was curly because even though it was cut short, waves slick with sheen glistened in the shop's morning light.

Taking in the full measure of the man, Miriam felt something in her insides stir. He wore the same Marine Corps uniform that had been her father's. Khaki shirt, left breast ablaze with ribbons detailing where he had been stationed, the medals he had received. Dark-green trousers, a cloth hat that folded into the tuck of a belt. Her mother still pressed her father's old uniforms every few months or so. She'd catch her mother laying them all out on her sleigh bed and staring at them for hours, before putting them away again.

Miriam knew she should answer this young man, but for the first time in her life, she had lost the power of speech. She figured if she spoke, she'd only stutter out some half word. She sat and stared at him, slightly open-mouthed and blinking. She felt a deep blush start and spread to her fingertips.

"So," the man said slow. He rocked back and forth on his heels, hands thrust in his pockets. "I've got to say, and I hope you don't mind. You must hear this all the time. But you have the prettiest eyes. They'd give Miss Diana Ross a run for her money. Say, I'm new to Memphis. Well, Millington. I'm at the base out there. Just made first lieutenant. Sorry. I feel like I'm rambling. I talk too much, Mazz always says. Mazz—Mazzeo—Antonio Mazzeo. Jesus, I was just making bee sounds at you. *Mazz. Mazz.* He's this friend of mine back on base. Say, what are you doing tomorrow? Saturday night? Sorry, you probably know tomorrow is Saturday. Don't need me telling you. Anyway. A few of us are going to the Officers' Club. It's nice, I promise. And there'll be other girls there. Sorry, other *women.* Girlfriends and wives. Not that I'm asking you to get married. Did I mention I talk too much? Say, is it always this hot down here? How you survive it?"

His shy smile, his nervous laughter, the way he ran his hands through the soft waves of his hair throughout his rambling put

Miriam at ease. Perhaps, just maybe, Cupid had struck them down both.

Miriam straightened in her seat, squared her shoulders. Tried to conceal the long exhale from her quivering lips. She bit her lip. Lifted a page from her novel and dog-eared it. "You in Memphis now. No more EJ," she said and rose from her seat. "The only white boy we listen to down here from Tupelo."

She pushed open the small swing gate that contained her behind the counter. She made sure to sway her hips as she walked down the crowded aisles of the tiny record store. Made sure to brush against the man's khaki sleeve ever so slightly as she did.

"Well," she said, pausing, calling out over her shoulder. "Ain't you coming?"

They spent the rest of Miriam's shift rummaging through Elvis records, telling each other their life stories, sneaking shy glances, falling in love. Talking Hemingway and Fitzgerald and Faulkner, they agreed how none of them, not a single one of those white boys, could write a sentence as good as Zora Neale Hurston.

He told her everything. How he had fled Chicago. Enlisted even to the surprise of his twin brother, Bird. But he had to leave that city. Had to. Bird, eventually, had understood. Both had been born the year of the bird flu pandemic of '57 that claimed thousands. But not their mother. Marvel pushed her twin boys out into a frigid November night, coughing all the while from the virus. He told her of how he had risen in the Corps. Arrived from the accelerated officers' program in Quantico, Virginia, to be stationed as a first lieutenant in Millington. Not a half-hour away. He had arrived in May to find Memphis in full bloom. Memphis in May reminded him of Coleridge's ode to Xanadu—stately pleasure domes were massive plantation houses with wrap-around porches on every tier, and the majesty of the Mississippi River could put to shame any sacredness of the Alph. Magnolias were white with bloom and as fragrant as honeysuckle. The air was thick with green. In the evenings, no matter the day, he could smell barbecue roasting in warm smokers, and on Fridays, the countless church fish fries permeated the moist humid air, made it crackle. There was music. There was always music in Memphis. Old gramophones and Cadillacs blaring, and oval-shaped wooden home radios were always, always on and at full blast, and he heard voices that would shame the Archangel Gabriel—Big Mama Thornton, Furry Lewis, the long, immortal wail of Howlin' Wolf. Jax noticed that niggas in Memphis strutted. Not that Black folk in Chicago didn't, but Jax could only remember the fierce wind of his city, images of Black figures bundled in layers of down walking slanted against the brute force of the angry wind off Lake Michigan. Here, Memphis niggas waltzed down the street as if in tempo to the music that was as omnipresent as God. Black folk loving every second of their Blackness. At night, he would head to Beale Street with the other single officers, eyes wide with awe—all the Black streets held nothing but Black bodies. Beale was filled with Black folk drinking whiskey and laughing and loving in dark corners and singing and drawing switchblades and tuning guitars and chewing tobacco and dancing. Cotton was knee-high. Green fields were tilled in neat rows of cotton overflowing white. There were fields of the inedible fruit—the crop that had brought his ancestors and the ancestors of every other Black person he ever knew, to this country to pluck and to pick without a cent, without acknowledgment of their dignity for four hundred years. Now that he had arrived in the South, he told Miriam, he didn't understand how anyone could ever leave it.

And Miriam told him everything, too: How she was helping to raise her baby sister, August—well, her half sister, technically, but her whole sister in every way that mattered. How her mother had turned militant in her quest for civil rights, for equality. She told him that if he loved Memphis, he would cherish Douglass, her North Memphis neighborhood. How their house—gorgeous, filled with antiques, and built by her own father—had turned into a haven for Black intellectuals, politicians, protestors. How, on a random Tuesday morning, Al Green himself had stopped by the house, and Miriam would never in her entire Black life forget how he and fourteen-year-old August banged away on those keys in the parlor. She told him about Miss Dawn, her quasi-grandmother— her leaning house, her sassy tone, her spells. Miriam told the young Marine in front of her that she had never been in love.

Miriam wasn't sure when exactly she learned his name that afternoon. But she must have. Because she went to sleep that night, and his name was the prayer she recited. His name morphing into butterscotch, twirling, performing acrobatic pirouettes in her mouth: *Jax. Jax. Jax.*

The very next evening, Jax drove her to the Officers' Club on base in Millington. After scouring both hers and her mother's wardrobe, Miriam had chosen a red sequined shift dress with a low back and a high slit. She paired it with black kitten heels and a small black envelope purse. Her mother knew about the date and let her go, quite happily.

"Young folk should always be together. Lord knows, not a soul on this earth could have stopped me from meeting your daddy," Hazel had said, helping Miriam sift through closets and chests and armoires for the perfect dress.

Her mother stopped then. Went over to the edge of Miriam's bed and sat on it, tired suddenly.

"I'll be home right at midnight, Mama," Miriam had said.

Miriam heard a honk. She opened the front door promptly at seven-thirty to find Jax at the curb standing beside what looked like a time machine, holding a small bouquet of African violets and staring at her, open-mouthed.

He made not a move. He seemed paralyzed, transfixed, as Miriam's kitten heels clicked on the pavement leading from her porch to the street.

She, too, was taken aback. Jax drove a sports car the likes of which she had never before seen. It was a color darker than the night around them. Once inside the car, she noticed that it smelled like Jax: musk, leather, cigarettes, and shoe polish. She took in a deep breath.

At the club, Miriam met Antonio Mazzeo, known to all as Mazz, from Chicago's North Side. He and Jax had been inseparable since boot camp, five years prior. Both still carried with them their Chicago accents—sharp *C*s and even sharper short vowels. They shared their love of the Cubs, of a Polish loaded with hot peppers, of summers in a city that dazzled emerald against the waters of Lake Michigan. Mazz belonged to the only Italian American family living in a hard Irish neighborhood. He could walk out of his family's fourth-floor brownstone where, below, the first floor held the family bakery that served cannoli and cappuccinos and hand-stuffed potato gnocchi, walk right out to see Ernie Banks at first. Jax and Mazz had formed a brotherhood in boot camp. Jax had been shocked—Mazz was the first white boy he had ever met that didn't either try to spit on him or kill him. Being spat upon by their drill sergeants instead, they felt a kinship—both hated for their bloodline and both hailing from one of the greatest cities in the world.

Mazz sat between Miriam and Jax at the bar, cheek resting in his palm, staring at Miriam as she sipped her wine and ranted on about the fact that every nigga in Memphis wants a record, but none of them a novel.

"Marry this one," Mazz said, raising a glass to Miriam before tossing back a shot of tequila.

Miriam blushed. She noticed that Jax shifted in his seat.

"I'm serious. I told him. Didn't I tell you? 'Get you a Memphis woman,' I said. Southern belles." Mazz let out a long whistle.

Miriam couldn't help but blush. "I can hear you, sir," she said.

"I *want* you to hear!" Mazz exclaimed. "Make a fine man out of him. If you can. Get hitched. Don't you people jump a broom or something?"

"You people," Jax repeated, grinning.

Miriam noticed that his lips, already so lovely, blossomed when he smiled.

Mazz took another shot of tequila. Rose from his seat at the bar.

"No, don't leave," Miriam protested.

"And with that, ladies and gentlemen, I leave you two fine people to your night," Mazz said, slightly slurring his words.

Miriam smiled, watching him go. He stumbled into a couple slow-dancing to an Isley Brothers song. Jax used this opportunity to draw closer to Miriam. With a deft movement, he dragged her barstool closer to his. She could feel the metal of his military badges and ribbons brush against her dress. The smell of him— leather and something she couldn't quite place.

"Oh!" Miriam raised a hand to her face to hide her laughter, only to find her hand suddenly being drawn gently down by Jax's.

"Don't ever do that," he said, his tone serious. "Don't ever cover up that smile. I think it may just be able to launch a thousand ships."

Miriam blushed again, and it spread like a small fire all over. Felt it in her toes.

"Come on," he said, rising.

"Where we going?"

Jax offered his hand.

Miriam considered it. She gave in, placed her hand in his.

"Let's go downtown. Show me around your city." Jax kissed Miriam tenderly on the cheek, then ran to fetch his car. The kiss was the softest thing Miriam had felt in her life. She stood waiting with her purse in her hands, again transfixed by the beast of a vehicle that Jax pulled up to the club's entrance. He hopped out, opened the passenger door, and looked at her expectantly.

"What kind of car is this?" Miriam asked, stepping toward the offered door.

"It's a Shelby," Jax said.

Miriam raised her eyebrows, surprised and impressed.

"A 1969 Shelby Mustang GT Three-fifty," Jax said with pride.

"She sure is something," Miriam said. She could hear the awe in her voice.

"I thought the same thing when I first saw you." Jax planted another kiss on Miriam's cheek before closing her door and running around to his side of the Shelby. He started the engine and shifted into first. "You look amazing in red, by the way," he said quietly, sounding almost shy.

In that moment, Miriam was certain that somewhere in the deep recesses of this earth, in some underground ocean-filled cave, there was a small but indisputable earthquake.

They drove to Memphis. Downtown was aglow with lights, and the streets were packed with people. The Shelby's windows were down, and as they drove slowly through the city, she could hear the strumming of guitars filling the night air, the music growing into a cacophony by the time they reached Front. The aroma of hot fried food permeated the night air.

"You're awfully quiet," Miriam said.

"Just taking in your city," Jax said. He downshifted into second and made a left on Front Street. "And taking in what Mazz said," he added.

Miriam blinked back confusion. Mazz had said a lot of insane things that night; she was struggling to remember what Jax meant.

They stopped at a red light where, to their left, couples were dancing to the blues music being played by street performers in the middle of Beale Street. They watched for a moment, then Jax turned Miriam's face toward his. "Why don't we do it?" he said.

"Do what?" Miriam asked. He could not mean what she thought he meant. But what if he did?

"Get married?"

Think, Meer. You don't know him. This is your first date. Love at first sight happens in the classics and usually does not end well. But Mama said she knew, just knew, about Daddy . . .

Miriam's thoughts were a tornado shifting this way and that, toward logic and away from it. But in the very pit of her, in her veins and arteries and sinews, she knew she loved this unknown man.

"Well," she said, turning to look back out the window rather than at Jax, "because we've known each other for all of a day."

"Thirty-two hours," Jax countered, pulling ahead as traffic started moving again.

"Thirty-two hours," Miriam repeated.

"And that's not enough time?"

"Not nearly," Miriam said.

"Right."

They heard the unmistakable wail of a trumpet. Someone on Beale was attempting to play Louis's "West End Blues" and, like everyone since Satchmo, was failing.

"Who's your daddy?" Jax asked suddenly, cutting through the trumpet's moan.

"Excuse me?" Miriam snapped her head from the window to look at him.

"Um. Say, that didn't come out right."

"You best not verbalize what foul mess you're thinking in that Yankee head of yours," Miriam said. "I'm a good Catholic girl."

"Sorry. I, I mean——" Jax stammered. "All I meant by it was that I would like to, um, ask for you. You know, formally. How do they say it down south? Betrothed?"

"You're serious?"

"I am."

Miriam shot him a look that could've intimidated Satan. "Why?"

"Why?" Jax laughed.

"I'm serious."

"Because you're the most fascinating girl—woman—I've ever met. And it'd be an honor. I think it would be an honor. And that's just fine if you need more time. Take your time. But I know. I just know. Can't really explain it. Say, sometimes you just know a thing. And listen, I'll be honest. I can't say I'm a good man. I'm not. I hung around some rough folk back in Chicago. I'm not sure I even know what love is, what it looks like. But I do know, what I know more than I know myself, is that I would spurn God for you. So. Who do I need to ask? For your hand?"

"My daddy dead," Miriam said. She went back to staring out the Mustang's window. "Beaten beyond recognition. Body thrown in the Mississippi. Never even knew the man."

"Jesus Christ."

"It's all right," Miriam said, considering. "My mama the one you've got to worry about."

CHAPTER 4

August

1978

A knock at the door caused August to stop playing the piano in the parlor. She growled in frustration. She heard the knock again. Then again. She threw her long braids over her shoulder.

"Fine!" she called out. "I'm coming. I'm coming."

She swung herself around on the piano's swivel stool, slid off, and skipped to the door. She threw it open wide and found herself taken aback by whom she saw there. A tall man stood before her in a uniform she thought looked familiar. He wore a thick, dark-green khaki jacket and a matching cap and trousers. A silver badge on both shoulders caught and reflected the July morning Memphis sunlight.

"We don't want anything you selling," she said.

The man laughed. "You must be August. Heard a lot about you."

August frowned, jutted out her right hip, and placed her hand there. She eyed the man. "Who told you jack all about me?"

"August!" Miriam appeared from behind her, her smile as bright as fireflies in an evening field.

"That's not how we talk to folk."

August pointed at the man, incredulous. "That's how we talk to *Yankees.*"

"Girl, go play outside."

"Oh, *sure*," August shot back. "Great idea. Let me go grab a Barbie—no, no, you right—let me go play in the street and suck my thumb and catch frogs and let this strange Negro up in our house."

"I can't hit you because Mama won't let me. I ask her every day," Miriam said.

"You said she had a smart mouth, but damn." The man removed his cap and placed it snugly underneath his arm. "May I come in?" he asked.

August cast her sister a side look. At almost fifteen, she already matched Miriam's height.

"Yes, of course. Welcome," Miriam said, with a rush to her voice August had never before heard.

"We really doing this, huh?" August threw her hands up. "Fine, come in." She waved. "There's the piano, the couch, the Victro—the old record player. That's a random cat that must have come in when you interrupted my piano practicing, a lovely gold rotary phone. You got a carpetbag big enough for all this?"

"August Della North, get yourself somewhere scarce, please, before I do it for you." Miriam's voice was a combination of singsong and a cat hissing.

August threw up her chin and bellowed, "Mama!"

"Oh my God, I'm so sorry," Miriam said to the man. "We weren't raised by wolves, I promise. Would you like something to drink? Tea?"

"We're pouring the thief drinks now? That's what we're doing?" August asked. She shook her head and then called out again, "Mama! Mama! Come here. Meer is over here giving sweet tea to a Yankee."

August heard her mother approaching from the back of the house, muttering to herself, "Lord, give me strength." August grinned at Miriam and crossed her arms.

When their mother came from the kitchen, she was dressed in her gardening uniform—overalls and a wide Huckleberry Finn straw hat. She had come from the back garden with a basket full of burgeoning okra and turnip greens. She held gardening gloves, caked with dirt, in one hand. She took a long look at the scene in the front room and was silent. Then she said, with cool finality, "August, go play outside."

She half-obeyed. There was a plum tree that rested along the left side of the house, right against the parlor's stained-glass windows. Its dark branches created a shady half canopy around the house, its fruit staining the surrounding ground a dark purple.

"I was minding my business," she whispered to herself as she climbed the plum tree. "I swear I was minding my business. Kicked out of my own house. And all I wanted to do today was play the piano." She reached a branch right underneath the window. "Perfect," she told herself.

And it almost was. The voices coming from the parlor would become muffled whenever a loud car's engine rolled down Locust Street. But August heard enough to know that her sister would be leaving Memphis.

"So, you want to take my joy from me? My firstborn? What a Yankee won't steal from a Southerner, God only knows." August heard the contempt in her mother's voice. "You want to take my Miriam from me? My sole daughter of Myron's."

August gasped, shocked that her mother was telling their business to a stranger, and a Yankee at that. She knew, of course, that she and her sister had different fathers—her mother had been open about that for as long as she could remember—but she'd never heard her mother volunteer that information to someone outside the family. Outside Memphis.

"My word, speaking of that August, did she not offer you some sweet tea?" August heard laughter well up in her mother's voice.

"That one. Spitfire. Acts like she was raised by wolves instead of a God-fearing Southern woman."

"I'm fine, thank you," came the man's deep voice.

"So, you come to take Miriam off me. My only proof I ever loved a decent man."

"August's father wasn't decent, I take it?" the Yankee asked.

"You wouldn't believe who that girl's father is if I told you, which I am not doing on this Sabbath. This Sabbath, I'm giving you an honor I doubt you can live up to: making Miriam happy for life. Now that's a bigger honor, a bigger responsibility than any of them shiny badges and medals on your shoulders."

"With all due respect, Miss Hazel——"

August raised an eyebrow. Miriam must have briefed him on the proper Southern etiquette for addressing widowed women. That fact, more than anything, told August that her sister was serious about this man.

The stranger in the Marine Corps uniform continued: "I am a commissioned officer in the Marine Corps. I have a steady salary, and I'm certain I'll make captain. When I do, we'll move to Camp Lejeune in North Carolina. Picked us out a pretty little house on the shore. I can provide for Miriam."

" 'I can provide for Miriam.' " August's mother laughed. "*Miriam* can provide for Miriam. Lord knows, I didn't raise a silly girl. It's not even so much she would be forsaking Southwestern——"

A silver pickup, its bed lined with tall fishing poles, careened down the street, obscuring the conversation in the parlor. "Damn it," August hissed. She cast a furious glance at the truck as it passed. "Niggas here stay fishing," she muttered.

"Will you *love* her, is what I'm concerned about," her mother was saying. "Treat her right? Do for her and care for her? Be there when she's sick and when she's lonesome?"

"You're an Edith Wharton fan, ma'am?"

"You're literate, then. Well, at least that's something. Wasn't sure what y'all Northerners were taught in school. Or if at all."

"I love her," the Marine said simply.

And at the very same moment, both August and her mother said the exact same thing—August whispering sharply into the leaves of the plum tree, her mother's voice low and threatlike in the quiet parlor.

"You better," the two North women said.

Seventeen years later, August would answer the phone in the middle of the night to hear her sister sobbing on the other end. Something Miriam rarely did: cry. Barely comprehensible. August had to strain, but she was able to make out the words *fight, black eye,* and *ashamed.* Even in her half-awake state, she could remember sitting in the plum tree, straining her ear to the stained-glass window, hearing her mother resign herself to her daughter's fate.

Lying in her mother's four-poster oak bed, listening to her sister's sobs, August silently counted the bullets she had left in the Remington, calculated how many hours it would take to drive from Memphis to North Carolina, reckoned how long she would be in jail for killing a no-good Yankee. If she should even bother with burying the body. Maybe she'd prefer to drive the damn corpse to the police station herself, toss it out the door, and scream, "Take this shit."

"Come home," August said. She was certain, felt it in her bones, that her mother would have said the exact same thing.

CHAPTER 5

Miriam

1995

The annual black-and-white Marine Corps Ball was an extrava-
ganza. The dress code was formal. Ranking Marine Corps officers
would don the Marine Corps dress blue: a blue jacket trimmed in
red stitching and paired with brilliant blue trousers that had a
matching red pinstripe running down the outer seam of the leg.
His sword was at his right side, the ivory handle of the weapon
shone like a tooth. As had been tradition for hundreds of years,
women wore black or white or any combination of the two.

Miriam's gold sequined train shone like celestial glimmer on
the pinewood floors of the Marston Pavilion. Camp Lejeune, in
Onslow County, North Carolina, was the largest Marine Corps
base on the East Coast, and the sprawling Officers' Club over-
looked the New River, with sweeping coastal views of the Atlantic. She and Jax approached the Tinian Ballroom, which was awash
in light. The ballroom had been christened for a Pacific battle

where, in a matter of days, the Marines devastated, captured, and occupied a tiny Asian island north of Guam called Tinian. Three domes too big to be considered chandeliers hung from the ceiling and gave the room a Romanesque gleam.

Miriam was exhausted. Most days caring for Joan, now ten, and Mya, seven, left her worn out by eight. Plus, she and Jax had stayed up late the night before hurling burning insults at each other. *You ain't a man at all. You need all them medals and badges, don't you? Can't be a man at home though.* Miriam had been clutching the note she'd found from his secretary in his fatigues pocket. And Jax. Sitting in a plush armchair in the dark, chain-smoking and smirking all the while. Tongue as good as forked. Laughter in his voice. *So what, I strayed? You let that boy do that to Joan. Having you for a mother is worse than having no mother at all.*

She had decided that morning to wear a gown the color of spun gold. The Marine Corps Ball was traditionally a black-and-white affair. Miriam didn't care. For once, she wanted to take charge, wear what she felt like wearing that night, answer to no one.

The dress was heavy. The sequins were hand-stitched. The gown had a dramatic side split and nothing for a back. It was held together by a small clasp at the base of the neck and the sheer will of the gods. The dress had been her grandmother's creation. She remembered her mother gazing at it fondly when she'd passed it on to Miriam, wrapped in blue tissue paper and stored in a tight trunk to keep out moths.

"My mama made this for me. I wore this the night Myron came home from the war. We had a right fine meal out on Beale . . ." Hazel had said, drifting off into nostalgia. Miriam would pull out the dress from time to time but had never worn it before. Wanted to save it for an occasion that would honor the last time it was worn.

"You look like a goddamned fool," Jax whispered. He clutched her arm with more force than was necessary to help her keep her balance as he steered her into the elegant, elaborate ballroom.

Everyone in the ballroom—Marines with their wives in long black and white gowns and jacketed waiters holding trays of champagne—all seemed to crane their necks as one as Miriam walked across the floor. The lively chatter cut out, replaced by gasps from some of the Marines' wives. Even the music stopped for a moment. The band fumbled at their instruments as the couple continued walking to their assigned table. Not a sound could be heard apart from Miriam's ruby red heels clicking along the pine floor.

Miriam whispered, "You're hurting my arm."

Jax ignored her—her and the hundreds of shocked eyes that followed their progress across the room.

Then, a Chicago accent, thick with sharp *A*s and crisp *O*s, broke the silence. "Well, well, well. Look at the couple I brought together." Always the bachelor, Mazz stood alone next to their table, holding a tumbler of whiskey, swaying a little already from the booze. Ever the spitting image of a young Marlon Brando, he looked sharp in his Marine Corps dress blues. He was as tough as he was handsome. Had scorpions as pets in the Gulf. Smoked cigars or chewed tobacco. Scoffed at cigarettes. Said those were for women and children. He was what the Marines called "Old Salt." He was the finest marksman on Camp Lejeune, and though a rank below her husband, Mazz commanded almost as much respect.

The orchestra resumed a lively waltz, and people turned back to their conversations.

With one strong tug, Miriam broke free from Jax's hold on her arm. "Antonio," she said and, in the Italian way he had taught her, planted two soft kisses on both Mazz's cheeks.

"Miriam," Mazz said. Then, nodding toward Jax, "I still can't figure it out. How in the world you get you a woman like this?"

Miriam, lifting a champagne flute from a passing tray, let out a bitter laugh, threw her head back, and finished the glass in a few swift gulps. She handed the empty glass to Jax, who took it without looking at her.

"I'm going to the ladies' room," she said then, not making any effort to conceal the disgust in her voice.

"Don't you go starting the next Troy on me, Meer," Mazz called out as Miriam left. "I'm too fucking lit to hold my rifle, swear to God."

Clutching at her train, and praying she wouldn't trip and fall on her gown on the way to the bathroom, Miriam didn't turn back.

Brooke Sanderson, wife of First Lieutenant Billy Sanderson, was applying lipstick the shade of a rotten plum to her pursed lips in the long vanity mirror. She stopped and stared when Miriam walked in. Brooke was dressed in a long, black satin gown with embroidered white gardenias that ran from the one shoulder in a long line down to the hem, her hair curled all over in tight ringlets. The picture of a perfect first lieutenant's wife.

"Well, where on *earth* did you get that dress?" she said.

There were two types of military wives, in Miriam's opinion—those who supported their husbands and those who thought they, too, were Marines. Brooke was squarely in the latter set. Attended every officer's wife function—high teas and luncheons and charity drives and golf outings. She ran the Camp Lejeune Toys for Tots Christmas program as if she were Britain's prime minister during the war. Miriam thought her the most entitled white women she had met—uninteresting, her life so intertwined with that of her husband's that she was no longer distinguishable as a woman.

"Oh, Brooke," Miriam said with indifference. "Hi. It was my mother's, actually. Brought it with me from Memphis." Miriam took her own lipstick out of her matching gold sequined purse and began applying the bloodred color to her full lips.

"*Memphis?*" Brooke asked. "I didn't know they had nice things down there. Figured everyone would be running around in overalls." She shrugged and lit a cigarette. Exhaling, she looked Miriam up and down and said, "You celebrating tonight?"

"Aren't we all?" Miriam said warily, using a tissue to dot the corners of her mouth.

Brooke rolled her eyes. "Oh please. Making major is a big thing, and my Billy still only a first lieutenant." She sighed. "But we'll get there. Major. Whew. I'm *sure* I'd wear a dress like that, too."

Major. Jax hadn't told her. Miriam's hand froze in midair. The large bathroom shrank to the size of a dollhouse in that moment. Her breath caught in her throat, and Miriam felt as if she were a tiny grain of sand falling into a tightly coiled seashell, never-ending in its brutal swirl. Suddenly, instead of her own shocked reflection and Brooke's half-surprised, half-smug face in the mirror, she saw the worn pages of the Brontë she'd been reading in the old record store on Cooper Street in Memphis. She saw Jax, too—a tall, dark, beautiful stranger trying to get her attention for the first time.

What had happened to *that* man? To her marriage? Miriam didn't rightly know. All she knew was that she hadn't prepared for how lonely marriage could be. Jax always off at training, months-long deployments God knows where, training for war. And then, one came. And off he went, leaving her alone. Once more. Miriam hated the large Victorian they'd moved into after their wedding seventeen years before, with its spiral staircases and secret nooks and crannies, its creaking floors. She hated the space of it at night, after she had put the girls to bed, how her footsteps echoed in the hallway. She had no one to talk to in North Carolina. She missed Memphis. When Jax returned from the Gulf, he returned even more distant than when he had left. Hardly speaking a word, and when he did, it was to argue. They fought about the phone bill—sky high because of her late-night long-distance phone calls to August. They fought when Jax thought his meat overcooked at dinner. They fought when she found the scraps of napkins with women's phone numbers scrawled across them in lipstick not her shade. And now this: the fact that some uppity white woman in a bathroom knew more about her husband than she did. Miriam was done. She was done with being unhappy all the damn time.

"You must be proud," Brooke said, eyeing Miriam in the mirror.

"Ecstatic," Miriam said and smiled wide.

Back in the Tinian Ballroom, Miriam found Mazz nursing his glass of bourbon, feet perched atop a chair, smoking a cigar. She scanned the room.

"He's talking with the colonel, right over there." Mazz aimed his cigar at a crowded table.

Miriam took a seat. "Any more champagne?" she asked.

"One of those nights, huh?"

"Yeah. One of those." Miriam didn't realize she was shaking until Mazz placed a hand on top of her forearm. "I'm done, Mazz," she spat out.

Mazz stared at her.

She nodded. "I'm done," she repeated. "It's not even about the cheating, right?" Miriam laughed. "I'm considering paying her. She's doing me a favor. *Come take this off my hands.* And I've tried. Lord knows, Mazz, I've tried. To be a good wife. A good mom—" Miriam broke off. "Give me your bourbon if I can't get any champagne."

Mazz raised his hand in the air and signaled for a waiter.

Miriam scoffed. "White folk a trip."

Mazz faked being shot in the heart. "I'm getting the drink for *you.* Aren't *I* the slave here?"

Miriam laughed in spite of herself, accepting a glass of champagne from the waiter.

"There we go. There's the old Meerkat back."

"It'd be real nice to have the old Jax back," Miriam said, throwing her eyes in her husband's direction.

"You shouldn't have worn that," Mazz said suddenly. "I know it's not my place. Shit, I'm drunk. But damn, Meer, that was a right low thing to do to a man."

Miriam rolled her eyes. "This was my mother's dress. I'll wear what I want——"

Mazz interrupted, holding up a palm. "Those red shoes broke him, Miriam. Fuck the dress. I mean, no. It's gorgeous. You know what I mean. Why'd you have to wear *those*?" Mazz seemed angry. Miriam felt both defensive and confused—Mazz had defused many a fight between her and Jax over the years with his humor, the way he seemed never to take sides while somehow being on both their sides. She watched him shift in his seat, take a puff of his Cuban. His eyes were unfocused; he seemed not to be angry with her, but with something she could not see.

"I want you to understand something," he said. "First and foremost. A commander has the authority and obligation to use all necessary means available and to take all appropriate action to defend his unit and other United States forces in the vicinity from a hostile act or a demonstration of hostile intent." He rushed through the words, like the way Miriam used to say her prayers as a child—memorized so deep she hardly had to think about their meaning.

"I quoted that direct from the United States Marine Corps Laws of War. Jax followed orders. He used all the means he had available to him to defend us in that fucking daycare, and that's what he fucking did, all right? I won't hear anything else but that. First and foremost. The rest . . ." Mazz trailed off.

Miriam was quiet, watchful. What daycare was Mazz talking about? How many of Jax's secrets would she have to find out in a twenty-four-hour span?

"The Gulf was hell, Miriam. War really *is*. And it was scary. Shit, I was fucking scared. I'd never seen someone get shot before. Stabbed? Sure. That's Chicago. But I can tell you I grew to know fear like a sister when the shots rang out and Jenkins got hit." Mazz was staring, unseeing, at a distant spot on the table. The orchestra was playing an upbeat melody, some couples swaying together on the dance floor.

"And we were all so young, Meer. That's the thing. None of them boys over the age of thirty. Not a one. When Jenkins got shot, you know who he screamed for? His mother. Over and over. Mama! Mama! Had to stop calling mine 'Mama' for a while. How the hell you explain that to a sixty-five-year-old woman who refuses, to this day, to speak English? *In bocca al lupo.*"

Miriam could see Jax across the room, throwing his head back in laughter at something another Marine had said.

"We rode out that day, Jax in command," Mazz continued. He had always been a natural storyteller, born out of his sense of ease with other people and himself. Right now, though, he seemed nearly unaware of his surroundings, in a state different from his usual one, in which he catered to his listeners and drew belly laughs. Miriam understood: He wasn't telling this story for her.

"He had just made captain. I was his first lieutenant at the time. We'd been sent in to save this army unit that was pinned down and taking heavy fire. We knew because we could hear the shells from inside the Humvee. A bullet from an AK makes a kind of whizzing sound. But then it's gone, the whizzing, and it gets replaced by a dull, droning horsefly sound. The truck lurches, right? Imagine this pile of Marines in a heap, all tangled up and cursing. Then more shots. Gunfire. Closer and closer. Funny. I remember it made me think of throwing Chinese firecrackers at the sidewalk as a kid.

"Jax could tell we needed a joke," Mazz went on. "He gave us one. Something about if this made us pussies, we couldn't have lasted a day on the streets of Chicago's South Side. I can't tell you how much we needed that laugh. Then he spreads a map across his knees, shows us what we're gonna do, and we ride out."

Miriam was looking at the table now, too—neither of them seeing it. Mazz's voice had dropped, both in pitch and volume. She would have had a hard time hearing him if it weren't for the fact that she seemed to hear nothing in the room but him now. Neither Mazz nor Jax had ever talked about the specifics of what they'd done and seen. She was no longer in the ballroom, dressed in gold, surrounded by the rustling of gowns and the clink of glasses. She was in that truck in the Gulf, hearing the pop and crack of gun-shots.

"The truck came to a full stop, and now we're not individuals; we're a coordinated tactical weapon of destruction. We're on foot, snaking the neighborhood, see the two army Humvees ablaze in the street. I'm looking left and right, seeing that the city of Khafji is just that, a fucking city. Filled with apartment buildings, cafés, human beings. Who would send a tank through an occupied city, tall apartment buildings lining the street? The United States Army."

Mazz shook his head. "Only branch worse is the fucking Air Force. Anyway, I follow Jax, and we got twelve Marines behind us, all trailing Jax. The building we enter is low, single story, and in the dark night it's the same color as bone. Windows on the north side of the building all blown out. Bullet holes peppering the east entrance.

"We're all behind Jax, clustered like a fucking bomb. Then we start clearing rooms. There's a long, narrow hallway with a series of side rooms sprouting out like veins. Patient rooms maybe, I don't know. All I was thinking was *Il mio dio, we've got to clear each fucking one.* We did. M-Sixteen first, body second. Bang. Another door blasted open. A swirl of M-Sixteen laser lights. A few seconds of silence. Repeat.

"But the fourth and final door would not open.

"We're exhausted by this point. Sweating. Jenkins, this young gunner—didn't look like he had ever been inside a woman, peach fuzz above his lip—moves back to take a wider stance, swings his right arm back with the ram and hits the door. All five foot ten, two hundred pounds of force, and the damn door still does not fucking open.

"Jax hollers out at this point: 'This is the United States Marine Corps! Open the fucking door!' Nothing. But we can feel the sons of bitches in there, hiding. Breathing. I swear, I hear a gun click. It was so hot in that fucking hallway it felt like I was in a womb.

The men getting real restless now, crowded in that dark hallway, the perfect storm for senseless death.

"Then a pop. From within the room. Quick. Subtle almost. Everybody starts screaming, 'We're taking fire. We're taking fire!' We crouched like spiders. Look at each other. Quick glances to make sure no Marine was down. But one was. Jenkins. Closest to the door at that point. The bullet sent him careening backward. He begins to moan. Low, steady. 'Mama.' That's what he's moaning. *Cazzo.* I can still hear it.

"So, we tell him to shut the fuck up. We don't want to give away our position, and Jenkins's screaming is like a homing beacon for the enemy. We were all kind of losing it at that point. Jenkins on his back, crying out for his mama, his God.

"I don't know if it was then when Jax noticed that the door didn't reach the ceiling. That there was a slap of window right on top. But that Jax did what he had to do. Grabs a grenade from his belt. Throws that son of a bitch in a perfect upward arc through that top window above the door into that fucking room, shouting, *'Ukhrug barra! Ukhrug barra!'* and to the rest of us, 'Get back, get back!' I remember thinking he'd thrown it just like Fergie Jenkins—it was that well aimed. In the aftermath of the explosion, we saw movement from inside the room and shot."

Mazz paused then. Raised his eyes from the table and looked at me head-on for a moment. Then he noticed his glass was empty and waved it in the air. An obliging waiter hurried over.

"How the hell were we to know that the room was full of kids, Meer?" he said. His voice was louder now, closer to his regular pitch. "A girl, 'bout Joan's age now, holding fort. Protecting her siblings. We just shot the first thing that moved. The room was dark as shit, dust and debris floating in the air. The power cut out from the artillery shells long before. You ever seen something happen so fast you only realize what you saw in hindsight? It wasn't till after that I realized it wasn't another army, their guns, that had moved. It had been a tiny palm held up in plea. And even through the Oz green of the night vision, we could all see the bright red of a single tiny shoe. Attached to a brown foot, a bit of the tibia sprouting from the ankle, it lay on the floor alongside a crib.

"It was the red shoe that broke him. We entered the room. All the kids were dead. Most of them in more than one piece.

"I found Jax afterward, walking in circles by the burning carcass of the army Humvee we had been sent in to save. Where his M-Sixteen should've been—strapped to his chest, the metal crossing his heart like a crucifix—was the red shoe. The child's foot still inside. I tried to pry the foot out of Jax's hands, but he wouldn't let go. Kept mumbling about how Joan is mad about *The Wizard of Oz*. Said he'd just given her a pair of those red shoes for Christmas . . ." Mazz took a long drink from his tumbler.

"And I wear red shoes tonight," Miriam said. Her voice sounded stronger than she'd thought it would.

"And you wear red shoes tonight," Mazz repeated. He took another drink.

Miriam sat back. The story was horrifying. It was. But she was no stranger to fear. Terror. Grief. Rage. She thought of Jax sitting in his armchair in the early hours that morning, black coffee in hand, saying with a bitter coldness, "Having you for a mother is worse than having no mother at all."

"I'm glad," Miriam said.

Mazz cocked his head.

"That nigga will remember the night I leave him."

CHAPTER 6

Joan

1995

I awoke to the sound of a tornado. I heard the crash of something heavy downstairs and tossed off my many quilts, looking over at Mya through the stack of L. M. Montgomery and Addie books that were piled on the nightstand between our matching twin beds. The room was dark but for the pink nightlight Mya insisted be left on every night. I went to Mya. She lay fast sleep in her bed, snoring. Whatever earthquake roared in our house, Mya would sleep through it. Our room had a slanted, vaulted ceiling and a giant bay window that faced the street. I used to sit at that window for hours when I was younger, gazing at the stars, convinced Peter Pan would appear, teach me how to fly.

I loved our house. Victorian style and three stories, to Mya and me, it was an exact replica of a dollhouse. We charged the other kids who lived on base dollar entry fees to explore the uneven floors and the hidden butler's pantry and the unexpected maid's stairway that led to back bedrooms. The attic was a buck-fifty. "The Secret Garden House," Mya and I called it. Mya had been afraid the house was haunted. But I'd say, *What them dead white folk going to do? Turn off the lights?* Still, Mya had insisted that the pink nightlight above our stack of books be turned on nightly. Stamped her feet, in fact. So, we left it on every night. I never let it slip that I hoped the pink light might, just might, let me catch the moment my toys came alive.

I heard another crash. Sounded like a skillet hitting the floor. I crept to the door and closed it quiet behind me, so as not to wake Mya, so as to let my dolls come back alive and talk of things to come. At the top of a spiral maid's staircase that descended down into the kitchen, I saw Wolf. She was the color of snow and about the same size as me when stretched out, nose to tail. Her black-tipped ears went upright as I approached. She paced the top of the staircase, agitated.

"It's just me, girl."

Wolf relaxed when she saw me. Settled into herself, resting her massive head on her large front paws, and gave a tired sigh.

I scratched Wolf's ears in the way she liked, then made my way down the stairs, careful to tiptoe on the carpeted part to mask my approach. I tucked the folds of my long, pale-blue nightgown into the crook of my arm. The light at the bottom of the stairs grew brighter as I crept down. I found my perfect perch, one I'd used many times before, where shadow met light, where I could catch a glimpse into the illuminated kitchen and where the thick banister kept me masked in shadow.

I understood why Wolf had stayed at the top of the staircase.

The fights between my parents had escalated over the year. A few times, the police had been called. Not by us, never by us: the neighbors. The noise of it all. Their shouting could shake the house. It isn't any wonder they were called. The banging of pots; the smashing of china. The police, deferential to my daddy—he was a high-ranking Marine Corps officer, after all—would knock before entering, and my parents would quiet. Daddy pressing an

angry finger to his lips, a snarl like Wolf's still curling over them
as he ever so slowly let the officers in.

It looked like a storm had blown through our kitchen. The refrigerator door was open, and food had spilled out. Heads of lettuce, green tomatoes on the floor. Pots and skillets hung at odd
angles from the rack in the center of the ceiling. The big silver pot
my mama resurrected every Christmas to cook chitlins lay on its
side on a burner. It rocked slightly to and fro.

I heard my parents before I saw them, heard the unmistakable
alto of my daddy.

"Say, you just *had* to wear that dress. You looked like a goddamned fool tonight."

My mama's bitter laugh. "I'm a bad mother, right? Might as
well be a bad wife. Get off of me!"

My parents barreled across the kitchen toward the open refrigerator as one chaotic force, a swirl of sequins and Marine Corps
dress blues. Daddy still wore his blue jacket, the ribbons on his
jacket gleaming in the kitchen light. Mama's back hit the edge of
the refrigerator door hard, and I saw a frightened look in her eyes
as she twisted like a cyclone from the pain of it. Mama threw herself onto the island to stop herself from falling. And Daddy was
her shadow throughout, in a boxer's stance, bouncing on his toes,
waiting to strike. I held my breath, hands balled into fists, as if I
were his opponent in the ring. I had heard my parents fight before. A light sleeper, I often woke to the sound of them shouting. My father cursing, my mother crying. But I had never before
seen my father *hit* my mother. I did not think that kind of chaos
was possible. The truth shocked me, but I couldn't deny it. There
it was in front of me: My father was capable of dark, terrifying
things. He had hit her. Maybe he had before. The casual way he
followed her, the boxer's stance. Maybe that's why my muscles
were tensed: I was ready to hurtle down the rest of the stairs and
throw myself in front of my mother.

But Mama was a force. She ran around the kitchen island in
her gold sequins, creating distance between them in a matter of

seconds. With the quick reflexes of a rabid animal, she picked up a plastic Heinz mustard bottle that was among the disarray on the floor and squirted the bottle's contents straight into my father's face from across the island.

The yellow spray reminded me, ridiculously, of the arc of a jump rope at its height. It slid down Daddy's perfect uniform, the cheap yellow seeming to make no sense on his formal blues. For a moment, I thought of a parallel world where parents finished a glamorous evening eating messy late-night hamburgers, playful and teasing.

"Have your whore wear black and white!" my mom screamed.

Daddy stumbled backward into the open fridge, yelling like a wounded animal as he swiped at his eyes. More noise than Mama made when she hit the refrigerator door, I thought distantly.

Mama paused, put down the bottle, and just as quick, ran to my father and asked, "Are you okay, baby?"

Daddy flung out his arm.

Whether Daddy aimed purposeful or not, whether he struck in fear or in anger, the fact remained that his fist met my mama's worried left eye with a right hook that sent her flying. Mama fell in slow motion, her sequined dress looking like a thousand fireflies twinkling in a summer southern field.

Daddy walked over to the heap on the floor that was Mama. Where he found a dishrag, I didn't know. In the chaos of the kitchen, everything happened so fast. He bent down over her, and I thought, with a rush of fear, that there might be blood he needed to wipe up. But then I saw: Daddy used it to wipe his own face. He was squatting now, hovering over Mama.

"You let that boy do that to Joan," he said. "Like I said: Worse than having no mother at all." And he walked over her. Walked out the kitchen into the unlit hallway that led to our den. There were yellow stains dripping down his shoulders. As I watched him go, his back looked like the back of a stranger.

I crouched, frozen, in my hiding place. I don't know how she did it, but after a minute, I saw Mama crawling on her belly like I had seen Marines do in training. Crawled until she reached the wall where we had our telephone. An arm shot up and fumbled for the cord. Failed. Faltered. Attempted again. I strained with her, willing the phone to fall into her hand. The third time, she got it. She was able to turn herself so that she lay half upright, half sprawled out on the kitchen floor. Her left eye was swelling up, but her right eye was what scared me. There was a fear and desperation there I'd never seen in anyone, especially not my mama. I couldn't see what numbers she was pressing into the phone, but I knew it couldn't be 911 because she went past three digits.

"August?" I heard Mama say. Then she started to sob.

CHAPTER 7

Miriam

1995

It took some effort, but finally Miriam managed to grab the bottle of Pappy Van Winkle off a high shelf in the kitchen. The kitchen mirrored the parlor in that it also had a high-beamed, conical alcove. But where the parlor was dark, the kitchen was bright and cream. Wood-paneled walls painted the color of buttermilk. Her father had hand-painted purple lilacs, clusters of purple lavender, and hummingbirds on the walls, too. Miriam remembered there were dates hidden in discreet black cursive among the flowers: January 1, 1863; December 7, 1941; August 14, 1945. And eye-level and hidden within a bouquet: June 6, 1943, her parents' wedding day.

Miriam's father had built the kitchen to resemble the intimacy of an old Italian restaurant. There was a huge butcher-block counter that took up an entire length of one wall. Pots and pans of all shapes and sizes hung from the high ceiling. The north wall was built with brick, and there, he had put the stove and the near-walk-in butcher's fridge. Instead of a traditional kitchen table, he had built a breakfast nook complete with a U-shaped booth. A curved bench around the table held green, tufted-velvet cushions that Miriam remembered felt like sitting on air.

Miriam walked to the booth, where her sister sat on an emerald cushion, chain-smoking Kools. Miriam said nothing. She knew her sister well. An arched eyebrow or an upturned corner of the mouth was evidence enough of her judgment. But it was well past midnight. All the children asleep. What was the real harm?

Miriam poured August's drink first. Poured a finger of the rye into her short, wide glass. Miriam eyed her own drink next, measuring a finger and then adding another ample splash. "Oh, why not?" she said, taking a seat across from her sister in the booth.

"Where'd you get this whiskey?" August asked.

Miriam winced as she sipped. "Stole it the night of the ball from the Officers' Club."

"You didn't."

"I did," Miriam said and took another sip.

"Don't make that a habit," August said.

Miriam raised an eyebrow. "Didn't I see another bottle of rye up there?"

August took a sip. "It's for cleaning!" she snapped.

"What?" Miriam laughed, spitting out her drink.

"For when I need to clean out the men in my life," August said. Just when the sisters were about to bicker, August would usually say something that sent Miriam into fits of hysteria, ruining any chance for a long-lasting argument. "And, you know, for cleaning out my throat," August added.

"Girl, when's the last time a man been up in here?"

August paused, her glass held midway to her lips. "A real one? Shit, not since our daddies."

Miriam cackled long at that one. She set her drink on the table and held a hand up to cover her Cheshire cat grin. "You heard from Derek's daddy?" she asked. If August could make any conversation funny, Miriam could make any moment carry the seriousness of a man's last breath.

August almost spat out her drink. "I didn't tell you? That nigga dead. Died in a knife fight in New Chicago. The Lord giveth, huh? Girl, you been gone a long-ass time."

"You shouldn't speak so of God. Or of the dead." Miriam knew she shouldn't be so critical of her sister when she herself, at times, doubted God. His Judgment. His irrational decisions. But Miriam was an older sister; she lived in criticism, if only because she wanted the best for her sister, wanted her life to be better in all ways from hers.

Miriam thought back to the moment she'd pulled into the long driveway of the house that afternoon. Pulled in front of a house more familiar to her than the blood running through her veins. She had made it home. On her own. Save for the grace of God and, most surprisingly, the kindness of an old white man. Miriam knew that God was a trickster. As He gave, He took. He gave her one hell of a mother, took a father. Gave her two children she'd cross the Sahara for, gave her this black eye, took her husband, her dignity. God was a duende. A sprite. He could take the form of anything He wanted. Maybe He had done so back in Sugar Tree.

Miriam saw distaste spread across her sister's face.

"Who needs God when I got Al Green?" August said. "You know, he still preaches. Hand to God. Not five blocks away. Won't sing nothing but gospel now, though. Ain't that a bitch? Most beautiful voice on this earth, not five blocks 'way, and we can't even hear him sing 'Belle.' "August took a sip and responded to Miriam's judgmental raised brow with "Listen, Meer. I like believing in niggas I can at the very least see." She held her glass of rye and motioned it in a circle. "And I haven't seen a good man in ages."

"If we don't got God, Aug, who the hell do we got?" Miriam asked. She tried but could not contain the irritation in her voice. She hated that her sister did not share her faith. Miriam attended Mass because her mother did. She felt her faith was something bestowed upon her, something hereditary, something inherited, something that kept her close to her mother, who had left them all.

August laughed for a long time. Then she held up her glass. "We have this here whiskey."

They clinked glasses.

"You always got something smart to say," Miriam said, chuckling herself, deciding to let it go. It wasn't like she went to Mass every Sunday herself. She wasn't exactly in a position to preach, and she definitely didn't have the energy to fight. At least not this one.

The dinner that night had been difficult. Without needing to discuss it, Miriam and August had sat down in the middle of the newly formed family, their bodies creating a barrier between Derek and the girls.

When Miriam had taken Joan into the bathroom, she dropped to one knee, undressed her daughter with the deftness only mothers possess, and simply held her, for a very long time, neither one of them saying a word.

At the center of the round dinner table was a tiny crystal box. Joan had been quiet throughout dinner, so Miriam opened the box and encouraged Joan with a nod to take one of the cards inside.

Joan hesitated for a second, but then took the card. Her eyes widened as she began to read the prayer written in gold on it. " 'Do not neglect to show hospitality to strangers, for by this some have entertained angels without knowing it.' Hebrews thirteen-two," she read.

"How fitting," August had said. "I reckon I'm cracking up several thousand angels right now. Somebody hand me my Emmy!"

Mya had let out a shrieking laugh and slapped her hand on the table, shaking the plates of lamb cooked in red wine, red buttered potatoes sprinkled with parsley, and steaming candied yams.

"My, do you even know what an Emmy is?" Joan had asked.

"Do *you*?" Derek snapped. It was the first time Derek had addressed Joan directly. Words chosen like a weapon. Silence was a gun. And when it went off, when it was fired, the entire table fell silent.

Miriam and August exchanged looks, then each woman's eyes went to her respective child.

Miriam watched Joan put the card back slowly, carefully, in the glass box and close its lid. Joan then narrowed her eyes until they were mere slits set in her face. "I know more than you think," she finally said. Then she crossed herself three times and picked up her steak knife.

Miriam was brought back to the present with a suddenness that made her jump in her cushioned seat.

"Gunshot," August said. Then: "You'll hear those often. Girl, it's like when you left, you took the last of Motown with you." She took a drag from her menthol. She had smoked it down to the filter. Smoke and the echo of the gunshot hung thickly in the air. "Shit, I saw a girl last week on Chelsea. Not fourteen years old. On the corner, girl. *Working* it. You hear me? Crack may as well have been a virus for all what it's done here."

Miriam finished her two fingers' worth of rye in a single shot, throwing her head back to take the full weight of the whiskey. Her cheeks were flushed, she could tell. The gunshot had sounded uncomfortably close. The last time she heard a gunshot, she was Joan's age: ten. It had been a .32 then, too. And she had been with her mother.

"Am I a bad mom, August, for coming here? Bringing the girls?" Miriam bit her lip and twisted the long gold rosary around her neck as she always did when she was nervous.

August fumbled in the folds of her kimono and brought forth her pack of Kools and her lighter. She took her time, removing a fresh cigarette from the pack, placing it on the perch of her full lips, tilting her head toward lighted flame, cupping expert hand over the flame, lighting the cigarette, and inhaling and exhaling in a long stream of smoke.

"You're only a bad mother if you don't feed them," August said through plumes of smoke. "Speaking of, what you going to do for work? They hiring secretaries down at the police station."

"The same one kill my daddy?" Miriam exclaimed.

"Touché, trick," August said. She shook her glass back and forth quickly, signaling to her sister that she needed more.

Miriam rolled her eyes. She poured her sister a hefty amount and measured the same for herself. "Nah. I'm going to make Mama proud."

August's eyes bored holes into Miriam's. "You *aren't*," she said, awe in her voice.

"I am. I brought my transcripts. I'm not a complete fool. I brought what mattered."

"And they going pay you?"

"I called. The lady at the admissions office said she'd do what she could." Miriam raised her glass in a toast.

"Well, don't that beat all?" August clinked her glass against her sister's. "Another nurse in the family. I know Mama would be proud, Meer. Real proud."

"It'll be hell," Miriam said, but she smiled. She put a worried palm to her forehead and held it there while she exhaled. She was going to go back to school, at the age of forty. The studying alone would swamp her. The forthcoming long nights at the library. And all the other students would be so young and hungry and ambitious. Miriam was just plain hungry. She knew she needed to provide for her girls. And something deep and almost animalistic, instinctual, in her did not want Jax's money even if it were offered. She wanted to do this on her own.

Her mind went to a fight long past, when Jax had spat out a vicious question she had no true answer for: "Where the hell you think you going go, how far you think you going get, with two babies, no degree, and a Black face?" Miriam doubted she had the answer now. But she knew she needed to try to find it.

Maybe it was the whiskey, but there was a sudden heat in her chest when Joan's soaked pant legs came into the frame of Miriam's mind. *How will we survive?* she thought to herself. *How on earth?* She was jolted from her worry when she felt her sister's sudden, hard grasp on her forearm.

"Gotta be better than the hell you just left, Meer. Gotta be."

"We best keep that boy away from Joan."

August stiffened in her seat.

"Don't act like that," Miriam said. "Might as well say it out loud." She swirled her whiskey in her glass. "I'm worried my Joanie may just kill your boy."

CHAPTER 8

Miriam

1988

She was pregnant again. This time it was early fall, and the Memphis nights were exquisite. Most of the trees had turned to copper—the sunlight catching in the gold medallion leaves of the trees. She and August sat out on the front porch, sweet tea in hand, and Miriam was thankful for the cool night air. The breeze shook the sunflowers her mother had planted years before, that somehow had survived the first Memphis frost and had now grown tall as titans. And without the death of her mother hanging over her pregnancy, this baby seemed lighter, easier. Miriam was sick of grieving. Sick of seeing her dead mother all over the house in Memphis. Miriam saw her as if in the flesh, standing in the kitchen over a pot of something hot and boiling on the stove. Or once, she thought there was someone in the backyard, and she swore she saw her mother there, among the tomatoes, straw hat on and everything.

When Miriam had been pregnant with Joan, she finally understood why her mother would sometimes take out her father's uniform, press everything, lay it out on the bed, and sob quietly next
to it until she fell asleep. When Hazel died, all Miriam had left
was the grief of her. So, she saw her all the time. Saw her in the
delivery room. For twenty-six hours Miriam had sweated and
heaved and pushed her first child out of her insides, screaming all
the while, "Mama, it hurts!"

The baby had been a girl.

"Joan," Miriam had christened her daughter.

"And she saw things others couldn't," she'd said simply to Jax
when it was all over.

And now, Miriam had come back to Memphis to give birth for
a second time. Jax was away at officers' training, a yearly sojourn
for any high-ranking Marine Corps officer. He would miss the
birth of their second. But Miriam had been adamant that her second daughter be born in Memphis, too.

Miriam, though she missed her husband, was thankful to be
back home with her sister and her young nephew. Joan loved
the house too, her tiny body explored the house like a calico kitten, always hiding in the crannies of the antique furniture. August had given birth eight years before, to the first son in the
North household in generations. She spoke little of his father,
and Miriam, not wishing to upset her sister, asked few questions.

From their spot on the porch, the sisters looked out across the
street at a pecan tree in the neighbor's yard, swaying gently with
the breeze. They sipped their drinks, though August's sweet tea
was laced with whiskey. She was draped in a new silk kimono Miriam had gotten her.

"How you feeling?" August asked.

Miriam didn't answer. How her sister asked, the tone of her
voice—as if her sister were approaching a weak, injured feral
animal—reminded her of the night of her wedding.

August, almost fifteen years old at the time, had been standing behind her, wrapping Miriam's long curls into tight pink rollers. Miriam wore a long silk nightgown with a thousand white cranes outlined in emerald sequins throughout the long folds of fabric.

Their mother sat on the edge of the quilted bed of the girls' room, watching. Al Green had been crooning from the record player. "How you feeling?" Hazel had asked. She wore concern on her face like foundation.

"Mama," Miriam said, sighing, trying not to roll her eyes in exasperation.

"You know she in love, Mama. Though, Lord knows why," August said.

"I love y'all two crazy girls, Lord knows why," her mother had replied, a coy smile on her face. Then, after a pause, the smile evaporated. The concern was back. "Meer, y'all hardly know each other."

"I know I want him," Miriam said.

"Being the wife of a Marine is a hard, hard thing."

"So is being alone." Her mother was silent. Miriam regarded the large sapphire resting atop her left ring finger.

"You'd drown for sure," August said, laughing.

"August!" Miriam hissed. "If anything happens, I'll come home, Mama."

In the soft glow of the girls' room, Al Green's warm voice filled the air like yeast rising.

"My lovely, beautiful daughters, both of you can always, always come home," her mother had said, swiping tears from her eyes.

Now Miriam felt tears prick the corners of her eyes as she looked down at her pregnant belly in the porch swing, wondering if she'd always think of this house as home. If her future children would. Her sister sat next to her, gently kicking out her feet to keep the swing in motion.

"I wonder if the pecans are ready to pick," August said. A few had fallen in the wind and bounced around the neighbor's gnarled tree's roots before settling in the dark thicket of the lawn.

"How's school going?" August had gotten accepted to

Southwestern—now called Rhodes—the spring before and had thrown herself into her studies.

"All I do is read and write, it seems. I can read a novel by the time we finish this bottle." August drank.

"You still not talking to God?" Miriam asked. Why was she this way? This critical of her lovely, brilliant sister? The only one in the family not a believer.

"About what?" August said, spitting the words out in a staccato bitterness.

"You know it's not His fault Mama died."

August swirled the ice in her glass, stared into it, took a sip. "Who the hell else's fault is it?"

A bang—the massive yellow front door had opened, the wind catching it with a force that flung it against the side of the house and back again.

"What on earth?" August began. "Derek, bedtime was hours ago." She stopped speaking just as abruptly as the door had opened.

Miriam had to angle her head since August was so much taller, but she finally saw Joan.

Joan was naked from the waist down, the top of her Kermit the Frog pajamas disheveled and part of it caught in the curls of her hair. Thin streaks of blood trickled down her brown, baby spider legs. Her eyes were wide as saucers but dry as bone, staring through the twilight and autumn wind.

"My God," August whispered. Her glass fell then, toppling into the folds of her kimono and soaking the cushions of the porch swing.

Miriam did not remember standing up, but she must have moved like lightning, because she was suddenly on her knees on the porch floor, her arms around Joan, trying to absorb her daughter's body into her own, whispering, "Oh honey, oh honey, oh honey," as if it were a spell that would make everything all right. *She's three*, she kept thinking. *She's only three years old.*

August found the wire hanger in Derek's room. One end twisted, slick with blood.

A week later, Miriam and Jax sat in a pediatrician's office in Midtown Memphis. She wore a pink suit with big black buttons that ran down the front, lace gloves, her hair pinned up. She had wanted to appear as respectable as possible. Within the chaos of the week, the Department of Children's Services had visited the house, had taken Derek away for counseling, for state-mandated therapy, taken him away for months. What if the same were to happen to Joan? It was a thought too frightening to bear. So she put on her Sunday best. Made sure Jax did the same. He wouldn't let her adjust his tie in the morning dawn. Swatted her hand away without a word. Miriam noticed the sweat dripping from his thick, close-cropped hair, as if he had sprinted from the plane. He likely had.

He had taken leave from officers' training school the moment Miriam called. Took a helicopter from a discreet military facility, hopped on a military flight, and landed in Millington a day later. Entered the ancestral Memphis brick home, swung open the wide yellow door and scooped up his daughter. Spoke to no one but her for days. Kept stroking her soft, tight-coiled curls. Whispering into them, *My Joanie. My Joan of Arc. My brave Joanie girl.*

They were ten minutes early for the appointment. Miriam had made sure. Told August to wait in the car. Take Joanie for an ice cream, maybe. Or eggs, since it was still so early. They shouldn't be longer than an hour.

Miriam had seen awareness spark in her sister's dark brown eyes as she spoke. Looked like amber shining. Miriam didn't have to say more. She had reached into the car window. She gave her sister's hand, on the Cadillac's steering wheel, a reassuring pat and followed Jax into the hospital. She didn't need to look back. She didn't need to verbalize her worry: *What if they take her? What if they say I am an unfit mother and take my daughter? Get her out of here. Get her the hell away.* Her sister had understood: That amber gleam in her eye flickered as she sped away, Joan strapped into her car seat in the back.

Dr. Seth Cobb was a petite man with long, slender fingers and a large forehead accented by glasses with thick black frames. His office was in the sixth-floor children's ward of the Mount Zion Baptist Hospital, the same Memphis hospital where both Miriam and Joan had been born and where Miriam's mother, Hazel, had worked as its first Black nurse.

The doctor was sitting in a plush tufted-leather chair with an array of degrees framed behind him, arranged on the wall like an offering. Joan had been seen by him earlier in the day, and before, on the night of the rape. Miriam and Jax now sat across from the man, who held his small chin up as he spoke, as if he were looking down on them.

Miriam twisted her gold rosary, while Jax, next to her, sat completely still. He wasn't in uniform, but a crisp white Oxford shirt and pressed trousers.

Miriam withdrew teeth from lip and blurted out, "What are the next steps?"

"Her hymen broke. She has some scarring, but she will heal. I'll send you home with some antibiotics for that."

My God. My baby, Miriam thought. "She's allergic to penicillin."

The doctor poked his chin out even farther as he reached to examine some notes in front of him. "What happens when she takes penicillin?"

Miriam didn't like his tone. There was doubt in it. Like he didn't believe her. But she knew damn well what her firstborn was and was not allergic to.

"She breaks out in hives." Miriam's voice was strained. She spoke slowly, trying to be polite, cordial.

"Ah, yes. There are others. Not to worry."

"I'm worried about my child, Doctor. About the trauma of it all. Will she remember this? For the rest of her life? Have to carry *this* around with her? We want . . ." Miriam took a moment to craft her sentence. "We want the best for our daughter. We are good parents."

Dr. Cobb shrugged. "She won't remember this," he said flatly.

She couldn't believe it. "And why do you think that?" Miriam asked. She gave up on pleasantries, did nothing to mask the contempt in her voice.

"Because the girl is only three," he said, blunt, so matter-of-fact.

Miriam cringed. How he had said "girl."

"Look." Dr. Cobb folded his hands neatly on the massive desk in front of him. "I see a lot of cases like these. Too many, in fact. Abandoned children. Bad homes."

It took all of Miriam not to stand in that moment. But for the life of her, she couldn't help but hold up a lace-gloved hand. "My father is Myron North. The first Black homicide detective in this city. My husband is a captain in the United States Marine Corps. This *suit*?" Miriam grabbed at her collar. "Vintage Chanel. That *girl* wants for nothing. Nothing." Miriam's hand shook with fury.

"Now, I'm not saying that's the case here," he went on flatly, as if she hadn't spoken, as if he hadn't heard one word of Miriam's emphatic proclamation of her family's humanity. "I'm talking in general, understand."

Miriam realized, with relief and horror, that her worst fear—Joan's being taken away from her—was no more than fantasy. She doubted that this man would ever give a damn about the life of a Black child.

He continued, nonchalant, seemingly unfazed, his dry tone never breaking. "And she's young." He waved a hand. "It won't affect her. At least not mentally. She'll be sore for a few days. I recommend warm baths. Oatmeal baths. There will be some discomfort, of course. Urination may be painful, but the meds will help with that. Given her age, I will prescribe a very small dosage of pain medication for that. Bring her back in if the pain worsens or you see any blood in the urine. But it would be rarer than Halley's comet appearing thrice in a season," he said. "A three-year-old remembering her own rape."

So help me, God, Miriam thought. *Do not kill this white man. Compose yourself. Get it together. Ask him about counseling.*

Just as Miriam opened her mouth, Dr. Cobb stood up and said, "Have a great weekend, folks," then opened the door for them to leave.

CHAPTER 9

August

1988

August could almost hear her mother's voice saying, "Don't you go stalling that car now, August. Be easy with her. That's the last gift Myron ever got me." The 1950 Cadillac Coupe de Ville was the color of fire. August wondered if that made her more of a chariot or a bomb today.

August made a slight right down East Parkway toward the Mount Zion Baptist Children's Hospital entrance and saw bright November sunlight. She checked the rearview mirror to see if the turn had disturbed Joan. She wasn't asleep. She hadn't made a sound the whole ride, but her eyes were open, looking out the window into the middle distance, her head leaning against the side of her car seat.

August had half-obeyed Miriam. Instead of ice cream, she had taken the girl to nearby Rhodes College. Had walked her along the campus green, had pointed out the large oaks, the ivy covering the alabaster stone of the school buildings. August hadn't even known where she was going until she was already in the school's parking lot. She felt as if she'd been driven by some unconscious force within herself, something that was reminding her that it wasn't just Joan's or Derek's futures that were on the line. It was hers, too. Her goal of following in her mother's footsteps.

As August walked the green, holding on to her niece, she thought about how the picturesque November day in no way matched the shame of the situation. The ivy looked like gold coins climbing up the tall buildings. The trees' orange leaves glistened in the slight wind, giving the trees the appearance of sparklers igniting. To August, the day looked like a goddamn celebration.

God certainly had a sense of humor.

August drove toward the light, scanning for her sister and brother-in-law. The least she could do was drop them off, keep Joan safe by her side for the duration of the appointment, then pick them up, neither of them in any fit position to drive. With Derek gone, the house had been deathly quiet while she watched Joan.

"I need a motherfucking medical fucking doctor to look me in the eye and tell me my daughter going to be just fine," Miriam had said that morning, bleary-eyed and half-comatose at the breakfast nook. August had never heard her sister curse. Never before heard this kind of flatness in her voice. Devoid of life. Joan, all the while, had attached herself to her mother's hip like a blood tick.

August brought the Caddy to a complete stop outside the entrance, engine idling. She scanned the horizon. A row of hickory trees graced the western side of the hospital in a neat line.

She caught sight of her sister coming from a smaller, side entrance to the west of the main doors. It was hard to miss her— Miriam was steady approaching her due date. She was following Jax up to where the sidewalk met the pavement. August signaled right. She eased the car into first and made her way across the parking lot.

Jax turned then, not toward August—he hadn't seen her car yet—but back toward Miriam. In a moment, she had caught up with him. He was saying something August couldn't make out. She squinted in the morning light, cursing herself for having left her sunglasses on the goddamn kitchen table at home. The sun was blinding, reflecting off the trees with gold brilliance.

She shifted the car into second and pressed on the gas a bit. She'd never liked the damn Yankee much no way, and she didn't like the way he was gesturing at her sister now.

She was nearly there. Then—a quick movement. And Joan started screaming, a terrible, desperate sound. August's foot slipped off the clutch and she stalled out the car.

Jax's right arm was outstretched as if he were reaching for an Olympic torch. Except, instead, his hand was clenched hard around her sister's neck. And he was squeezing it. August saw her sister's feet kick out. The nigga was lifting her off the ground!

"God's"—and August uttered the same exact curse she had used when she found her mother dead in the garden—"cunt!" She fumbled with the ignition. Tried to start the car again, but because God was an angry one, it stalled for a second time. "Fuck!" August screamed.

Jax was still choking her sister.

"Fuck this," August declared, unstrapping her seat belt. She left the driver's-side door wide open. Keys still in the ignition, she sprinted toward them. She could see that Miriam had her hands over Jax's in an attempt to pry his fingers loose.

A few feet away, she realized she may be tall, just a hair shy of Jax, but she didn't weigh nearly enough to punch this man in the face, and it feel anything more than a slap. But Jax had his back to her. She could tackle him. Use the weight of her running to propel her human basketball of a self into him.

And she did just that. Shoved her body into Jax's back with everything she had.

Jax fell.

So did Miriam.

But August was there to catch her, break her fall. She allowed herself to fall to the ground, and let her sister topple over her. She made sure her sister's midsection was protected, bracing her hands to receive the full weight of Miriam and the baby.

How she had catapulted her frame to both subdue Jax and save her sister, August would never truly know. But she wouldn't thank God for it. Not a chance. He had allowed all this to happen, August figured as she lay on the cool asphalt, her sister on top of her, heaving and gasping for breath. Because what kind of God lets an auntie leave her screaming niece in a car?

What kind of God would make a Black woman choose a thing like that?

What kind of God would allow her sister to stay with a man like this?

Later that night, Miriam calmly explained to August that Jax was her husband. That he had never done this before. That he would get better. They all would. The doctor had said Joan wouldn't remember her rape. Maybe she wouldn't even remember Derek. This visit. They would all recover from this. Jax hadn't been himself. The stress of it all. The shock. The shame. "Men, you know?"

August heard and knew none of it. Knew only that God was an angry one. So were all the men she knew. August was sick with it. The whole mess.

Later that night, in the lonely quiet of the dark house, after everyone else had gone to bed, August couldn't stop hearing Joan's screams. Echoing through the parking lot, projected out the open driver's-side door of the Coupe de Ville.

That Joan. August needed for that white doctor to be right— maybe she wouldn't remember this. Any of it. Maybe she wouldn't even remember being left in the car.

The sound of Joan's screams rang in August's memory. She took the bottle of whiskey down from the kitchen shelf and drank until she couldn't hear anything but her promise to herself—*that girl ever asks you for anything, anything at all, you give it.*

CHAPTER 10

Joan

1995

After dinner our first night in our Memphis house, Mama brought me and Mya to the quilting room. The back part of the house was split into two wings—east and west, with a long hallway connecting the two. It met in the middle with the bathroom Mama had cleaned me up in earlier that day. The dark hallway looked vaguely familiar. I threw my head to the left and made a promise to myself that I would never go farther than that connecting bathroom. I would never go to Derek's wing of the house.

Mama led us right down the hallway, where there were two rooms—the quilting room on the left and the bedroom my mother would sleep in on the right. When Mama opened the door, I saw large quilts, big enough to cover our two twin beds twice over, hanging from the walls of the blue-wallpapered room. The room was lined with them. Farther inside, I saw a small anteroom in a corner with a curtain that half-concealed a massive bronze Singer machine, complete with foot pedals.

Mya ran to the bed underneath a grand marigold-yellow quilt fitted with a blue diamond as its center eye. This left me with the bed closest to the bay window, the bed underneath the emerald-green quilt in the Tree of Life pattern. It was our family tree, branching out in beautiful leaves with names sewn into them; I saw "Hazel," "Della," "Myron," and names I didn't know, like "Sarah" and "Clyde" and "Arletha."

My mama held my hand and used our grip to motion at the Tree of Life quilt. "You see your middle name, Joan? You were named after your great-grandmother Della, who made this quilt."

Mya had climbed up on her twin bed and jumped on it, testing its bounciness. "I like it here!" she exclaimed between jumps.

"Your Grandmommy Hazel made some of these, too," Mama said. "That yellow one, over My. She refused to buy a sewing machine. She made them, all of these, by hand. She'd say, 'What slave woman had a sewing machine?' and she'd go back to stitching." She got a hitch in her voice whenever she spoke of her mother.

"Thank." Mya jumped. "You." Jump. "Ancestors." Another jump. "For picking cotton." Jump. "So we don't have to!"

"My, I'm about to make you go pick a switch if you don't get down from that bed."

We both knew this threat was a joke. Mama never hit us. Even when it was warranted—like when we broke her set of jade elephants playing with them like army men—her big eyes would get so wet and sad that Mya and I would apologize right away. Maybe she knew we overheard all those fights with Daddy. Maybe she knew there was only so much little girls could handle.

A quilt of mesmerizing geometric pale-blue squares hung above a chestnut chest. Mama nodded toward it. "She made that one for you, Joan. Started it when I called and told her I was pregnant. My—I swear. You best stop jumping on that bed!"

Later that night, tucked underneath piles of quilts and blankets, Mya and I heard the muted voices of Mama and Auntie August. It came in waves, their laughter. Then pauses of long silence. A shout. A bottle banging on a countertop. More laughter. Someone softly sobbing.

Even though the room had two beds, Mya had left hers to snuggle up to me in mine, something she did whenever she was scared but didn't want to say. Wolf was too large to fit on the twin with Mya and me already sharing it—though, Lord knows, the dog had tried. She had lain down on top of us, an eighty-pound weighted blanket of fur, and begun licking Mya's face.

"Wolf, stop," Mya said, pushing Wolf's massive head away from hers.

"Wolf, down," I commanded.

Wolf whimpered in response but obeyed. She curled herself into a ball and slept on the floor as close as she could get to the bed.

"Your forehead is so big," Mya said. She tapped her forefinger on my forehead like sending out a line of Morse code. "It's like a fivehead."

I pinched her as hard as I could. "Shut up and go to sleep."

"It's just like Daddy's forehead."

I kicked her, not too hard, underneath the covers. "Go to sleep," I shushed her.

"You look like Daddy, but I look like Mom, so I'm the pretty one." My brow arched and I laughed. "Is that right?" I asked.

"Yeah."

"That's fine by me. I'm the smart one."

Mya twisted in the covers, taking most of the blankets with her. "Sometimes." She paused. "You are *kind of* smart." She took her sweet time saying "kind of."

"God, I want a brother."

"You think we'll see him again?"

"Who?" I asked.

"I thought you were the smart one!" Mya's voice was sing-songy, mocking.

I didn't want to think about Daddy. Daddy: the violent villain.

And yet, I missed him like a limb. Missed even the smell of his hands. Shoe polish for his military boots he'd polish every night, and cigarettes. Those Kools.

"We should go exploring tomorrow," I said, changing the subject.

A sudden boom shocked us all. Wolf was up on all fours in less than a second, hairs raised from the back of her neck to her tail. She growled low.

Mya grabbed my arm, dug in with her nails and shook it. "What was that?" she hissed. She had always been afraid of storms. Howls of wind would send her running to Mama's lap or Wolf's mane.

Mama and Auntie August's voices stopped for a moment, then resumed.

"Shh, it's not a storm," I said to Wolf.

"I don't like it here no more," Mya said. "I changed my mind." Then: "What the boy do to you?"

"Nothing."

"You won't tell me?"

"I won't."

"You will." A pause. Wolf settled back down next to us. "I'll kill him if you want."

"My!" I said.

"I can. Sneak into his room when he's sleeping. Whack him in the head with a pot."

I laughed. Mya giggled. Elbowed me hard in the ribs. I pushed her back, gently.

We lay there for a moment, quiet. Turning toward her, I said, "Don't you ever go in that boy's room. Do you understand me? Not for anything." I tried to sound as stern, as serious, as possible. Mya had to know that she could never, for any reason, ever, be alone with that boy.

Mya's eyes reminded me of the deer we saw back at that rest stop: wide and wondering.

"Do you hear me?" I asked. "My. This is important."

"Yes," she said, echoing back my serious tone.

"Good. Now scoot over. I can't sleep with you sweating all over me."

"Well, *I* can't sleep with your forehead being so shiny and bright," Mya teased. "It's like the moon."

"Just think of it like that darn nightlight you're so obsessed with," I said. "Really, you should be thanking me."

In the morning, the kitchen smelled like home—like flour and butter and bacon frying. Mya and I watched our mom and our aunt getting breakfast ready. It was eerie; they moved the same. The motions of their hands, their hips—they even flicked their wrists the same way when tossing a tomato slice into batter. Auntie August was just the taller, darker version of Mama. It was all a bit bewildering.

I had always been the dark one. Mya was an exact clone of Mama. Skin the same shade as butter pecan ice cream. They were bright. Their hair obeyed under flat iron or pressing comb or hair dryer. Mine did not. My hair was a thick forest of unruly curls. It did not listen to comb, nor to my prayers to God. Both Mya and Mama were small, petite slips of women. I was taller than Mya because I was three years older, but I likely would always be taller. Everything about my body was long: my legs, my arms. When Mya was mad at me, she'd call me the Scarecrow from *The Wizard of Oz*. And my dark skin—Mama never treated me different from Mya because of it, bless God. But she didn't have to. The neighbors did. My teachers. Girls, Black and white, on base. The people who worked at the grocery store. The parents handing me slightly smaller handfuls of Halloween candy. All those confused double takes, the outright stares. The pity behind their prolonged looks came next. Then the disgust.

And now it came with such clarity, watching my Auntie August drop green tomatoes into sizzling hot grease, that I took after my aunt. And she was a vision. Her skin was the color of late evening. I imagined drawing her. I wanted to get the length of her limbs just right, the curve of a high cheekbone. I wanted to put her on paper. Have her live there. Proof of dark beauty. I wanted the world to see and to be ashamed.

She started humming over the hot stove. Her voice, even softly humming a tune, sounded like a church bell ringing. My mom didn't know, but Mya and I had stayed up late one night watching *The Color Purple*. If Auntie August wasn't Shug Avery herself . . .

I didn't know where Derek was, and I didn't ask. Likely, still sleeping.

As we ate, Mama said, "Y'all girls take this pie down to Stanley's when you're done. It's just down the street; you can't miss it." She wore an apron over her housedress, and her hair was still piled high in rollers. She was covered in flour. She set a lemon meringue pie down in front of us. It took everything in me not to stick a finger deep in its center and bring its sweetness up to my mouth.

"Take Wolf with you," she went on. "She needs a good walk. And you tell Mr. Koplo it's from me."

"Girl, Stanley done died," Auntie August said. My aunt stood over the stove, tossing the last of the fried green tomatoes back and forth in bacon grease, not taking her eyes off the pan.

"No!" Mama crossed herself, then pressed the cross at the end of her gold rosary to her lips.

"Same month as Mama," Auntie August said. "Ain't that something? But his son run it now. Good stock. Look just like him." She flipped a green tomato over in the skillet.

"Why didn't you tell me!" Mama shouted.

"Girl, you was eight months pregnant. Mama had just died. Wasn't that enough hell?"

Mama sighed, turned to us. "Well, take it down to Stanley's anyway and say it from the North family, and hopefully, his son will know why," she said.

"I want to eat it," Mya said.

August laughed.

"I made us our own pie," Mama said.

Mama's pies had been famous back on base. She'd pass them out as Christmas gifts to all the neighbors, our teachers, the mailman. During the holidays or any one of mine or Mya's birthdays, our kitchen counter became caked with flour and meringue and branches of blackberries for the cobblers.

"Why?" I asked.

"Why she'd make us a pie? Are you crazy? They're delicious," Mya said, hitting me on the shoulder.

"No," I said. "Why we got to *deliver* a pie?"

Mama sighed. I could tell she wanted us out of that kitchen.

"Because that family done your mama's daddy a good deed back in the day," August said.

"What do you mean 'your *mama's* daddy'?" I asked.

"If y'all don't get out of this kitchen," Mama said.

Mya slid out from the booth and attempted to balance the pie on the top of her head.

"August, get my children before I do."

My aunt turned from the stove to see Mya's balancing act. "Well, at least the oldest got some sense," she said, and returned to cooking.

"Mya, if you drop that pie I spent all morning on . . ." Mama warned, ushering us out of the kitchen. I could hear in her voice that she was trying to conceal a smile. Wolf was already by the door, tail thumping against the Persian rug.

"Mother, hush. You raised us right," Mya said in a strikingly accurate British accent, pie still balanced atop her head.

Mama opened the front door for us, shaking her head.

Wolf bolted out toward the two calico cats perched on the porch steps.

"Don't burn my city down," Mama called out when we reached the sidewalk.

"It's *our* city now!" Mya shouted back in that same British accent.

"Where the hell did you learn that?" I whispered, then made

the sign of the cross. I was convinced that if I crossed myself whenever I cursed, it would cancel out any sin.

Mya turned sharply, almost dropping the pie. "*Mary Poppins!* How can you—? Don't you remem— You sat right next to me and watched it, child!"

I rolled my eyes. My mom had been right; we could see the butcher's shop from the sidewalk in front of the house, on the corner of the next intersection. If we turned to our right, we'd be there in a few minutes and back. But if we turned to our left . . .

Mya and I exchanged knowing looks.

"Right then, old chap, hold this," Mya said as she handed me the pie. She whistled—something I'd never learned to do—and Wolf left the cats she had chased up a pecan tree and came to us.

"We still got to deliver it," I said.

"Yes, yes, hush hush, old sport," Mya said and attached the leash to Wolf's collar.

At the end of our street, in the opposite direction of Stanley's, where it dead-ended into blackberry bush, there was an old pink house. It was the largest on the street, bigger even than our home in Camp Lejeune, but the oldest by far. The crumbling Southern plantation leaned heavy on its foundation, like a Black woman exhausted from a day of picking cotton. It was pink—or it had been when the house had been built, likely hundreds of years ago. Now the pink had faded to a dull mauve, cracking and bubbling at the base of every column on a porch that wrapped around the house. Originally painted white, the porch, too, was peeling and faded. A hawk's nest was perched on an upstairs windowsill.

Mya whistled in wonder as we approached. I felt like I was in some ancient Southern tableau and that, at any moment, a ghostly Confederate general would appear on the porch steps, smoking a cigar and declaring that the damned nigger-loving Yankees would be licked by Christmas.

Instead, a woman the color of the muddy Mississippi River's banks sat on the porch steps. Her long locs were piled atop her head and wrapped in an intricate kente cloth. She wore a flowing blue dress as faded as her house. Twin wicker baskets rested on a lower step in front of the woman. As we walked closer, I could see the baskets were full of greens. The woman took long-stemmed legumes, snapped the ends off in a quick motion, and threw the pieces into their respective baskets.

As soon as I saw them, I knew I had to sketch her hands. They were exquisite. Her long, dark-brown fingers captivated me, entwined as they were in a fluid dance with the green beans. I couldn't tell her age—she looked both young and ancient at the same time—but it was obvious, from her dark skin reflecting the morning light, that she was beautiful. *Maybe Memphis won't be so bad after all,* I thought. *All these dark-skinned women around me. So much to sketch. So many colors to paint.*

We stopped near the bottom of the steps, and Wolf sat down, almost as tall as Mya, even when sitting. Hands are the hardest thing to draw. But this woman's hands, with their ancient veins and hardened knuckles—I knew her hands would be my *Mona Lisa,* Cezanne's *Oranges,* Monet's *Water Lilies,* if I could get them just right.

"You two Miriam's girls?" Her voice was pure Memphis. It sounded like the gunshot we heard the night before—sharp and yet slow, echoing far into the darkness of that night.

"How do you know who we are?" Mya asked.

The woman seemed surprised. "Y'all Norths all look the same. Hasn't anyone ever told you that before?"

"I'll give you this here pie if you let me come and draw you," I said without thinking.

"Joanie!" Mya exclaimed. She pulled my arm, and I about near dropped the lemon meringue.

"Hush," I whispered.

The woman chuckled and tossed another broken bean into her basket. "No need for all that. Why don't you pick some blackberries 'round back and bring me back a cobbler? Draw me all you want if I get some."

"Them your blackberry bushes?" I asked. I motioned with my head toward the left of her house, where the street dead-ended.

"I reckon so," she said, "and yours now if you bring me some of your mama's cobbler." She paused, threw a bean in a basket, and said, "Why you want to draw me anyway?"

"I like your hands."

"My hands?" The woman gestured with her right, holding a long green bean. "These things? Well now, I suppose they *are* rather magical."

"When you snap, can you make my toys dance?" Mya asked.

"What now, honey?"

"Mary Poppins can. And she's *real* magic," Mya said.

I pinched Mya's arm. "Don't be rude," I said, twisting her skin.

"No, your sister is right. Gotta prove it. My magic," she said.

"Can you make a magic carpet so we can fly? Or can you make it nighttime right now?" Mya shrugged off my pinch, jumping up and down in anticipation of the magic she was about to witness.

The woman rose from her seat on her porch steps. She brushed off the remaining beans that stuck to the front of her dress.

Mya and I, and even Wolf, stepped back a bit. I imagined the woman would fling wide her arms, throw back her head, and chant some nonsense that would turn the sky instantly black. Instead, she stood there on her front steps and stared at me for a long time. It felt like I was looking at a solar eclipse—I knew I shouldn't face it head-on, but I wanted to see the phenomenon through.

"Bury something of that boy's," she said.

My stomach lurched. There was no question she meant Derek. But how, *what*, did she know?

"Hair works best. A comb. Bury it deep in red earth. Do this at midnight. Tell no one."

"And then?" I asked, trying to sound brave. "What happens then?"

The old woman smiled. "Then you'll know Miss Dawn *real* magic."

Two years after I stole Derek's black comb from our one shared bathroom and buried it deep in the backyard while Mya stood over me holding the flashlight and chanting Hail Marys, two years to the day after my hands were caked in fertile Memphis clay, that boy was in jail.

CHAPTER 11

August

1995

August's shop was full that Friday. In the far back of the split-level house, off the kitchen, there was a door that opened onto a sunken basement that, with three small steps down, led into August's beauty salon. August had taken old record covers and decorated the walls with the faces of Diana Ross, the Jackson 5, Stevie Wonder, Earth Wind & Fire. Lined against the west wall was a large basin sink for the shampooing and, in front of it, four black leather chairs with reclining backs. These seats were always, always full. Miriam could bake, but August could style. Cut, curl, condition, cornrow—she had a gift. Could make the most tore-up, ashy woman in North Memphis come out looking like Miss Diana Ross in the flesh.

A screened-in back patio attached to the basement also served as the shop's waiting room. A few seats were stationed there as well for the women sitting underneath gigantic astronaut helmet hair dryers, waiting for their sets to dry. The back screen door served as the shop's entrance, so the women wouldn't have to come through the main house to get to it. A sign above the screen door, lettered in a frank black font, read, AUGUST'S, and underneath, NO CHILDREN, NO MEN, & WE EAT WHITE FOLK HERE.

Damn, August thought as her fingers softly kneaded a customer's damp hair. *Should I change the sign?* Mya flitted in and out the corner of August's eye. It had been two weeks since they arrived, but the girl had figured out how to work the jukebox in the corner the first time she entered the shop. August heard the unmistakable opening chords of Aretha's "Respect."

Well, at least the girl's got taste, she thought. *How the hell we survive off my shop money is anybody's guess. Mya eats like a man. Shit, I hope Meer comes up with something, and quick.*

She had two women waiting underneath dryers; the one she was shampooing that moment; Jade and her regular press 'n' curl waiting for her on the settee; and she knew Miss Dawn would be in any moment. August did okay for herself and Derek with the shop money, but there had been months when bills had been paid late or the lights turned off. She qualified but had refused to go on food stamps. Pride. She almost laughed out loud now. Counting Wolf, her household had grown by three humans and one canine in a single morning.

"That feels good."

The woman underneath August brought her back to reality. August smiled. She knew her shop was a blessing. The women of North Memphis knew this, too, and came to the shop in droves. August's only day off was Sunday. She'd enter the kitchen on a Saturday night, far past midnight, sink into the plush kitchen bench, and fall asleep there. Not even make it down the hall to her bedroom.

But August could not help but think about what she'd given up. Her dreams of going to college, perhaps even following and furthering her mother's dream of having a doctor in the family. Sure, she had gotten pregnant, and early. Most girls in Memphis did. But she knew, just knew she could have done it. Gone to Rhodes, finished. Gotten her degree. Lived. Provided for her son.

Her son—who, years before, had put an abrupt stop to August's college plans. The very night of Joan's rape, Children's Protective Services had shown up to the house on Locust, and an officer had pried Derek from August's arms while she frantically bit at him. Her son. Whom she'd lost twice now—first, for a month after Joan's rape, and again, two years later, when he'd broken a classmate's arm. He'd been returned after only six months that time, because August had quit Rhodes and proven to CPS that, with her hair salon, she'd be home full-time to watch him.

August was suddenly aware that Mya, all seven years of her, had straddled the jukebox in her shop like it was one of those penny mechanical horses in front of Piggly Wiggly and was singing along to Aretha. Comb in her hand to mimic a microphone.

"Joa-nie!" August called out over Aretha's voice. "Get your sister!"

Mya bellowed out Aretha's famous lines.

They may have been poor—the lights may have been turned off in the middle of a dinner of turnip greens and pigs' feet; Miriam's two girls sent to hunt for candles, crawling like cockroaches in the darkness—but they were North women. They laughed long and loud whenever they could. They laughed often. They let their hair down in August's shop.

Miriam and her girls, running from a broken man who beat Miriam in order to feel whole. Yes, August was relieved her sister had finally left before Jax killed her. But what now? After that first dinner, Joan refused to speak to Derek at all, wouldn't even acknowledge his presence most times. It made for awkward, sometimes silent family dinners. But then Mya would blurt out something funny—"sis-boom-bah! The sound a sheep makes when it explodes!"—and even Joan would put a hand up to her face or her stomach to stop herself from giggling. At least that: the laughter. *At least that,* August thought.

August salved conditioner into the woman's hair, wrapped her head expertly in a towel, and told her to go sit out on the porch under a dryer for twenty minutes.

"My head's a hornet's nest, dear chile, help it."

Wiping her hands on a towel, August heard Miss Dawn before she saw her. The music, now James Brown's "Please Please Please," must have muted the small bell over the door.

Miss Dawn was August's favorite customer. She lived just down the street, in a home Joan and Mya had christened "Jumanji." A huge willow grew right inside it, sprouting from the foundation itself.

Miss Dawn would come in early every Friday afternoon promptly at one o'clock, before the masses of Black women descended upon the shop. She'd sit for her standard twist and leave the shop with her locs done up in an elegant sweep, calling out to Miriam's girls, "Y'all best have boyfriends next time I see y'all," which would send blushing Joan and Mya into uncontrollable shrieks of joy.

"Why, Miss Dawn," August said, her arms outstretched to embrace the elderly woman, "you early today."

"I was bored, chile, up in that house, bored to death," Miss Dawn said, kissing August lightly on the cheek.

"Might as well come here see what y'all up to . . ." Miss Dawn paused.

Mya, somehow now off the jukebox, was using a broom to simulate James Brown convulsing onstage at the Apollo, belting out his beloved blockbuster hit. Joan played backup and mimicked fanning her sister.

". . . and them girls," Miss Dawn continued with a raised eyebrow.

August shrugged her shoulders and shook her head. "Life," she said.

"Life," Miss Dawn agreed.

Joan was suddenly in front of them, her eager brown eyes beaming up at Miss Dawn's ancient ones. Mya was still acting out James Brown moves to the delight of the other women in the shop, Miss Jade fanning her with an old church program.

"I would so very much like to show you my latest sketches," Joan said. Then she curtsied.

"Girl, you think Miss Dawn a queen or something?" August said, taken aback but not unamused.

"Yes," Joan said seriously, no hint of shame or embarrassment in her voice. "Yes, I do, Auntie."

Miss Dawn's arms were like the branches of the tree that grew up the middle of her home—strong and sinewy, ancient and elegant, long and brown. She laid one long one across Joan's shoulder, pulled her close, and leaned down so that their foreheads were touching in a quiet, private embrace.

"Well, hell," August said. "I've known you my whole life, and that ain't how we say our good mornings."

"You hush. Me and this girl got some scheming to do. Fetch me those drawings, chile. I'd like to see," Miss Dawn said.

Joan was gone in a flash, her footsteps echoing down the house's long, tangled corridors.

Miss Jade, another loyal client, chuckled at the exchange as she sat waiting in a 1950s-vintage fainting chair for a silk press. Jade had been with August since her shop opened. She had been a friend of her mother's, had helped raise Miriam. She'd run the numbers game in the neighborhood since there had been a neighborhood, it seemed. Always wore a blond mink coat worth a small fortune. Carried a small pistol in her Coach purse. Pearl-handled. Miss Jade looked like anyone's worried aunt or pushy grandmother. Always wanted her press 'n' curl. Or a set. Never deviating. But August had refused outright to put a relaxer in Miss Jade's hair. August was wise. The woman's hair had grown an entire foot since August had started working her magic.

August had tried to get Miriam to place a number with Miss Jade a week back, when they had sat drunk at the kitchen table.

"Are you insane?" Miriam was wide-eyed. "We're broke."

August had laughed, smacked her hand down on the table. The giggles had overtaken her. It was hard for her to breathe. But she choked out, "Meer, you Catholic, but you still a nigga!"

"It's time for bed, sister."

"Um, excuse me, Miss August," a soprano voice said, stepping in from the back porch, "but I been waiting out here thirty minutes. You know I got a date tonight."

Mika was August's least-favorite customer, but money was money. And August wasn't so high and mighty that she wouldn't take Mika's. Shit, she needed it now more than ever. A young thing, not more than thirty, Mika would strut into the shop, head bandaged in a silk Gucci scarf, heels on the tiled floor making the same sound as her long acrylic nails on the linoleum counters. And the sound of her voice. God! August didn't know a Black woman could sound so like a white one.

Yes, Lord knows, August needed the money from Mika's booked weave appointment, but it took all her strength not to walk out the screen door onto the patio and shake Mika like the crybaby she was. Instead, she asked loudly, "Why? Ain't it with a white man?"

The shop roared. Broke out into applause and laughter that lasted a long time. Reminded August of *Showtime at the Apollo*.

"Tell it, August," a middle-aged woman shouted from underneath a dryer, waving a pink handkerchief in the air to emphasize her point.

"Lord have mercy," Miss Jade said.

"I was with a white man once," Miss Dawn said, stunning everyone in the shop. "Oh yes, chile, let me tell you. I killed him many years ago."

If the shop had erupted before, this was the next great aftershock. Every woman in that shop was clutching herself in laughter. Even Mika cracked a stubborn smile.

Jade said from the settee, "Y'all ain't right up in here."

Just then, Joan came rushing back, her arm slung around her sketchbook. August swore she hardly saw the girl long without it.

"No, no, I'm coming, Mika. Give me a moment, hun," August shouted over the uproar.

But the shop wasn't done with Mika yet.

"When he unveils that tiny sauerkraut, don't you just want to bite it off?" a tall, bright woman in line to be shampooed asked loud, hair this way and that.

The framed record covers on the walls shook with the laughter. Laughter that was, in and of itself, Black. Laughter that could break glass. Laughter that could uplift a family. A cacophony of Black female joy in a language private to them.

Joan settled into a seat next to Miss Dawn, her sketch pad open.

August patted Miss Dawn's shoulder. "I'll let you two ladies get to it. Duty calls," she whispered, then rolled her eyes in Mika's direction.

Right as August turned to Mika, for the smallest of seconds, out the corner of her eye, she saw herself: Her own face was drawn in intricate penciled detail in Joan's sketchbook.

She was taken aback—by the image of herself, so lifelike, and by the fact that a ten-year-old had drawn it. *She has the gift*, August considered. Like how she herself had the gift of song. *Isn't that something? How the gifts can travel.*

August loved it all. The chaos. Mya jumping onto furniture like all of it was some horse to mount. Even the poverty, the uncertainty. What had happened and what may yet happen between Derek and Joan, she would worry about another day.

Only a few remnants of the laughter remained, now dwindling giggles and suppressed glee, like a symphony in diminuendo. Eventually, a soft quiet descended over the crowded shop. Women went back to reading their *Essence*s, their *Jet*s, their novels. Miss Jade checked the time on her watch. Even the girls settled down, bored, finally, with the jukebox. August saw Joan had finally put down her sketchbook in order to help her sister down from the jukebox.

August began to hum, slow and deep, matching the pitch of laughter that still echoed in her ears. Her voice grew louder, syllables forming words. A song as familiar to the women in the little shop as daughters are to mothers, sisters to sisters. Mya, without having to be told, paused the music coming from the jukebox. Miss Jade joined in. So did Mya. Miss Dawn. Joan. All of the women in the shop. August felt she knew the words better than she knew herself, most times. And when she hit that high note—that high C—even Mika nodded her roller-adorned head and sang along.

Maybe it was the fact that they were all together again—North women underneath one roof. Maybe it was seeing Joan's drawing and the rush of love and protection that had welled up in her in that moment. Wanting Joan to always cherish her gift made her want to honor her own. August couldn't rightly explain it herself, but she figured her mother would have been right proud. So, maybe she did it for her.

How sweet the sound that saved a wretch like me.

Part II

CHAPTER 12

Joan

1997

The honk of a car horn sounded in the driveway, startling us all. Auntie August lurched forward with a start, and coffee spilled from her cup. Mya had been in between bites of cheesy grits but paused with her spoon midway to her mouth. I sat next to her with my sketchbook in my lap, and my pencil swerved on the page. Derek had one hand on the refrigerator door and another holding a pint of buttermilk.

Two years. It had been two years since my mom, Mya, Wolf, and I had filed into our white Chevy Astro van filled with all we had—each other. We arrived at Grandma Hazel's house exhausted, hungry, AC broken, hair untamed, remembering every sin a Black man had committed against us.

My mom was still in the bath. From my spot in the kitchen booth, I could hear the water running. She would soon start her day by rushing off to class with a half-eaten bagel stuffed in her mouth. She had gotten into Rhodes College, the same college and the same nursing program her mother had attended. Mya, Mom, and I would sit at the kitchen table on Sunday evenings and finish our respective homework. Mama had even snagged a part-time job at the college library, shelving periodicals and sorting microfiche far past the library's closing hours. It wasn't much, but it was something. I had never seen my mom so busy and so content.

The morning had been a typical one. I had been sketching the vase of flowers on the kitchen table, but my mind was elsewhere. It was summer vacation, and I planned to spend mine drawing as much as possible. In the two years since we moved to Memphis, even my hate for Derek could not blind me from the beauty of my new city, my new home. I had never seen summers so lush and green, never been this hot before in my life. Back at Camp Lejeune, we had the cool of the Atlantic that touched our brows, chilled our sweat even in the midday. Here, the ladies in Douglass did not leave the house without a paper hand fan with a church program printed on the back. We climbed trees to escape the heat—me, Mya, and the cats. Too hot for the stone of the porch, the cats had moved to the magnolia in front, the plum tree on the side, and lounged sleepily from branches, and we followed.

I wanted to paint it all. The church fans, every color of the rainbow. The women of all shades who had come to Auntie August's shop not for their usual presses, but for the relief of cornrows and Bantu knots and box braids. I wanted to draw Mya and the cats in the green trees.

Now that school was out and there was no math homework for Mama to hound me about, my goal for the summer was to compile a series of sketches of women from the neighborhood I had grown to love. My weekly sessions on Miss Dawn's porch had added to my skills as an artist. I had pages and pages of her hands moving this way and that. Only if the weather would allow, the heat being near-suffocating, I'd take a whole easel and sit out there for hours with her. Seemed as if we could talk even Wolf's ears off. Often, Wolf would place her huge head in my lap and sleep like that.

Drawing was my refuge. I could escape into my sketchbook. I didn't see much of Derek because I chose not to. Yes, he was there in the house living with me. But I behaved as if he were a house cat I didn't much like and who did not much like me. If he entered a room, I left it. If he spoke to me—rare—I hissed back. There had been more than a few Mexican standoffs in our kitchen. Always soundless. Dinners, the one meal all five of us shared together, were tense and awkward. My stomach twisting so that I'd lose my appetite. Most nights, I'd ask to leave the table and retreat to the front porch, bringing my plate of food with me. It was hell batting off the cats and the flies and the bees and the birds that all seemed to want what was on my plate: mashed potatoes with gravy, turnip greens, candied yams, neck bones smothered in hot sauce. I'd swat them all away and scoop quick mouthfuls as I brought out my sketchbook, rested it on my knees, and began to do what I loved most. If I concentrated on the sketch at hand, Derek would fade into the background of my life.

The car in our driveway honked again, longer this time.

"Nigga, go," I said.

"Hear, hear," Mya said, her British inflection slightly muffled through her mouthful of grits. But behind Mya's humor, her eyes were ice cold. She'd asked me that first night we arrived, and not one time since, what had happened between me and Derek. She didn't need to know the details to know whose side she was on. Mya could annoy the shit out of me the way only younger sisters can. Her constant jokes. Always checking my forehead. The way she looked over my shoulder while I was doing geometry homework and shouted out the correct answers in her Mary Poppins voice before I got even halfway through understanding the question. But she'd fight Satan for me, tiny fists balled up and unafraid.

"Joan," Auntie August said with a sigh. She sounded tired. The coffee had spilled down the front of her robe, and she reached for a paper towel.

Derek took one long pull from the pint of buttermilk and then placed it back and closed the refrigerator door.

"Goddamnit, Derek, don't go," Auntie August said.

During the school year, boys with pistols bulging from the back of their jean waistbands had showed up at our doorstep each morning promptly at seven-thirty to escort me, Mya, and Derek, their young new recruit, to the Douglass High School. The middle school and elementary were located just a block away. It had become the most dangerous block in North Memphis. The night before we first went to our new school two years ago, Auntie August had sat me and Mya down while Mama was in the shower and told us frankly that in the time since Mama had up and left with our Yankee father, the Douglass Park 92 Bishops had controlled our new neighborhood and the surrounding hoods of North Memphis: Douglass, Chelsea, New Chicago. I had a feeling Auntie wanted to add "no good" to her description of Daddy, but she stopped short. She sucked on a Kool and continued explaining calmly that we should never wear red, never wear blue. Stick to neutrals. Always. An affiliate of the Bloods, the Douglass Park Bishops wore red bandanas hanging off their back pockets or tied around still-growing biceps. They shot people, she said. Children. Asleep in their beds.

Mama would sometimes say Memphis had changed since she was last here. There were just as many abandoned lots, payday loan sharks, and liquor stores as churches now, peppering the city where once had stood pillars and monuments of Blackness— Clayborn Temple, Sun Records, the Lorraine Motel. I'd overheard Auntie August telling Mama that most white folk had fled to the countryside in the early part of the decade, to the cotton fields of Shelby County and its white-only schools. Sometimes I thought the gangs were a blessing in a way. Made Memphis Black. Utterly. Black men and women ran these streets without a white person in sight—a relief. If Memphis were alive, gangs would be both her red and white blood cells—killing and healing and repeating.

Earlier that spring, Kings Gate Mafia, a subset of the Crips, crept north and rolled on Derek's new boss, Slim. Everyone in the neighborhood knew that Slim was high priest of the Douglass

Park Bishops, but even he could not dodge bullets. Slim's house was across the street from ours. Back in May, a black Lincoln had pulled up slow in front of Slim's house, and three almost-boys, barely men, hanging out the windows, AK-47s extended, had shot every living thing inside Slim's one-story midcentury Southern home: Slim, his mama, his grandmama, and a German shepherd that had protected the family and the block for six years. Wolf had played with her.

Once we were sure the bullets had stopped, we'd all gone out on the porch in our pajamas. It was late at night, but even in the moonlight we could see that the pecan tree in Slim's front yard, the one we had climbed and whose nuts we had gorged ourselves on countless times, had been ravaged by the volley of bullets. Auntie August smoked a Kool and drew her kimono around her tighter when the breeze picked up. Mama's hair was tied up in a pink silk bonnet. She twisted her gold rosary in her fingers. Mya wiped sleep out of her eyes with the sleeve of her nightgown. Derek, wearing a long flannel, muttered curse words under his breath. Eventually we heard sirens. Watched the bodies, draped in white sheets, being carried into ambulances. The police cars and ambulances lit up our street in an eerie red glaze. I don't remember any of us saying anything until, finally, I had seen it all—Mama asked my aunt for a cigarette.

Another honk from outside, then a bunch more in rapid succession.

"Nigga, leave already," I said. I knew the car outside, a tan-colored Chevy, belonged to Pumpkin. Knew Derek was likely to run around Memphis with him doing God could only guess.

Derek kissed his mother lightly on the cheek and walked out, but not before calling from the parlor, "You got a smart mouth, girl."

"I got a nice left hook, too," I shouted back.

"Joan!" Auntie August said again.

I looked down at my sketch. The vase of purple violets suddenly looked rotten and pathetic, like bruises overflowing from an urn. Damaged life spilling out of death. I felt hot tears coming on against my will, a burning rage born from utter powerlessness. I closed my sketchbook and got up. Our kitchen table was doing nothing for my art.

I shrugged. "What he going to do to me? Sorry, what *else* he going to do to me?"

"Why won't anybody tell me what he did?" Mya asked and banged one end of her fork down hard on the table.

"Eat your grits," Auntie August said.

"I'm going to Miss Dawn's," I said and as I traced Derek's steps through the parlor and out into the morning light, I thought about curses and combs.

CHAPTER 13

Hazel

1937

Hazel took cautious steps as she made her way to Stanley's. It was only a block way, but not only was the ground like quicksand, but she was also wearing her father's too-big work boots, which made it extra hard to balance. She might be only fifteen, but she imagined that even when she was fifty, the boots wouldn't fit.

The flood that winter had washed away most of Memphis. Old folk in the neighborhood said it was as devastating, as deadly, as the quake that had flattened the Delta city back in 1865. The Mississippi swelled with heavy rainwater, and with one last heavy thunderstorm, the river finally busted, flooding the surrounding tributaries at a rate no one had envisioned—and thus, no one was prepared. Entire neighborhoods and the people who lived in them were swept away in the rising brown waters. In a matter of hours. It was a force of God. The end of days. Families scrambled atop their roofs and held up signs that simply read, SAVE US. And some were saved. Boats usually used for fishing in Wolf Creek were out-fitted to save as many of the thousands of Black folk perched atop their homes in North Memphis as they could.

Hazel's father had taken one of those boats out and never come back. One of the families he'd saved had found her and her mother afterward, wrung their hands as they told how he'd climbed onto their roof to help pass their string of toddlers to the waiting hands in his fishing boat, the floodwaters rising around him. Over his head.

Two months now without her father, the ground was still mostly mud. It gave way so that folk slipped and slid in it, got their cars stuck in the thick of it. Folk got to calling it "Memphis mud." Hazel hadn't wanted to go out into the mess at all, but her mother wanted meat that night—flood or not. And when Della Thomas wanted a thing, she got it.

Della was the best seamstress in Memphis, Black or white. Women would come from all over to sit in her parlor and get fitted for dresses that would stop traffic on Beale, make married men slip off their wedding rings for the night, make women feel like gods.

Hazel took down her mother's appointments for her in a large ledger book, surrounded by rolls of tulle and intricate lace by the yard, and all around the room were fat tomato pincushions stabbed with pins and needles. In a corner of the parlor sat a black Singer as big as a piano, with foot treadles and even the turn-of-the-century spinning wheel on which her mother had learned to make yarn; her mother loved an antique. Della may not have been able to read, but she could guess a woman's corset size just from looking at her. Was a wonder with her seamstress's ruler. Didn't even need to memorize the numbers as she went.

Hazel had grown up helping her mother in the parlor. She'd take payments and fill out the customers' dress orders. She could sit for hours watching Della tighten a corset around a waist or piece together a quilt. Hazel didn't think of her mother as work-ing; she thought of her as an artist creating. She saw the pride with which her mother made her stitches, as tiny as they were, how they became a dress that would be worn and loved and remembered. After the morning appointments, Hazel delivered finished gowns to the large mansions along Poplar and modest print dresses to the mothers along Chelsea, with a quick curtsy and without much conversation exchanged. Hazel loved the bridal appointments in the late afternoons best. The bride would hardly stand still for her fitting, twirling in the silk, admiring herself in the mirror, smiling for no, and yet every, reason. Hazel would sit in silence nearby, attaching floral lace appliqué to the bride's veil. The white brides would eventually notice Hazel with a start and say, *Well, my, I didn't even know a little Negro child was here!* But the Black customers would coo *Little brown church mouse* in a way that made her feel she belonged. It wasn't that Hazel was shy; she was just observant. She preferred watching and learning from her mother in silence rather than interrupting conversation, announcing herself.

With her mother's skills so coveted, Hazel had always had fine things, especially clothes. It wouldn't do to have her sitting in the parlor not looking the part, and besides, it made her feel more adult. She was accustomed to lace pinafores and silk stockings and satin pantaloons—not to the rubber men's work boots her mother had taken out of the closet for her that afternoon before Hazel set out.

"These were your father's," she'd said, holding them up high like they were a pair of prize catfish. "He picked a life's worth of cotton in them," Della huffed, maneuvering one boot onto Hazel's foot. "Come on, girl. Step in them. Push hard. There you go. Step back. Let me look at you."

Hazel had turned fifteen the previous November, and she was both proud of and a bit embarrassed by her thickening body. She found herself stumbling into furniture she previously could easily slip between. Her widening hips had knocked over many a helpless lamp. Her eyes—doe's eyes, like her mother's—were a deep dark brown that could turn emerald in certain lights, in certain euphoric moods. On the cusp of womanhood, she glowed, dark eyes contrasting with the lovely butter pecan color of her skin.

"You look like your daddy," her mother had said, a catch in her voice.

"Really?" Hazel asked.

Her mother looked away. "Now, where's that list you wrote?"

"It's here in my pocket, Mommy." Hazel held up a scrap of paper.

"Get everything on there, every single thing, you hear? And you come back quick," Della had said, pushing Hazel out the door with a gentle shove and her usual forehead kiss.

Hazel maneuvered around pools of water as she made her way to Stanley's. The family-owned deli was a two-story redbrick building on the corner of Chelsea Avenue and Pope Street in the North Memphis neighborhood called Douglass, where Della's family had lived since emancipation.

Stanley's was a staple in the neighborhood. Even though folk called it a deli, people went there to buy most things: fresh okra, fishing hooks and live bait, ice-cream sundaes and freezing-cold Coca-Colas. A long glass case spanned the length of one wall and displayed chicken thighs and beef sausages. A gilded Victrola in the corner was constantly playing the soft moans of Blind Boy Fuller and Bessie Smith and Memphis Minnie. Shelves were stocked with saltwater taffy, tins of sardines in oil, bottles of molasses. A small garden in the back grew tomatoes and okra and muscadine and sweet corn. Stanley could be found either behind the counter or out front, stooped in front of his sign, boasting in chalk that he had the best melons for a mile.

Stanley was white and foreign and Jewish, but he was beloved in their Black neighborhood. Everyone liked him. His deli had a colored section, but the sign was more decorative than anything. The shop was too small to section off, and given that most of his customers were Black, Stanley never did make a fuss about it. Even the old Baptist ladies forgave him his Judaism, unable to resist his beef ribs. No one knew why he'd chosen Memphis or how he'd even heard of it all the way in Germany, yet here he was for going on ten years now. He talked sometimes of a storm brewing in his homeland; perhaps because he was a butcher, he could smell death.

During the crash of '29, Stanley's deli did not go bankrupt. This simple financial fact infuriated white Memphis. They could not understand that smart planning and the sheer fact that humans will always need bread were the reasons Stanley's did not have to shutter. It did not matter; the Klan shuttered it for him. Set fire to the building one night. The next day, all of Douglass, thousands of Black hands, came out to help Stanley rebuild, brick by brick. Even Hazel, just eight years old then, had swept ash from the foundation.

So, when Stanley closed up shop on Friday nights for *his* Sabbath, the neighborhood would fry catfish in their front yards instead. And when Stanley refused to sell pork, the neighborhood did not understand his reasoning, but they did not argue with it. They made the slightly farther walk to another butcher, on Chelsea, for their pigs' feet, hocks, and salt pork without complaint.

"Ah, the quiet rose is here," Stanley said when Hazel pushed open the door of the deli. He stood, tall and slight, in a blood-stained apron behind the glass display case showcasing the chicken gizzards he had just butchered.

Hazel heard music as she reached into her pocket to pull out her grocery list. Memphis Minnie's voice poured forth from the Victrola.

Hazel heard the chorus of Minnie's 'When the Levee Breaks'.

She scoffed. *How fitting*, she thought, wiping her feet on the doormat. She walked to the counter and was holding up her mother's list to Stanley when she paused. A voice, alto, full of vibrato, was singing along to the music. It was the most beautiful thing Hazel had ever heard. It sounded like a man had swallowed a nightingale.

A tall, unknown boy stood at the Victrola. After spending years delivering mended dresses to countless households in North Memphis, Hazel just about knew every face in Douglass. This boy was new, foreign. Hand in his pocket, his back to Hazel, he tapped his foot to the music and sang along in a way that made Hazel forget herself for a moment, forget the grocery list, the many scheduled appointments in her mother's shop. All she wanted to do was stare and listen.

Stanley must have seen the change in Hazel. He smiled knowingly and cocked his head toward the boy. "Go on. Say hello." Stanley's thick German accent made his words seem more like commands than a friendly suggestion.

Hazel's eyes widened, and she sucked in air. Bit her lip and twisted her long gold rosary.

"Go on," Stanley said, gently taking the list from Hazel's hand. "I'll get these things for you."

Hazel watched Stanley start to climb the ladder along his high shelves to retrieve a sack of flour. Watching him felt like watching sap trickle down a maple.

Just as slowly, she turned to the boy and took the full sight of him in. He was the color of indigo. Hazel had never seen somebody that midnight dark before. Her eyes scanned the long length of him. She fingered her rosary as she admired the graceful shape of his head and his long and lean shoulders. She caught glimpses of his face as he turned his head this way and that, eyes closed, singing along. Small flashes of thick lips and high cheekbones and peach fuzz on his chiseled chin. It was hard not to melt there on the spot. Hazel took him in like he was a tall glass of lemonade on the hottest of August days.

Hazel exhaled, steadied herself. Approached. Thought better of it. Withdrew. Took a step back, then another.

Every hair on Hazel's body rose: Her back had hit something, someone. That was unexpected. The deli was small, and she was sure no one else had come in—but who knows? The dark boy, just the sight of him, had mesmerized her. She was caught in his gravity, thrust out of her usual, discreet watchfulness. She hadn't heard the small bell over the front door chime, announcing a new visitor. She hadn't seen the police officer—white as a clam, wide as a fence—push open the door and enter the deli. Hadn't seen him remove his cap and cock his head at the sight of two Negro children in the white section of a Southern establishment.

But she did hear—and jump—when his deep voice rang out over Memphis Minnie's, "Girl, have you lost your ever-loving mind?"

Girl. Hazel tensed. It was instinctive. She knew, without having to turn around, that the man was white—which was just a synonym for a death warrant in the South.

In a flash, the boy had spun on his heel and was on her, tugging at her sleeve, pulling her to him and away from the officer. His eyes—big, dark pools—seemed to plead with hers.

Come to me, his eyes said. *Come to me right this second.*

"Stanley, you let niggers dance up in here?"

At first, Hazel let herself be pulled by the boy. The tug on her sleeve grew more insistent, and she felt herself being led away from the danger. Hazel knew she should keep going, fold into the embrace of this new, dark boy, handsome as the night. Knew he was safety. This boy would be her blessing, her salvation. A minute ago, she would have given anything to have him turn around so she could see him in his full beauty.

But something in Hazel pulled back against her retreat, made her hesitate. It was the same force that swiveled Lot's wife's head around; the same longing, the same nagging desire within Anna Karenina as she watched that train approach, breathless and defiant. Whatever it was, Hazel succumbed to it.

She did something then that was unheard of in Memphis—unheard of anywhere in the South without death following like a shadow. Hazel looked at the white man. Full-on. She twisted her head around and threw her eyes directly at the large white man behind her. Beheld him without bent head or lowered gaze or blinking eye.

He was, indeed, large. His uniform was stretched to its limit around his midsection. His face, clean-shaven. A tuft of curly black hair protruded from his cap.

Hazel's frank stare must have startled the man. She saw him recoil. Saw him reach to his side, unholster his baton.

"Girl, I'm going to ask you again if you've lost what nigger mind God gave you." The police officer started to swing the baton in loose, threatening circles.

There it was again. *Girl.*

Nigger, Hazel did not so much mind. Perhaps because she used it herself, albeit affectionately, with only the closest of girlfriends, albeit without the sharp, hard *r* sound the officer had used. But *girl* had always sent Hazel into a silent rage. Ever since she had noticed at a very young age that white folk used it to address her mother. *Girl, you did a wonder on this lace.* Or *Girl, you got my linens ready?* Della, a grown and determined and brilliant woman, reduced to *that colored girl in North Memphis who makes them fancy dresses.*

The boy pulled her sleeve harder, and Hazel could feel his urgency. But she stood her ground. It took everything in her not to bare fangs. Hiss at the officer. Spit in his face.

Out of the corner of her eye, she saw Stanley put both his feet along the edges of the ladder and slide down it—all ten feet—in a swift, singular second. When he reached the floor, he casually picked up a spare broom that rested against a shelf and slowly approached them.

"Don't mind her," Stanley said, slightly out of breath, in his thick accent.

The boy, with a final tug, pulled Hazel close to him. Her eyes were still locked on the officer, but Hazel felt the fight leaving her as unexpectedly as it had come. The boy's scent was overpowering. He smelled like leather and orange peel.

"I've got you," the boy whispered into Hazel's ear. "I've got you."

Perhaps nothing else would have made Hazel drop her gaze, but she melted at the brown butter of his voice, leaned into him, looked into his eyes instead. His eyes were an entreaty. They simply said: *We need to leave.*

"Stanley, why on earth you got niggers dancing in here? Even got nigger music on. And here I thought the flood was the end of the world."

"They're just kids," Stanley said.

He took a few steps toward the officer, broom in hand. Added, "Her daddy died in the flood."

"Let's go," the boy whispered. His eyes were pleading.

Hazel relented. She nodded her assent.

The boy took her hand, led her toward the door. He made delicate steps, maneuvering around the shop's table and chairs. Putting as much distance between them and the white man as possible.

"The fuck a dead, drowned nigger got to do with the price of tea in China?" the officer said, voice rising. "And where the fuck y'all going?"

The boy did not pause in his long, steady strides to the door. He did not pause when they heard the unforgettable sound of a wooden broom handle hitting bone. They reached the door just as the officer said, bewilderment and contempt in his voice, "And what the fuck do you think *you're* doing?"

The bell over the door chimed as the boy opened the door wide and pushed Hazel through it. "Go!" he shouted.

She ran. Hazel obeyed for the sole reason that she heard the boy's steps right behind her.

Her father's boots made her stumble when she took a hard right on Chelsea. But she continued on, dodging puddles the size of small ponds. She heard the boy's deep breaths behind her, heard his splashes in the muddy water. Hazel kept running.

They ended up at the dead end of Locust Street. It was dark green with heavy southern foliage—bush and bramble, willows and magnolias hundreds of years old grew in a thicket of unkempt brush. Pecan trees lined both sides of the street.

Hazel put her hands on her knees and panted. "I love this house," she said when her voice came to her.

A colossus was before them. Pale pink. Rain and weather and time must have faded the original brilliance of the color. But it was still elegant in its ghostliness—it must have been built long before the Civil War. It leaned slightly on its foundation. White columns tall as trees held up a wraparound porch. Blackberry bushes just beginning to flower graced the north side of the house.

"Are you crazy?" The boy was hunched forward, still catching his breath. "You could've gotten us strung up from a tree."

Hazel stood up straight. She saw beads of sweat trickle down from the boy's temple to a dark crevice in his neck. "Girl," she said.

"What?" He held a hand up to shield his eyes from the sun and squinted.

"He called me 'girl,'" Hazel said. "I don't like that."

The boy's eyes grew wide. They reminded Hazel of a morning glory opening. "*That's* why?" His tone was incredulous. "*That's* why we almost died? Shoot, Stanley just may be dead already."

"Don't say that."

"Why not? Jesus, I heard Memphis women were crazy, but this beat all. That was a *police officer* back there. We could've been killed. And all because you don't like being called 'girl.' Jesus Christ on a cracker."

Hazel crossed her arms, frowned. "You started it," she said.

The boy shook his head. "Now, this is going to be rich."

"With your dancing."

He straightened up, put his hands on his hips, and stared at her. Hazel realized he was a full head taller than her. Looked like there was no end to his growing.

"No one else was in there," he said, shrugging his shoulders. "And I like music."

"You like music. Who don't? We live in Memphis."

"We don't have music like that in Georgia."

"That where you from?"

The boy nodded. "We got here right before the flood. Hell of a time to move, huh?" He looked at his feet. "Sorry about your daddy," he said to his shoes.

Hazel looked down at her own boots. Her eyes felt hot.

"Heard about what he did," the boy went on. "Saving all them families when the fire department had laughed. Took out his fishing boat—just a skiff, what folks say—and headed out. Drowned saving the drowning. And that's more than God did that day. You must be proud."

"Mm-hmm." Hazel was determined not to cry in front of this boy.

He looked at her in surprise. "You're a quiet gi—"

Hazel jabbed him hard in the shoulder—the only part of him she could reach—before he could finish.

"Ow!" He rubbed the spot where she hit him. "It's true. Memphis women crazy. You might be more dangerous than any flood." He smiled, and Hazel couldn't have looked away if she'd tried— which she didn't.

The boy extended his hand with the same gentle gesture he'd used in Stanley's. She noticed the lines in his palms. How long and intricate they were. She wanted to trace her finger along them, discover where they led.

"Maybe we should try this proper. Hi. I'm Myron. Myron North. It's been an absolute pleasure getting to know you," he said.

Hazel blinked. She regarded his hand for some time. The hand that had been her safety raft, her compass. Instinct rose inside her for the third time that day. She knew if she took it, this hand, she would be opening the first chapter of a book that would span her lifetime.

Her chest expanded and contracted with a long breath. She steadied herself. Raised her head to meet his eyes. "I'm Hazel," she said, and placed her hand in his.

Suddenly, a window in the second story of the pink house opened. A young woman in her twenties—with the loveliest brown arms Hazel had ever seen—had thrown it open. She wore a silk nightgown the color of a nectarine, and her head was a nest of short, messy locs.

"If y'all don't go ahead and get married and get off my lawn, so help me God," the woman shouted. Then, more to herself than anyone else, "But don't nobody ever listen to Miss Dawn."

CHAPTER 14

Hazel

1943

Hazel's round tortoiseshell glasses kept slipping down the bridge of her nose. The almost-quilt in her lap consumed her attention. Technically, she was still piecing, not quilting. Quilting would come last, after Hazel had stuffed thick cotton in the middle and chosen a good, solid color for her quilt's backside. Right now, she was piecing together the front side of her patchwork quilt in an assortment of robin egg blue and sea foam green.

She bit her bottom lip as she worked, smearing her red lipstick across her teeth. Her mother was attending to a customer on the other side of the parlor. Della was on her knees, pins in her mouth. She was affixing a knee-length lace hem to the end of Mrs. Finley's white linen dress—a rarity. Ever since the war broke out two Decembers past, lace had been harder and harder to find. And more expensive. Only their rich white customers wore silk stockings now. The orders for new dresses had dwindled, too. Deliveries of new silks and chiffons had turned to deliveries of steamed, pressed handkerchiefs. Now when Hazel answered the phone and took down appointments, they were for simply mending dresses her mother had made the season before.

"Right there, not an inch higher," Mrs. Finley said sharply.

"Mm-hmm," Hazel's mother said through what Hazel knew were clenched teeth.

The tall, broad-shouldered blonde was one of her mother's most exacting and most loyal customers. Mrs. Finley was known throughout the Black neighborhood as one of the direct descendants of Nathan Bedford Forest. There was talk that she herself sewed her husband's Klan robes, not daring to take them in to any seamstress. She had also convinced the entirety of the Women's Board of the Memphis Botanic Garden to start coming to Della's shop. This fact and only this fact had saved Della's business when others had closed during the Depression. And when Hazel's father had died, this white woman, for what it was worth, overpaid her monthly bill by a whole five dollars. So Hazel knew that she had to be on her best behavior whenever Mrs. Melanie Finley stepped into the shop for a fitting. It was her mother—always a proud woman—who more often needed the reminding.

"Mama, we got that two-o'clock with your favorite customer," Hazel had said at the breakfast table that morning.

"When's the last that Remington's been cleaned?" her mother asked, as she poured grits into Hazel's bowl.

"Mama!"

"You right. Her death should be slower than all that."

Hazel laughed, shook her head.

Ever since Hazel turned eighteen, her mother had started paying her a small salary for managing her bookings and making her deliveries. Hazel had spent not a cent. Stashed every dollar her mother gave her in a blue-striped hatbox she kept high in her closet. She was twenty-one now; the box wasn't full yet, but close.

She was saving for Myron. For the both of them.

For the past six years, ever since that day at Stanley's, Hazel and Myron had met every Friday in front of the deli, ordered two butter pecan ice creams, and walked hand in hand down Chelsea until they reached Locust and the ancient fading mansion at its flowering dead end. Miss Dawn, the mysterious new owner of the leaning house, begrudgingly let them sit on her wide porch swing. More often than not, she would open a window or door and yell at them they should go ahead, get married, and get their own damn house to live and love in.

"Maybe she's right," Myron had said one Friday toward the end of their senior year at Douglass High.

They'd been together for three years at that point. Hazel's head was in his lap—their customary position atop Miss Dawn's porch swing. Myron held a branch of honeysuckle over her head. It was 1940, and the talk of a war in Europe was gently kneaded into the evening gossip shared on front porches. Honeysuckle was in full, delicious bloom. He broke off flower from stem and, with a gentle pinch, pulled a droplet of nectar toward Hazel's open mouth.

"About what?" she'd said, after swallowing the nectar.

"Getting our own house."

Hazel propped herself up on her elbows. "You want to buy a house?" she asked.

"No," Myron said.

Hazel relaxed. She sank back into her comfortable position. Closed her eyes. Felt the heat of the Memphis day on her cheeks. They were both only eighteen. Hazel knew her mother wouldn't let her get married to some neighborhood boy not a cent to his name no matter how much she was in love.

"I want to *build* you a house," Myron said.

Hazel's eyes blinked open.

"You heard me, gi—"

Hazel grabbed Myron's hand, still holding the honeysuckle branch. Bit him. Not too hard. But she made sure teeth sank into flesh.

He pulled back his hand.

"Woman!" Myron exclaimed, but Hazel knew he lived for her

love bites. She noticed that even after they were married, they didn't behave like the married folk Hazel knew. Often, Myron would chase her around the house he built for her, Hazel's laughter filling the home, until he had successfully tackled her on their four-poster bed. Sometimes, Hazel would stay up waiting for Myron after a late shift, and they'd sit at the kitchen booth over cigarettes and drink coffee and talk of things to come.

"Are you serious, Myron?"

"As serious as you beating on me."

Hazel rolled her eyes.

"Nah, I'm serious," he said. "Why not?"

Hazel was quiet. A hummingbird flitted about the blooming magnolias. "How do you know?" she said.

"Know what?"

"That I'm the woman for you. That you the man for me."

"Sit up," Myron said, his tone suddenly serious. He nudged her with his knees.

"No, I'm comfortable."

"Hazel Rose, you look at me now," Myron said. He raised Hazel's head with the tip of his index finger. "You remember the first thing I ever said to you?"

" 'You all kinds of crazy'?"

Myron gave a small laugh. "It was 'I got you.' I meant that. You hear me? I meant that."

For a few minutes, the only sounds were the hummingbirds and the gentle breeze blowing through the magnolia leaves. Then Hazel said, "I never told you what else I did that day."

Myron tilted his head and took a long look at her. "I'm afraid to even ask," he said.

"I went back to the deli."

"You did what?" Myron's tone turned sharp.

"I went back. Later that night. I waited 'til midnight. Snuck out. There was a single light on, so I knew Stanley was in there. I knocked quiet as a bird, but he heard. Came out the back holding a frozen lamb's leg to the side of his face. He opened the door and let me in."

"What happened then?"

"I gave him one of my lemon meringue pies," Hazel said. But she had also done something else that day back in 1937, done something that would have gotten her killed in the South: She gave Stanley a kiss. Planted the tenderest of kisses on the left side of his face, bruised and purple as a melon.

Under the honeysuckle above Miss Dawn's porch swing, Myron and Hazel had made a decision. They would start saving for their future house.

A month later they graduated, and Myron became a Pullman porter, where he'd been for the past three years now. His huge frame suited him for the daily haul of white folks' luggage at downtown's Union Station. He worked the overnight shifts because they paid more. Teased Hazel that he didn't mind being called "boy"; he knew he was her man.

Which was why confusion, heavy as down, blanketed Hazel as she looked up from her quilting to see Myron, breathless, standing before her. He had burst through the shop door, not bothering to knock or ring the buzzer—something he had never done before. He also was never late to work. And yet, there he was—tall and dark and splendid in his uniform.

"My—" Hazel began, but Myron held up a finger, cutting her off.

"Lord, I know you didn't walk up in my house to shush a grown woman," her mother said. She was still on her knees in front of Mrs. Finley, but she had stopped pinning the lace hem in place.

Mrs. Finley's mouth was frozen in the shape of an *O*.

"Myron, what's going on?" Hazel said, placing her quilting to the side and rising from her seat.

"What on earth is this boy doing here?" Mrs. Finley said, emerging from her stupor.

Della sighed. "That's Hazel's sweetheart. We know him, Mrs. Finley."

"But I don't. And I don't want him here." Mrs. Finley hugged her chest as if she were Eve in the Garden, suddenly nude and exposed. "Get him out. I want him out of this shop."

Della raised her eyebrows. Hazel couldn't help admiring how her mother was able to embody contempt, albeit restrained, even from her diminutive position on the floor, head bent upward toward the white woman. "Pardon?" she said.

"Mama," Hazel said warningly.

"Pardon?" her mother repeated, louder now, standing up to meet Mrs. Finley at eye level.

"We'll go outside on the porch," Hazel said, turning toward the door.

"No!" All three women started at the urgency in Myron's voice. "I'm sorry, but I think your mama should hear this," he said.

Hazel's heart seemed to drop into her stomach. She reached for him. "What's going on, love?"

"This boy can't be in here," Mrs. Finley said, her voice rising hysterically. She seemed disoriented by Della's reaction, confused by the upset of power dynamics in the parlor she had visited so often. "I don't want him here," she repeated.

For a moment, the shop was still. Della and Mrs. Finley's eyes were locked in a standoff, Hazel holding her breath. No one moved.

Then Myron dropped to one knee.

Mrs. Finley screamed.

"Lord on earth," Della shouted, waving a hand to silence her. "Can't you see he proposing? White folk don't do this?"

Hazel looked down at Myron, realizing in a dazed way that he'd been holding his right hand behind his back since entering the parlor. Now he brought forth a tiny crimson lacquered box. Held it up to her.

The fog that had overwhelmed Hazel when she first met Myron in Stanley's deli now wrapped around her again like a heavy quilt. And even though they did not own a record player, Hazel swore she could hear the unmistakable voice of Memphis Minnie.

She ignored all else but him. Ignored Mrs. Finley in her periphery, shouting something and clutching her pearls. She even ignored her mother throwing strips of lace into a basket with angry finality and directing Mrs. Finley to get the hell out of her shop if she was so afraid of Black love.

Hazel couldn't hear Myron's words over the music playing in her head. But she did not need to. She saw his mouth moving fiercely. It seemed like he was speaking an avalanche of words. She heard not a one.

The red box was light as a baby bird in her hands. Hazel held it for a moment, watching Myron's lips. The front door slammed; Mrs. Finley must have gone. Hazel passed the box to her mother without looking away from Myron's face, feeling relief sweep over her once it was out of her hands. She hadn't even bothered to open it, look inside. See the pear-shaped sapphire there. That would come later. Instead, Hazel swept up the fabric of her skirt, fell to her knees in her mother's front room, and took Myron's face in her hands. Choking back sobs, she scolded him. Berated him. Told Myron he was a damn fool to waste all that money on a ring. Didn't the man know she was his? Didn't the man know he was hers? Didn't he know this fact if no other?

I got you, remember? Remember? Such a damn fool to waste all that money. A shame, the whole thing. And supposed to be saving up for a house. Why, dear God, did she belong to such a damn fool?

What Hazel did not find out until later that afternoon—the three of them eating blackberry cobbler in the kitchen, her mother having decided to cancel the rest of the day's appointments—was that as Myron knelt there on bended knee, concealed in the inside pocket of his jacket were his draft papers.

The two were married by week's end. Myron gone to the front the following.

CHAPTER 15

August

1997

The morning had been trying. She was tired from lack of sleep, and she needed a cigarette. She didn't even want to think about the number of appointments she had that day. August loved doing hair. She loved owning her own business and making Black women happy. But she didn't feel much like doing hair that day. Something deep within her urged her to get back into bed and sleep.

She had groggily made breakfast for everyone: grits with sharp cheddar, salt pork fried hard. She heard the water running in their one shared bathroom in the middle of the house and knew Miriam was up and getting ready to go to her summer nursing school classes. There was a mound of dishes in the sink. August sighed, and got to work washing them.

It was Saturday in the summer. Summer meant August's shop was full almost every day. It was hot—a humid, sticky, wet heat akin to the inside of a baked cornbread roll. The asphalt simmered and sizzled come late July. An egg could cook on the sidewalk. Mirages appeared distant and shimmering on the horizon. The nearness of the Mississippi made the humidity an enemy of most Memphis women. They needed their edges and curls tended to more often in the sweltering heat that words could not describe.

The argument that had ensued between Joan, Mya, and Derek lingered in August's mind as she cleaned the dishes in the sink. Joan had run off to Miss Dawn's—anger painted on her face like one of her artworks. A short walk, August had assured herself. The drive-by shooting had occurred the spring before, and tensions in Douglass seemed to thicken the already-heavy air. Kids didn't play in the streets all day and night like they were wont to do. Mothers called their children in by sunset, shouting from screen porches, a whole hour before the streetlights came on.

August understood that the summer meant blood. School was out. The heat was driving folk crazy. Intermittent gunshots could be heard throughout Douglass at all hours of the day. Late the night before, she had heard the phone ring. She heard Derek's footsteps squeak across the old hardwood floors. She heard the click of the pearl-handled receiver leaving its hook on the rotary phone in the hallway. She could hear only one side of the conversation, and it was muffled at best. But she had heard enough.

Words like *retribution* and *choppers* and *trunk* and *body*.

Laments like *We can't let this shit just go, mane, unchecked* and *We hit back soon, mane, soon and with all our niggas* and *Fuck, mane, in front of my goddamn house, it's a warning.*

August heard the final declaration of *Let's show Orange Mound how real niggas live.*

Heard the antique phone receiver slam down.

When Derek walked into the kitchen that morning, August had felt a pain in her rib cage, on the left, where her heart was. Every day, Derek looked more and more like his father. He was tall and dark and brooding. And every day, just like his father, he bored deeper into crime.

At first, it was petty stuff. August remembered the apologetic phone calls from Stanley informing her that Derek had lifted a honey bun or a can of Coke or, once, a pack of Kools. Things had been hell ever since Derek attacked Joan back in '88. He broke a girl's arm not two years later. For little to no reason. Broke it like a wishbone in the middle of his fifth-grade class.

The state had taken him away for a second time after that. The white folk at the Department of Children's Services made plain the third taking would be permanent. A counseling program had been mandated—a revolving door of therapists and psychiatrists and social workers had all declared the child "problematic," "aggressive." One counselor going so far as to write "dissociative personality disorder" down on one of Derek's countless evaluation forms.

August didn't know what to think. Only what she had to do. The state had made clear that Derek would need twenty-four-hour "surveillance." Constant, consistent monitoring and care. Monthly surprise home visits from state evaluators.

She'd agreed to the state's strict terms. What choice did she have? Let strangers, detached white doctors, raise her son?

That night, she'd packed up her college textbooks—packed up her dream of attending Rhodes like her mother before her, of perhaps even becoming a doctor—and, like winter sweaters, stowed them away in her dead mother's armoire. Went to the shelf in the kitchen Meer could never quite reach without straining, found the nearest bottle, and sat that whole night with the whiskey and her thoughts and her sobs. But by the time morning light had streaked into the kitchen's windows, she had a plan.

Hair—the idea had hit her like a drunken husband. Singing, she knew, was not an actual plan. She knew she had a voice that could shame most angels, and she also knew she wasn't classically trained. A single session with Al Green when she was all of six does not a Nina Simone make. And shit, she wasn't prepared to go hungry for a gift that mostly annoyed her. She thought about sewing, turning the house into Hazel's childhood home, but the thought of mending white women's clothes almost made August spit out her drink. No. If she had to serve, had to work for her bread and butter, then, goddamnit, she'd serve her own.

Years of piano had made her fingers nimble and athletic. She had been the family's informal hairdresser, pressing and setting her mother's curls faithfully every Sunday evening. Had done up Meer to look like Diana Ross in the flesh. Hair it would be. A shop in the house. The basement in the back was the perfect place. Hardly used, off the kitchen. She could make a separate walkway around the side of the house easy. Lay a few stones. Use the last of her mother's small inheritance to buy the chairs, the dryers.

Yes, August thought to herself with the kind of clarity that drunkenness brings. *Yes, I can do this. Shit, I gotta.*

At dawn that morning, donning her kimono and swaying from the whiskey, August had headed out into the back garden her mother died in and searched for stones for her new path. Around midmorning, she fell asleep in the same spot where five years before she had found her mother.

Derek was returned for the final time six months later, and though violence seemed to hum just underneath his skin, CPS hadn't been called again. Within a year, August had become the most coveted, the busiest, the best hair stylist in all of North Memphis. She hoped more than anything that her mother, wherever she was, was proud.

Lost in her thoughts, August realized she had washed the same pot four times now. But she couldn't get the morning's events out of her head. Pumpkin pounding his car horn a few minutes after Derek walked in. He was coming to collect his new protégé. She knew Pumpkin well. Seventeen years old, the same age as Derek, Pumpkin was short and a bit thick and a golden-brown color; his nickname had stuck. He'd come to the house and walk Derek and the girls to Douglass. She let him. What choice did she have? She remembered the fierce argument with Miriam. It was their first in years. August remembered how it had come to screams.

"I'll be goddamned if I get my girls messed up in this," Miriam had said, pounding a fist on the table.

August was taken aback. Her sister rarely swore. When she did, August knew Miriam was not herself. But August struck back with her tongue: "Your God is dead, Meer. Where the fuck you think we live? This the hood. Our house is the hood now. There is a gang war in this place. They shoot children walking to school now." August had stumbled around the last sentence. The word caught in her throat, and she fought back tears. "And not no one gives a single goddamn. Not no one. Not the police. No one. They'll shoot them for wearing the wrong goddamned color, Meer. Think about that. Think about how absolutely fucked that is."

"And so, what? We go along with the crazy?" Miriam had yelled. "We let our children walk to school hand in hand with gangsters? Not my girls."

"My child is a monster, Miriam!" August's voice, a natural alto, had shaken the rafters themselves. She had called her sister by her full Christian name, not her pet name. Something August couldn't ever remember doing before. "They already *live* with a gangster!"

Finally rinsing the pot, August now thought about the kiss on her cheek Derek had planted before running out to meet Pumpkin. The "I love you, Mama" none of the girls heard him whisper in her ear.

"Nigga, go," Joan had said.

August had felt Derek's kiss long after he'd gone. Like every man she had ever known. She put the pot back in the soapy water and began scrubbing again, worried about everyone she loved around her.

CHAPTER 16

Hazel

1955

Hazel stood at the kitchen sink scraping scales from a catfish. She had cleaned and filleted five already, gutted out entrails and lined the fish on the counter to her left, face-up, their glassy eyes open.

She wiped her brow with her forearm, shifted her weight. She would make sure to take a seat, have a rest in a few. Myron was always on her about it. *Only you would be frying fish hotter than hell outside,* he'd said to her that morning, kissing her forehead. *Stubborn as anything. Nine months pregnant in August in Memphis. Stubborn as all hell.*

She smiled as she reached for another catfish. Silver fish scales caught the light and reflected the colorfully painted walls, turning Hazel's sink into a rainbow of colors. She remembered Myron adding the finishing touches, flowers blooming on the walls against the warm buttermilk backdrop. Few knew he could draw. It was something he had hidden even from her—until, one day, doing the laundry, fishing in his pants pockets for loose change, she had discovered a napkin with an exact copy of her sleeping face on it.

How Myron survived the war was anyone's guess. Hazel had received weekly letters from him, now a Marine Corps private, alluding to his location—Normandy, the Ardennes, Buchenwald. The atrocities at each, the details of the carnage, Myron never included. Only his love for his new wife, his desire for the touch of her.

They had waited—Hazel insisting throughout the years, stopping Myron's kisses at a certain point—so that, on their wedding night, the boy who had grown into a man was waiting for her. All Hazel could remember, after he had removed her lace gown and laid her down on a quilt her mother had made for them, was that a man and a woman together, loving, reminded her of butter pecan ice cream.

When Myron had come home from the war in '45, he had promptly begun work on his long-awaited wedding present. In the two years he was gone, Hazel had been true to her word, filling her hatbox to the brim with everything she saved. She remembered him standing on a small ladder in their new kitchen and hand-painting lilacs and lavender, hiding dates in the bouquets— birthdays, their wedding date.

Hazel fell into a reverie as she scraped the fillets, her mind on her wedding day. The rush of it. A different kind of shotgun wedding. Her mother had canceled her appointments for the week. Della had ripped the lace straight off Mrs. Finley's dress order. She spent her nights applying Mrs. Finley's lace to Hazel's wedding dress. Stayed up that entire week muttering to herself that her baby would have the best on *her* day.

Miss Dawn. Word of Myron's proposal and his draft papers had traveled like a winged messenger to her doorstep. The next day, Douglass awoke to the sound of the cowrie shells in her long braids jingling in the Memphis morning air. She wore a long print dress of a kind of fabric no one there had seen before—a West African batik the color of the sea. She walked straight into their house, not bothering to ring the doorbell. A simple toss of her long braids laced with shells and dove feathers was sufficient announcement. When she entered Della's shop, Miss Dawn declared in a voice raspy with age older than her thirty-odd years that the wedding would be held in her backyard. And she'd not hear of anyone but her paying a dime for it.

But what even Miss Dawn couldn't have foretold was that her money didn't end up being necessary. All of Douglass had pitched in. The men smoked hogs slow for days and brought over vats of neck bones and jars of pickled pigs' feet, and the women brought warm loaves of cornbread and saucepans full of candied yams and strawberries as big as rubies embedded in pies as deep as mines.

Hazel remembered cupping a hand to her open mouth when she first saw Miss Dawn's backyard. Where the fields and fields of baby's breath came from, Hazel was too stunned ever to ask, but the white fluff covered everything. Looked like snow had fallen in one particular spot in the South in early June. An old, cracked gazebo became the altar. Turned-over milk crates padded with quilts from her mother's front room became seats.

Stanley had given her away. The morning after Myron proposed, Hazel set out early for the deli with determined steps. She pushed past the line of women already gathered to purchase their thin-cut turkey slices, their hand-churned butter and fresh, warm sourdough bread. Hazel issued "excuse me, ma'am" after "pardon me" until she reached Stanley, who had one hand around a can of pickled beets while the other held up a bouquet of river trout.

"Miss Thomas," Stanley said with surprise in his voice.

"It'll be 'Mrs. North' soon enough," Hazel said, breathless and beaming. She held up her left hand. No one could miss the sapphire perched on her ring finger.

She heard the cries from the women behind her:

"Girl, don't you see this here line?"

"God bless the child, maybe she's crazy."

Stanley's eyes misted over, and he looked like he was struggling to compose himself. "Now isn't that good news," he said, and packaged the trout and handed it to the annoyed waiting woman. Took the grocery order from the next in line but kept his eyes on Hazel throughout. "Good news," he repeated.

"Mr. Koplo." Hazel's bottom lip quivered. She grabbed at her rosary, twisted it in her fingers, and bit down on her lip hard to keep it from moving uncontrollably.

She thought about telling him about Myron's draft papers. How he was being shipped off to Stanley's own homeland to fight in a war . . . No. The look on Stanley's face stopped her. So did the terrifying thoughts of war. No, she decided. Not today. She would think about the war when she was a wife. For now, on this morning, she was a bride-to-be.

"Mr. Koplo, will you walk me down the aisle?"

Della had thought it just right that Hazel should ask Stanley. When Hazel returned from the deli, her mother was in the front room. "The only white man on this earth I trust," she said and went back to sketching the pattern for the wedding dress.

Hazel began gutting another catfish. In the ten years since the war ended, the only thing missing from her and Myron's life was a baby. They had their work: Hazel had her own loyal customer base now, and Myron had joined the police academy. But they wanted children desperately, had built bedrooms for two or three, but month after month, the blood came—faithful as a tide. Sometimes Hazel would despair, feeling she'd failed them, but Myron wouldn't let her blame herself. "It's just not our time yet" was his constant refrain. "One thing's for sure, though—our baby's stubborn as her mother, making us wait till she's good and ready. And when she is, we'll be ready for her, too." He kept the faith for them, always working on some project around the house while Hazel sewed and stitched just about everything under the sun—quilts, curtains, tablecloths, pillow covers. In a way, the house had become their child for those ten years. Until the beginning of this year, when Hazel missed her cycle for the second time in a row.

Hazel paused with a cold fillet in her hands, let out a long sigh.

At first, she'd thought it was the grief. Della had died earlier that winter. Unexpectedly. Hazel shuddered, remembering how she'd discovered her mother slumped over her Singer, in the midst of mending, of all things, pants for Myron. A heart attack took her. Died before Hazel could tell her she was pregnant.

Hazel shook the thought from her mind. *No more death, now, ya hear? No more,* she chastised herself. There was a pain in her gut. Her craving for fried fish became overwhelming. She winced from the sharp stab of hunger and hurried in her work. Threw herself into it. She was going to clean and fry up this fish. Eat a big plate. Then take it down to Myron. Her love. Myron, who had just made homicide detective. The first Black man in Memphis to do so. She would take him this lunch. Have his baby in a week. God as her witness. Standing at the sink, scraping out fish guts, Hazel simply, understandably, didn't want to think about the fact that she was an orphan. Her only kin on this earth Myron and the baby inside her.

CHAPTER 17

August

1978

The night before Miriam and Jax got married, August decided that her wedding present to her sister would be the gift of song. Jax's recent first lieutenant rank had come with orders to be in North Carolina—his new wife by his side—by the start of fall. The two sisters were sitting in their bedroom, hair wrapped in rollers, when Miriam said, "Sing for me tomorrow, will you?"

There was a catch in her voice, and August could see desperation in her older sister's eyes. In all their years together, this was the only favor Miriam had ever asked of August.

August was aware of the power of her voice. Knew it was the cause of many a weeping man and a terrified woman. Knew she could calm animals with it, large or small, however feral. She preferred piano. If she sang, damn near all the stray cats in Memphis, the homeless, construction workers tending to the power line at the end of the block—all would gather on her family's yard and nap for hours. August hated to sing in church. The crying, the speaking in tongues, and the grown men falling to their knees terrified her. All because she had hit that perfect high-C note? *Folk are ridiculous*, August gathered. She thought God was more demon than anything, more trickster than Father, for bestowing this of all gifts upon her.

"Fine," August said. "But I ain't singing no church song."

Miriam laughed. "Don't matter what you sing. Church moves through you. That voice."

The next morning, August stood not far from Jax at the altar, both of them pointed toward the church doors, waiting. Jax was in his Marine Corps dress whites. August hated to admit it, but the stranger looked sharp. The Marine Corps emblem, an eagle perched atop a globe with an anchor struck through the globe's middle, dazzled in bronze buttons along Jax's collar and down his jacket front. And his dress whites fit him like a glove. He seemed nervous, quiet for once—which August preferred. But his eyes kept darting all over the church until the doors opened and Miriam and Hazel appeared.

Miriam looked ethereal in a layered tulle gown made to look Victorian, antique. Her arm was linked with Hazel's, who led her to the beginning of the aisle.

Stanley hadn't been able to do it. He was weak from his latest stroke, confined to a wheelchair. But he was there. Right before the wedding, he wheeled himself up to August, tugged on her sleeve. His speech had altered so much from the stroke, but his German accent had never lessened over all the years.

"*Umwerfend*," he said. German for "stunning."

August had kissed his cheek.

The old lace of Miriam's dress made a lovely sound as it swept the floor. As Miriam and Hazel began to walk down the aisle, August sang the first notes of "Do Right Woman, Do Right Man," almost in a whisper. Even with the veil, August could tell her sister was holding back laughter. Likely thinking to herself, "That girl. That crazy, crazy girl."

August's voice grew stronger. She added vibrato. Leaned in on certain notes, let up on others.

Hazel shot her a look that could have cut a block of ice.

August sang on.

"You lucky I love you," Miriam whispered to August when she and Hazel finally reached the altar.

Her mother's face was set in stone, but August could make out the birth, the beginnings, of a smirk.

"August Della North, your daddy turning over in his grave," Hazel scolded into August's ear before kissing Miriam's cheek and making her way to the front pew.

But it didn't much matter. The entire congregation was in hysterics. Not so much at the song August had chosen, but at how she sang it. A fifteen-year-old girl—fatherless, dark, tall—singing Aretha like Aretha should have sung the song.

The wedding had been short, bless God, August thought as she entered the Officers' Club an hour later. Catholic weddings were usually not longer than a traditional Mass. Miriam's had taken place in the morning—a Southern tradition—the reception held at three in the afternoon at the Officers' Club.

As August wandered around the packed room, she scratched at her thighs, though she knew she shouldn't. But the mosquito bites were plaguing her, and the lace of the stockings was agonizing against the frantic itch of the bites. August had been covered in them, layering bites over bites ever since she'd eavesdropped on her sister's proposal in that plum tree at the beginning of summer.

She looked around at all the people packed in the Officers' Club: dancing, eating, and grabbing drinks from the bar. August didn't understand it. Shouldn't they all be in black? Grieving a loss? Isn't that what this was? Some no-name Yankee nigga no one knew from Cain coming to take away her sister. *Camp Lejeune.* It sounded like a prison. *Camp.* Something told August it wouldn't be the summer camps she had been sent off to every July down in Mississippi, where she had learned to build a fire, catch and gut trout, use a compass—rituals her mother had claimed every God-fearing Southern woman should know as easy as the Lord's Prayer when she had driven her down in the family's Coupe de Ville. No, this camp would be different. Her sister would not be frolicking in unkempt bramble and unruly thicket, but August figured Miriam would indeed learn new ways of Southern womanhood.

But here August was anyway, dressed in a pale yellow, the color of one of her sister's lemon meringue pies, holding her petite junior bridesmaid's bouquet of violets, resting, glaring close-mouthed at all the people acting like there was something to celebrate today. Trying, desperately and discreetly, not to scratch at her bites. Or, at the very least, to scratch discreetly.

"You brought that house of the Lord down."

August turned her head to see Miss Dawn, who looked like she was traveling toward her on a cloud. Miss Dawn wore a white gown with cumulus clouds for sleeves, a single pastel cowrie shell hung from her long locs, piled high atop her head. She held a tiny porcelain plate painted with English tea roses and overflowing with red velvet cake. She forked cake into her mouth and nodded.

"Brought down the house."

Miss Dawn had known August her whole life. She'd even been there at August's birth. As Miriam told it, their mother, Hazel, did not trust the attendings and nurses where she worked at Mount Zion Baptist to deliver her baby. Not after Hazel's first delivery, when the white doctors and staff had to restrain her from setting the delivery room afire. In the middle of a late August night in 1963, Miriam ran from the family home and down the street to the leaning pink house at the end of the block, screaming for Miss Dawn to come and to come quick. Pulling her head back in from her bedroom window, Miss Dawn had sprinted back with Miriam and found Hazel on all fours near the clawfoot tub, a moaning and calving heifer of herself. Miss Dawn had placed a hand on Hazel's belly, another cupped August's crown, and she cooed and guided August into existence.

Miriam—eight at the time—stroked her mother's face with a damp towel. Placed soft kisses on her forehead. "I got you, Mama. I got you," she'd whispered over and over.

Miss Dawn speared another chunk of red velvet cake and pointed it at August. "You should sing more often, child," she went on. "God talks to every baby when they're born. Every single one. But I believe He talks to some a bit longer. Whispers something only He can understand, I suppose. Some magic bestowed to certain children. You one of them. You and the whole North clan, really. Though don't a one of y'all see it."

August moved like lightning. She pulled the fork from Miss Dawn's long fingers expertly. Her lips closed around Miss Dawn's fork, and she tasted the decadence of the cake.

Miss Dawn threw her head back and roared. "You Hera in the flesh," she said and pulled August to her breast. Because August was almost her height, and because August still held the fork in her mouth like a popsicle, Miss Dawn kissed the side of her cheek.

Then sunlight pierced the dark hall as the front door of the Officers' Club was thrown wide open. The midday light blinded August momentarily. Even Miss Dawn held up a billowy sleeve to shield her eyes from the imposing sun. A figure appeared in the doorway, but the figure was so slight it did little to block out the overwhelming sun.

"Where he at?"

The accent. August would always remember how sharp, how short the vowels were. She hadn't heard anything like it until a few weeks prior, when some Yankee in a beautiful Marine Corps uniform interrupted her piano practice that Sunday.

"Where he at?" the stranger repeated.

The door closed behind him, and August's eyes were able to adjust, able to take in the Chicago man.

He was the spitting image of Jax. Anyone could see that. Reading their faces was like reading a lineage: They looked like clones. The singular difference being height. This man, a whole head shorter, this twin, threw his head this way and that, scanning the room for Jax.

August did the same. She spotted the ivory Marine Corps uniform in the center of the dense dance floor. Jax spun her sister around to Stevie Wonder's "I Was Made to Love Her." Miriam's train was tucked into the front of her dress. They both were in a trance of new love and did not notice the flash of sunlight, the newcomer.

The wedding crasher.

She heard him over the twang of Stevie's harmonica, the laughter from the couples on the dance floor, the stomping of heeled feet. August's musical genius made her strangely acute to sounds, vibrations, echoes. And her formative years sitting in her family's plum tree and listening in on adult conversations had only strengthened her auditory prowess. She had an ear for all sounds. She distinctly heard the stranger's indignation over the roar of the music.

"I know for a fact this honky not touching me."

A middle-aged waiter in a white dinner jacket and a thick black bow tie that matched his sideburns had stopped the stranger from entering the hall further. He had his palm on the slight man's chest and shook his long, wavy Bee Gees hair back and forth fervently.

August heard, "I'm not telling you twice to get your white hands off me."

August saw a gleam of pearl. The man had reached to his left side and pulled out a pistol. Clenching the barrel, the stranger swung the pearl handle down across the white man's face, and down the white man went, his body twisting from the force of the blow the same way August spun jacks and marbles on the kitchen tile. August swore she saw a tooth fly loose as the waiter careened to the floor.

"Where he at?" the stranger demanded as he placed his pistol back into a holster hidden in his dark suit jacket. He adjusted himself, his cuff links. Straightened the tie at his collar, then rocked his neck back and forth, settling it back into a comfortable place. Dusted off his jacket.

The white man was still a heap on the floor. The slight man had knocked him out cold.

As he stepped over the waiter, like he was nothing but a dead cockroach on the floor, the intruder said something inaudible even August could not make out. But after all her years of living in the South, she didn't have to. She had seen the angry mouths of white men and women hurl this at her and her loved ones too often to count. The newcomer had spat out "nigger" as he stepped over the unconscious white man.

"And that right there," Miss Dawn said between bites of red velvet cake, "is Hades himself."

"Where he at? Where my twin brother at?" the man shouted over Stevie Wonder. He continued, "Bird's here now. Yessir. Bird's in town. Where my new sister?"

August knew he meant Miriam, but that did little to stop her from leaving her place by Miss Dawn, striding up to her new brother-in-law with the confidence of an Asafo woman riding off into battle, extending her hand, and declaring, "She right here. And she think you too damn loud."

The new siblings danced all evening.

Later that night, underneath piles of quilts her mother had made, the taste of red velvet cake still in her mouth, August thought that perhaps not *all* Yankees should be killed.

CHAPTER 18

Miriam

1997

Miriam was waiting in line to buy her second cup of black, sugary coffee of the day when she heard the news. Formerly named Southwestern, Rhodes College was a small liberal arts school in ritzy Midtown, built in gothic stone and covered in ivy. Miriam was enrolled in the same fast-track nursing program her mother had taken some thirty-odd years before. Both she and Joan would have the same graduation date.

The program was intense and all-consuming. When she wasn't in class, Miriam shadowed the nurses and attendings at Mount Zion Baptist Memorial. Miriam's pillow became whatever medical book she had open, her bedroom whatever private space she could find. She made her household study with her. Often, Joan and Mya would hold up flashcards of intricate anatomy and quiz her over dinner. Mya would call out, "By Jove, she's got it!" whenever Miriam got one right. Joan would clap, slow and deliberate and proud.

The college sent Miriam and her classmates to Baptist Memorial to change bedpans and dressings, insert IVs into waiting and needy veins, and hold the hands of the dying. She did this in fourteen-hour shifts, three days a week. Her hospital work was unpaid, part of what it took to get her combined bachelor's and nursing degrees.

Miriam knew she could not let her and her girls be a strain financially on August. After class, she would head to Rhodes and work overnight in the library, down in the bowels of the microfiche and microfilm storage. Gigantic shelves on sliding wheels, containing boxes and boxes of old archives, could be moved with the push of a button. Miriam would climb up a ladder and restock and relabel into the early morning hours. The job allowed her to contribute to the grocery and MLGW bills. She knew she had to apply for food stamps when she snapped at Joan for squealing with joy when they drove past a Blockbuster Video. Ashamed she couldn't spare the dollar for the Hitchcock rental, she had called her daughter selfish. But what child doesn't want to watch a movie? That is what broke Miriam. Where shame met motherhood. She had snapped at her child for simply wanting to exist as a child.

Miriam found herself snapping at Joan nearly every time the girl opened her sketchbook. Joanie wanted to draw everything. The dark floral wallpaper in the parlor, the curve of the piano's hutch, August standing by the stove chain-smoking her Kools. Didn't the girl realize the state of the mess they were in? How on earth was art going to save them?

When Miriam and her girls arrived in Memphis, their bank account and fuel tank were near empty. August was bringing in good money, but not nearly enough to provide for an extra three mouths and a wolf of a dog to feed. Miriam realized she had to do something. She was the elder sister; she had to provide for herself, her daughters; August, too. She applied for government assistance.

Without shame. She figured it was better than the shame of asking Jax, the man who had hit her, for a dime.

And Stanley's son, bless that man, never said a word. Must have inherited more than his looks from his late father. The only question Mr. Koplo Jr. asked when Miriam showed up with her stamps was if she needed help toting her bags home.

After a month of eating spaghetti or rice and beans, the food stamps were manna. *Thank God,* Miriam thought. She had cried then, after Mya and Joan had put away the groceries. She fled to the bathroom and ran the tap so that no one could hear. Cried for joy at a full-stocked fridge. No, she did not understand how Joan could live in some fairy tale, oblivious to the newfound poverty they now navigated. Why couldn't she be more like Mya? Present. Practical. Excellent already at math and science. Whereas Joan's A's centered on her poetry classes, her art, history—all subjects at which it would be a lifelong struggle for a Black woman to earn a cent.

After the food stamps came the pittance of the state's housing allowance, which Miriam dutifully handed over in full to August, who had always been good with money, who was in charge of the household's shopping. August tried to hide the relief in her face when Miriam handed her the very first check, but Miriam knew her sister. She knew money had been a storm cloud hanging over them all. Miriam promised herself not only that she would—no, *must*—graduate, but that she'd graduate top of her class.

The hospital had a small café solely for staff—doctors and nurses and medical students—if a coffee station and stale bagels counted as a café. But Miriam was grateful for the break in her shift. Grateful for the cup of hot hazelnut, her favorite, in her hands, as she waited in line to pay.

She had been on her feet for about eight hours. She had a six-hour shift at the library ahead of her, one that started at eight that evening. While she'd been showering that morning, she'd heard a car honk, summoning Derek. She shook her head and kept scrubbing. Miriam, too, was afraid of Derek, but what was to be done?

She did not hate him. Her faith stopped her from hating her own kin, but she felt a pang of pity whenever she saw him. Maybe the boy just needed a father. But didn't her children? All she could do was monitor Derek and Joan when she was home. And when she wasn't, both Miriam and August agreed Derek could never be left in the house alone with the girls. Could never enter the quilting room. The east wing of the house was segregated—the girls and Miriam occupied this space, with Derek and August on the west side of the house. The kitchen became the family's hub, the only room were Miriam allowed her girls to be with Derek, and always, always with supervision. It hurt Miriam to think of it this way, but think of it she did: Derek was a rabid dog, and her girls, though lionhearted, were still children. Miriam loved her sister and was grateful for shelter, but she felt a different kind of shame, a deeper kind when she would glance from Joan to Derek across the round kitchen table.

She slugged along in the trail of exhausted human beings on the front lines of fighting cancer and virus and depression. Twisted her gold chain rosary absentmindedly in her fingers.

"That boy's got your eyes."

"What now?" Miriam said. The voice had come from a surgeon behind her, someone she didn't know. He held a cup of coffee in his hands as well and gestured with his coffee back and forth between Miriam's face and the television mounted high on a wall.

The surgeon flushed at Miriam's confused face. "Oh, hell. I'm just joshing you. Been in surgery too damn long. No offense, ma'am," he said. "Y'*all* don't look alike," he muttered more to himself than to Miriam, going on about how he had a bevy of Black friends, some of his closest, in fact. Still confused, she looked more closely at the television.

The local news station was playing their daily five-o'clock roundup. Miriam saw one of her favorite anchors—a serious woman with a thick Southern drawl and hair piled high on her head—announce that there had been another drive-by shooting in Memphis. The war between Kings Gate and the Douglass Park

Bishops did not appear to be waning anytime soon, the anchor warned.

Annoyed, Miriam turned away. It wasn't necessarily a surprise that the doctor associated her with this news story, but it was almost enough to make her wish she hadn't come down for coffee. Almost. She was exhausted. As the line crawled forward, the news anchor continued the report. Apparently, a house in the south side neighborhood of Orange Mound, rumored to belong to a known leader of the Kings Gate Mafia, had been another victim in this summer war. In a tragic turn of events, the anchor said, he had not been home during the time of the shooting. Instead, his grandmother and his three-month-old baby boy had been riddled with a barrage of bullets from an AK-47. A Memphis police car had, luckily, been parked nearby and had seen a tan Chevrolet Impala speeding away. Miriam's neck tensed. Wasn't that car tan, the one that had picked Derek up nearly every damn day this summer?

Trying to act casual, she slowly turned her head toward the television. "After a short chase," the anchor was saying, "police apprehended two suspects: the owner of the car, a Ricky 'Pumpkin' Howell, and a second man, as yet unnamed." Derek's mugshot flashed across the screen. "Both men were arrested and are in custody now."

Miriam pushed her coffee cup into the surgeon's chest without taking her eyes off the screen. "Here. Be a dear and pay for my coffee, will you?"

She didn't wait for his response. She dug in her purse for her keys to the van and was out the café and down the hallway in seconds.

She drove as if the highway behind her were on fire. Broke the speed limit on I-40 and ran a red on Warford, but she still felt it took the duration of a Civil War battle to reach home.

Miriam finally reached the large yellow front door of her ancestral home and threw it open. "August!" she shouted. "Girls!"

There was no answer.

Miriam had always loved this time of day best—dusk. Aged

golden light reflected in all directions from the stained-glass windows in the parlor. But now the evening light made the house seem ghostly, haunted.

Miriam walked into the empty kitchen, still calling for her sister. She hesitated at the door that led to August's shop. She breathed in deep, steadied herself. She closed her eyes and whispered, "Hail Mary, full of grace," then exhaled, placed a hand on the knob, and turned it.

The shop was dim. Slowly materializing, Miss Dawn came into view like an apparition. She was sitting on the settee with both Joan and Mya in her lap. Miriam saw Miss Dawn smoothing Mya's hair and whispering and wiping away her free-flowing tears. Joan sat motionless and unblinking.

Miriam's eyes continued to scan the room. There in the dark, sitting in one of her wash-and-set chairs with her head in her hands, was her sister. The family Remington sat next to her. Two of Memphis's finest stood over August with pads in their hands, poised to jot down notes.

Miriam heard her sister say, over and over, more statement than question, "What has he done."

CHAPTER 19

Hazel

1955

The officer behind the counter did not glance up from the *Memphis Gazette*. Red wisps of hair swirled atop his head in a small tornado that receded toward his crown. His face, pale and peppered with freckles as red as his head, remained hidden behind a black-and-white print page announcing the Cubs' two-pointer opening day win over the Cincinnati Redlegs with a full-page photograph of Ernie Banks under the headline SAVIOR? The officer leaned into the paper fully, let out a long whistle.

"Shit. This just may be their goddamned year," he said.

Hazel cleared her throat.

The officer lowered the paper and glanced briefly at her with a flash of green eyes. "Twenty-five dollars," he said. He shook the paper, lifted it back to his face.

"Pardon?"

"Twenty-five dollars," he repeated without looking up from

his paper. "Cash. If you ain't got the cash, don't go wailing on me now; a check will do. Made out to the City of Memphis. But it's got to clear, understand, and that'll take a day 'fore we release him. So, he stays another night. Otherwise, cash."

"No," Hazel said. "I'm here to see my husband."

"Girl, what did I just get done telling you?" Annoyed, the officer placed the newspaper down on the counter the color of salmon innards and stared hard at Hazel.

The badge on the officer's uniform read "C. Barnes" in bold block letters. Hazel vaguely recalled Myron cracking a joke about a certain white officer who was as red as a barn and dumber and lazier than the beasts inside one. This must be him, Hazel reckoned.

For a moment, Hazel forgot herself. When she heard that word, *girl,* she instinctively searched around her for something heavy and sharp that would draw the most amount of blood, cause the most damage. Then she remembered that she was nonwhite and a woman and carrying a child and in Myron's place of work. She took a deep breath. Placed a hand on her extended belly. Began again.

"My name is—"

Barnes cut her off. "Twenty-five dollars, and you can take him home tonight. You ain't going to cry on me, are you? Lord, join those gals over there if you are. I ain't dealing with this today. You people just come up in here and cry and think that's going to do a damned thing about your situation without the bond note—"

"No!" Hazel had had it. She felt her hand leave her belly and become a clenched fist. She banged it on the counter, shocking even herself.

Barnes gave Hazel a look. He folded up his newspaper and began to rise from his seat.

Hazel took a step back. Gripped the brown bag tighter. She chose her words carefully, spoke them slowly. "I'm here to see Myron. Myron North. *Officer* Myron North. If you don't mind. Please."

Barnes blinked. Awareness spread across his face. Then, a grimace. "I'll be goddamned," he said, taking a seat. "You're North's old lady? I didn't know. I mean, he goes on and on about you. But I didn't. I didn't . . ." He concentrated on his hands. He fell silent for a moment, looking almost sheepish. Suddenly, he yelled, "Eugene!"

Hazel was startled and took another step back.

"Eugene! Goddamnit," he said, louder this time.

A deep, distant voice responded. "What?" The twang. It wasn't even a Memphis accent. Sounded deeper. More tonal.

Hazel stiffened. Her anger and anxiety had not quelled. And another policeman was coming into the room, one with an accent Hazel thought sounded exactly like one heard at a lynching. Or a rape.

"Goddamnit, Eugene, come on out here. Got somebody for you to meet."

"Jesus Christ," said the voice. "Give me a minute, will you? Got ink all over me from booking this nigger. Jesus Christ."

A short, squat man with gorilla-like arms—hairy, thick, meaty—walked around the corner. Ink fingerprints covered his white collared shirt, and Hazel saw smudge marks where he'd attempted to wipe them off. There was an entire right palm print on his left breast.

"Well, what the hell is it?"

Barnes tilted his red crown at Hazel. "Guess who this is?"

"I don't know, Casey," he said, his vowels seemingly elongated with annoyance. He barely glanced at Hazel before him. Threw his ink-stained hands in the air. "Mary fucking Magdalene."

"This here North's wife," Casey said.

Eugene paused. He took in the full form of Hazel then, her nine-month belly, her hair done up in a neat bun. "Well, I'll be. What's a girl like you doing with North? Dorothy Dandridge herself come to see us," Eugene said.

"I came to bring my husband some lunch," Hazel said. She held up the brown sack as evidence.

"I bet you cook as fine as you look, girl," Eugene said.

Hazel tried to hide the repulsion on her face by biting her lip. "Why don't you fetch him from the back, will you?" she asked as politely as she could manage.

Eugene did not move. He rested his stained forearm on the counter. "How on earth North get a pretty little girl like you?"

Hazel pursed her lips. Considered replying, but thought better of it.

"And got a pretty little girl inside you, likely," Eugene continued.

"Oh hell, Eugene. Go fetch him. Let this lady be."

"I'm just being friendly, is all," Eugene said, turning toward the redheaded Casey. "Ain't we supposed to be friendly to them now? Ain't that what the new captain say?" He swiveled back to Hazel. Then, hand outstretched, started walking toward her.

Hazel realized, the horror almost overtaking her, that this white man wanted to touch her belly. Was walking toward her to do just that.

At that moment, Myron appeared in his black-and-white Memphis Police uniform, and Eugene pulled his hand away, inches from Hazel. He backed up, though not without letting an ugly smirk twist his face.

Hazel let out a deep breath she hadn't realized she'd been holding. The sight of Myron in any uniform—his Pullman porter's, his Marine Corps dress blues on their wedding day, and now his police officer's uniform—had always made Hazel feel safe, calm, and proud.

Myron was a tall willow compared to Eugene. His thick-rimmed glasses reflected the indigo of his skin. Alarm was etched on his face. He walked quickly to Hazel and pulled her to him and asked quietly but firmly what in the entire hell she was doing there. She held up the paper bag.

"Lunch," she said.

Myron lowered his head and kissed Hazel softly on the cheek.

"Y'all know this is the jailhouse and not the courthouse, right?" Eugene said to them.

Hazel heard Barnes flap his newspaper, burying his head in it. Still, Hazel could feel his eyes sear through the paper.

Eugene watched them with his arms folded across his chest.

Hazel thought of her mother. What would Della have done here in this police station? Two white men harassing her daughter. She figured her mother would've set fire to the damn place. With the white men inside it. It was all Hazel could do not to spit on the floor as Myron steered her out of the station, his grip on her tight.

"You can't come here anymore," Myron said sharply once they were outside. It was sweltering on Beale. There was no breeze off the Mississippi, and the sound of cicadas, even at midday, was overwhelming. Myron led Hazel to a storefront with a wide awning, so she could rest in the shade. "Here," he motioned. Then added, "Never again."

"I understand," she said.

"This . . . this isn't the kind of place I want my wife in," he said, his voice softening. He took the brown sack from Hazel's hands with a tenderness meant as an apology. "What do we have in here?" he asked.

"Catfish po'boy. Some slaw."

"You're too good to me," he said.

"I know."

"I got a warrior for a wife." He shook his head and smiled.

"You do," she said, beaming.

"Never again, though," he repeated. He placed his hand on her abdomen, swollen with life, and gave a weak smile. "But we don't have to talk about this now, Hazel. Thank you for the lunch. How's my firstborn son?"

"*She*," Hazel said, "is just fine today, husband." Myron's hand stroked her belly as she spoke.

"It's a boy," he said. "I'm not sure how I could bring forth women into this world." He planted a tender kiss atop Hazel's forehead. One of the myriad tender gestures Myron made, and Hazel's favorite. "I got you," he said. "But never again, you hear me?"

"Myron, you're worrying me. What are you talking about? I've been telling anyone who'll listen my husband is Memphis's first Negro detective. I—we are so proud of you, love."

Myron tilted his head back and closed his eyes. "They won't let me arrest white folk."

Hazel stepped out of their embrace. "What?"

"They won't let me. I'm hot on a case. I can't talk about it too much, baby, while I'm here." Myron checked over his shoulder and continued. "But I know who it is. I know. Some white college kid enrolled at Memphis. Staked him out and caught him in the act. They won't let me arrest him. Told me to check my evidence again. They figure any john raping women in a colored neighborhood better be Black, too. Found some poor fella to pin the thing on. That's the way of it."

The heat was getting to Hazel. She felt faint. And hungry again. With all her effort, she pushed herself up on her toes to kiss her husband. The love of her life. They had survived a great flood and a great war. They would survive this, too. She leaned in close and adjusted his tie. "Come home to me," she said.

Evenings in Memphis were setting time. The heat finally breaking. Folk in Douglass were able to venture outside on their wide front porches, sit, and enjoy themselves. Men coming home from work at the Cotton Exchange or Memphis Sanitation or a cotton field called out to their neighbors, their brown arms waving in tired salute, children already glued to their ankles. Women the shape of peaches and pears and apples and in every hue of brown would be at the door, hands on hips, shaking heads at the scene. This was the time suitors were allowed to call. Young folk would be draped around each other, their legs intertwining in a tapestry, asking each other, *Do you love me?* Somebody usually brought out a guitar. Somebody usually sang the blues. There was talk of everybody pitching in for a jukebox, but the older folk would laugh that idea away, wheel out a Victrola, align needle to groove, and play Ma Rainey. Stray cats would appear at back doors, moaning for scraps, hardly heard over the gossip and the music. Cigar and barbecue smoke combined into a frankincense that had always hypnotized Hazel. But pregnancy had made the aroma nauseating. She couldn't stand it. So she sat at the window in her parlor instead, fitted with a cushion seat so she could quilt, look out the window, and wait for Myron.

She placed the tiny tomato cushion that held her pins and needles atop her belly, but the baby inside her was restless and kept kicking it off.

"We gon argue over the smallest of stuff. If you don't let me put this here," Hazel spoke to her womb, laughter in her voice.

She had reached the final stages of her quilt. When she found out she was pregnant, she had begun to work on the project immediately. She threw herself into it. Collected scraps around the house, went door to door to the women who used to be her mother's clients and asked if they had anything green. Even though she used the tiny gold thimble Myron had brought back from a shop in Germany, the tips of her fingers were still calloused from the thousands of tiny pricks she had taken. But she had waited her entire life to make this quilt. Her favorite kind: a Tree of Life.

The emerald fabric draped itself around Hazel as she bit her lip, pressing needle through cloth. She adjusted the quilting hoop in her lap. It was difficult to get comfortable with the sheer size of her front and the angle of the oval wooden hoop that held the quilt together.

"This quilt going to get done, you hear me?" In frustration, Hazel stopped fidgeting and spoke again to her almost child. "And

I'm going to get my shape back after you. Mmm-hmm. You heard me. Mama cannot be this thick forever."

Maybe it was the music, but Hazel did not hear the car engine idling in her driveway. Perhaps because she was focused on adjusting the cushions behind her back, getting her sewing hoop to sit on her lap just right, all while the baby kicking inside her, she did not see Casey Barnes get out of the squad car, tuck his cap in the crook of his arm, and climb the steps that led to her porch.

But the neighbors must have, because the guitar strumming ceased and Mr. Emmanuel's voice down the way died down.

Puzzled at the sudden quiet, Hazel glanced up from her work. Caught a glimpse of red hair standing outside the front door like an omen, the *Argo*'s black sail.

She thrust the quilt and her sewing pincushion to the floor and rushed to the door and out onto the porch.

The officer stood before her and muttered under his breath that Myron's squad car had been found in an abandoned salvage yard on Mud Island, his body, bruised and broken, found and pulled from the Mississippi a mile downriver.

Before Hazel could process this information, she was drawn to the demeanor of the man. The way Barnes avoided Hazel's eyes was all the proof she needed that whatever had happened to Myron, her Myron, had been no accident. Myron had been murdered. By members of the very force who had sworn to protect and defend and honor.

Earlier that day, cleaning out the catfish entrails, Hazel had grieved her mother. Hazel knew loss. Grief was all she had left of her mother. Nothing to be done about it but miss the woman. But that early evening on her front porch, Hazel came to know rage. It was not Myron's time. Nothing natural took her husband. No heart attack, no old age, no cancer. This white man had taken him. That, and only that, became Hazel's mania.

What Hazel did next she had wanted to do her entire life. She mustered everything inside her, let it marinate, soaked it up in the back of her throat, cocked back her head, and hurled a glob of spit at the officer's face. The spit landed just above his left eye and slid down along his nose like egg yolk hitting a wall.

Barnes paused for a moment. He gave a startled, nervous laugh. Nodded his head. Took out a white handkerchief and wiped his face. "You're lucky you're pregnant," he said.

"You're lucky I'm pregnant, too," she shot back in an alto she never knew she possessed, staring him straight in the eye with pure wrath in her heart. "Because if I had the strength," she said, raising a quivering arm to point at the large magnolia in her yard. "I'd hang you right there. Right from that tree. Watch your body rot. Picnic underneath it."

Snickering all the while, Barnes placed his cap on his head and slowly walked backward down the porch steps. Eugene was waiting for him in the driver's side of the idling car. His smile Cheshire cat big.

After they left, after Hazel sank screaming to the stone of her porch and had to be carried inside by the men and women on Locust Street who had come running, sprinting to her aid, something quiet and lovely happened.

All of Douglass—the teenagers in love, the tired workingmen, the even more tired womenfolk—all of them stood on the steps of the porch of the house Myron had built for Hazel, stood on the lawn, climbed up in the branches of the magnolia and found seats where they could. The people in the neighborhood stood watch that night. Stood there all night. Not a one saying a word. Stood watch over Hazel and her baby. Some of the men fetched their old war uniforms. Stood saluting the house. That whole night.

A week later, Hazel pushed her daughter out of her insides the same day the headline of the *Memphis Gazette* read, NATION HORRIFIED BY LYNCHING OF CHICAGO BOY EMMETT TILL.

Hazel had erupted when she read the news. Along with apple sauce, Earl Grey tea, and a piece of stiff cornbread, a white nurse had left the morning paper on Hazel's breakfast tray. Hadn't given it a second thought. Security was called into the delivery room, the same white nurse screaming for help. Guards had to restrain Hazel. They tied her wrists to the bed, avoiding her teeth and nails, which tore at the closest white flesh they could find.

The new mother had set fire to the newspaper. Watched it burn black on the floor.

"Miriam," Hazel christened her daughter. As close a girl's name as she could get to "Myron."

Part III

CHAPTER 20

Joan

2001

The beginning of fall in the South was something to behold. The summer heat—a slow-moving tornado—had finally left the area. Nights were a pleasant cool. We could sit out on the front porch unbothered because there were fewer bees, fewer birds, fewer cats even. Magnolias in Memphis, including the big one in the backyard, had blossomed their last flowers. The plum tree alongside the house had dropped its last fruit some time ago, but the area around the base was still stained indigo. The dogwoods and maples and cherry trees lining Poplar Avenue had a slight touch of corn husk yellow as if God had placed dabs of butter on each leaf, so that when a breeze caught, the trees ignited in soft flame. Fall in the South meant Midas came down and touched everything. The trees seemed to be made of gold itself. Leaves became copper coins catching in the wind.

It was the beginning of my junior year. Through the window

of my Honors U.S. History class, I could see a maple just beginning to turn crimson in the September wind. Mr. Harrison stood
at the front of the room, lecturing while covering the chalkboard
in his neat scrawl with details about Roosevelt's New Deal.

Mr. Harrison, a gruff man whose accent reminded me of an old
Confederate general, was a secret liberal and a devout Cubs fan. A
diamond in the rough in the South. I'd had him in tenth grade,
too, and in the afternoons, he'd let me sit in his room and listen to
the Cubs play the Cardinals, our archenemies. He was an acceptable white man, but not one I could trust. The man still taught
that the Civil War was over states' rights.

"Yes, the states' right to own human beings!" I had shouted in
the middle of one of his lectures last year, to stunned silence.

My mind wandered as he went on about the New Deal, walking up and down between the rows of desks. I loved history, but
truth be told, I wouldn't fully pay attention unless we were studying the Civil War or Stalingrad or the Battle of the Marne. Wars
fascinated me. How on earth could a sane man charge into a volley
of bullets—say, at D-Day? Weren't they terrified? The odds of sur-
viving something like the Marne or Shiloh were so, so small.
Didn't the men know that? Standing there, waiting for death?
Knowing they were walking straight into harm's way? Didn't they
know that it didn't matter who they were or whom they loved or
what else they'd gone through, bombs or bullets would take them
down just the same. *Like me,* I thought suddenly. *Like me walking
into Auntie August's house six years ago, when I knew what lived
inside.*

"Joan," Mr. Harrison said warningly. He had made his way
over to my desk and was looking down at my notebook, where I'd
been sketching the maple in one corner of the page.

"Sorry," I said. "I'm listening."

I felt guilty, hearing the frustration in his voice, and started
taking notes from the board as he returned to his lecture. We had
an agreement, my teachers and me. I would not draw in class as

long as I could access all the art classes Memphis had to offer a junior. What my school lacked in art supplies, I made up for in other ways, drawing on whatever I could—scratch paper, the back of exams—sifting through Memphis five-and-dimes with Mya, searching for brushes. My teachers knew I had a gift. Knew Douglass could not provide for this gift. So I was now enrolled in my first AP course—Art. I took the class on Saturdays, at the Rhodes College campus. Auntie August took me, since Mom was always working or studying. We'd drive our family's classic Coupe de Ville up North Parkway to the stone fortress that was Rhodes. I loved those rides. Auntie August would sing along to the radio, the pride on her face hard to conceal.

Today was only Tuesday, which meant another four whole days before I'd get to go again, feel the relief that being in a functional art room brought me. Douglass High simply did not have the facilities for the kind of art study I craved. I needed easels the length of rooms, canvases as big as men. I needed nude models of every race and gender and shape and size. Oils were expensive, and I wanted a rainbow's worth of them. A set of ten colors could run up to fifty dollars or more. And the brushes I needed were made from the tails of an unbroken pinto. My passion was not a cheap one.

A man named Professor Mason had been the broker of my art deal. A rather eccentric, tiny bald Black man the color of a camel, he'd slowly become a mentor to me. "What the hell are we doing if we're not letting someone with this talent into college classes, high school student or not?" I'd overheard him saying to a Rhodes admissions officer. And that was that. I was in.

I had never felt so respected. Even though these were college kids, and most of them white, and I was only sixteen, we all addressed each other as "Mr." or "Ms." And they offered helpful critiques and criticism of my work. "Try this brush" or "Have you tried etching? It may give you more freedom than you thought" or "You've got a knack for watercolors, Ms. North." The long hours I had spent working alongside fellow serious artists had garnered me enough respect to be allowed to choose the radio station while we all worked.

I chose the Cubs game. Each and every time.

Professor Mason had had enough one day. He stamped his cane down in a fury, went to a closet, and brought forth headphones, forced them in my face. "Use these."

"But Zambrano is pitching!"

His look was something fierce. I took the headphones.

And now, it seemed like U.S. History class was crawling by. I tried to focus on Mr. Harrison's lecture, but the maple leaf glittering in the sunlight vied for my attention, making me wish for the thousandth time that I could just be free to draw all day long.

I thought back to August, to one of our early morning Saturday drives to Rhodes. Auntie August had been singing along to Anita Baker's "Caught Up in the Rapture of Love," her voice more powerful, lovelier than even Anita's, reaching high notes and adding vibratos in places only a savant could.

"Auntie, how come you don't love the Lord?" I'd asked. I couldn't understand it. Auntie August never attended Sunday Mass with us. Instead, sleeping in and fixing Mama and Mya and me a large breakfast when we returned, famished. And though I would've loved to sleep in, just one Sunday, I felt it was my duty to go. Whatever ability I had as an artist, I knew I owed it to my Creator. Yes, I practiced at it. Drew everything I saw since I was old enough to hold a pencil. But that was my Catholic duty: to exercise this gift. As painful at times as that could be. I popped my joints in my hands, fearing already that arthritis would be a constant foe. It took me a year to master fingertips, another to master the veins in the hands. Shading them. Making them look real—like Miss Dawn's hands were there for the shaking—took me another year.

Auntie August had stopped singing and let out a laugh. "Philosopher Joan, you sure do know how to ruin the mood." She concentrated on the road, took a graceful left onto the Sam Cooper Boulevard ramp, then said, "What that white man ever do for me? Took my Mama away. That's what *He* did."

The way she had said "He," with such bitterness, made me mute. After a time, I said, "He gave you that voice."

She laughed harder then. "And what has this voice bestowed upon us, niece?"

"Well, I like your voice. I look forward to our rides, Auntie. All week."

She cut me a look then. Auntie August had a sharp tongue, but like Mya, she also had a sensitive side she hated showing. "You better be worth this gas money, niece. Better end up painting the Sistine Chapel or some shit."

I'd rolled my eyes and crossed my arms. "Not if Mama has her way," I said, unable to conceal the bitterness in my voice.

Mama's and my fights were becoming as legendary, as commonplace, as Auntie August's cream kimono. It seemed like every time I opened my sketchbook, there she was over my shoulder, telling me to put it away. When, once, I had said no, our yelling shook the house. Reminded me of Daddy.

"You sure do know how to ruin a good song, Joan," Auntie had said.

"Sorry, Auntie."

"Your mama just wants the best for you, is all," my aunt had said and exited the car off Cooper and onto North Parkway.

I stole glances around the room when Mr. Harrison's back was turned, sketching the angles of the desks and chairs and pretending they were notes on the lecture. Mama may have wanted what was best for me, but maybe she didn't know what that really was. Over the summer, she had looked over my shoulder while I sketched a vase of flowers, shaken her head back and forth, and said, "Girl, you are just like your father."

I didn't talk to Daddy much after we left Camp Lejeune. I hadn't seen him in the flesh since. He'd call for birthdays, the major holidays. He sent birthday cards, with platitudes printed in neat fonts, attached to gifts that never fit me: a charm bracelet, a Game Boy, a set of eyeshadow colors. I'd rather have had oils. Inks. Paper. Canvas. Pencils. I'd rather have had a *father*, frankly. The fact that he could leave us mystified me. Yes, we had fled in a van. But why the hell hadn't he pursued? Why hadn't he fought for us? Why didn't he ever visit Memphis? Why did he care more about his career than us, than me? Why had he given Mama a black eye? He had turned the thing damn near purple.

Mya still talked to him. I'd catch her on the ancient rotary phone in the hallway by the bathroom, twirling her fingers in the cord and whispering. I didn't blame her. How could I? She wanted a father.

I was satisfied to live without the lot of them—all men did was fail me. Derek was serving out his life sentence at the Riverbend Maximum Security prison, a stone's throw from Nashville. My Auntie August visited him every month. She'd return from the three-hour drive with bleary eyes and a depression that would last the week. The house would lose its magic in those times. Auntie August was a shell of herself. She'd do hair, but she wouldn't try her more exotic cuts or riskier styles. Her food would be almost tasteless, made without flavor or her usual, delicious finesse. She gave one-word answers to almost all our questions and went to bed early, hardly touching her plate.

The evening Derek was arrested, Mya and I had been sitting in the shop. Most of the clients had streamed out, and only Miss Dawn was left, getting her ritual wash and set. It was four years ago now, but I could still remember it clear as day. A loud banging on the shop's patio entrance had startled all of us. It was not the sound of a woman coming in for her treatment. Auntie August pressed a finger to her lips. She ran into the house, and when she returned seconds later, she was carrying a shotgun.

She'd rushed to the door, pulled back the curtain, and slowly opened the door to let in two police officers.

Mya and I ran to Miss Dawn and hid behind her chair. I did not like police officers. Neither did Mya. I was only twelve then, and all I knew was that they meant my parents' fights had escalated.

I remembered Auntie August asking, pointedly, if the two white officers had read her shop's sign outside and whether they had a warrant. How her face fell when they told her that they, indeed, did.

Later that night, we'd sat at our kitchen table shell-shocked and silent. My mom had done what she could—she made us all tea. Mya had fallen asleep with her head resting on Auntie August's lap. August's head was on the table, folded in the crook of her arm.

My mom had placed a brown hand atop her sister's shaking one. She reached across and grabbed mine so that we formed a half séance over the table. "We will get through this," my mom had said.

I snatched my hand back. "I've prayed for this night all my life," I said.

"Joan," my mom said, sharp, reproachful.

"He's gone," I said. "I'm finally safe. Free. We all are now."

Auntie August's cackle reverberated throughout the yellow kitchen. Felt like it shook the rafters themselves. "Free?" Her laugh was steeped in the same bitterness when I had asked her about God. "A Black woman hasn't ever known the meaning of that word, my love."

"Joan," Mr. Harrison said again, startling me back to the present. He was at the front of the classroom, a piece of chalk in his hand. "You're drawing again, aren't you?" He sighed but didn't sound angry. More resigned.

Damnit, I thought. I glanced down at my notebook.

"The New Deal" was written in my standard cursive . . . and nothing else. A lot of drawings of the room. The maple. Random half drawings.

I sighed, too. I would be in the library looking up whatever the hell "the New Deal" was before our next exam. *You're killing me,*

Teach. Give me war! I almost moaned aloud. *At least in a battle, people are fighting for something*, I thought. What was I fighting for, sleeping and eating and growing up in the Cold War being waged between me and Derek, and then between me and the memory of Derek? To get out with my dignity, I supposed. To get Mya through safe. To give Mama, despite our fights, a chance to make her own way, to become a nurse. To make sure Auntie August kept eating when she took to her bed.

My gaze shifted to the window again, but I was no longer studying the maple.

Mama had told us countless stories of Papa Myron. His love for his wife became a legendary thing in our house. Mama and Auntie August would mention his lynching infrequently, but it loomed large in all our minds. I wondered whether he'd ever been scared on the front. If he felt more scared there or when his fellow officers turned on him. A man who loved big enough to build Grandma Hazel the house we all lived in now—had he killed, when it came to it? It was easier to imagine that my *daddy* had. Harder to picture *him* ever being scared. Is that why he'd chosen the Marines, because he'd always been like that? Or was it the Marines that turned him angry and violent?

The wind picked up, working the leaf from its branch, and it fell out of sight. I shifted uncomfortably in my chair, thinking about how when Derek was still living with us, I sometimes felt a rage so strong I believed I could kill. Maybe I wasn't so different from Daddy. An unpleasant thought. Maybe he'd even made me this way, I realized, angrily. But my rage came partly from fear. That reassured me until I considered, with a start, that maybe that wasn't so different from my father, after all. When Derek got me angry, especially when we first moved to Memphis, it would take all of me not to break something—to pick up some antique in the house and throw it against the wall. I had to learn to control this rage. I would walk away, argue with myself. I'd leave the table and eat alone on the porch, cooling off. Why on earth could my father not do the same? What did my daddy have to be afraid of, anyway?

"Joanie!"

I snapped my head to the front of the room, confused. That wasn't Mr. Harrison's voice—and nobody in that classroom ever called me "Joanie."

Mya had appeared. In the classroom's doorway. Her hair was disheveled. Auntie August made sure our hair was neatly parted and combed every morning, but Mya's looked undone now. Her eyes were large and—my heart sped up—she was crying.

But Mya could not have been there; that was not possible. Mya should have been in Orchestra, her first-period class at Douglass Middle. The middle school was located just a block down the street from Douglass High. But there she was, breathless, scanning the crowded room for my seat. I could see the middle school Orchestra teacher, Ms. Oakley, behind her. The students sat in curious silence, all eyes on my sister.

I stood up. Mya ran to me. She nearly knocked me over. She buried her face against my shoulder, and I felt hot tears dampen my shirt.

"My, talk to me," I whispered in her ear. "What's wrong?"

I didn't know if she would be able to talk; her shoulders were convulsing in sobs. But everyone in that classroom, everyone on that floor—shit, every soul in North Memphis likely heard Mya as she tilted her head up to look at me and wailed that planes were dropping from the skies and that one had hit Daddy's work.

CHAPTER 21

Joan

2002

I'd been taking art classes at Rhodes after school this fall, just like I did during my junior year. Rhodes displayed all the art students' work in a small show each year, and last spring mine was included for the first time. I was the only high school student featured in the showcase. I don't know for sure, but I had to think that was part of the reason they'd offered me a full ride for the following year. There was no way I'd have been able to go otherwise—it was a dream come true. And *that* would never have happened without Professor Mason. *You got grit, girl,* he'd say, standing behind me as I painted. He'd stroke his long white beard and repeat it: *You got grit.*

One Saturday, he asked me to stay behind.

"Joan?"

Students were filing out of the now-dark studio and into the fading fall light. I was bent over my large portfolio, packing up my pencils.

"Professor Mason?"

He leaned on an intricately carved ebony cane. He threw up a free hand. "Call me Bartram."

"I'm not doing that; Mama would fillet me." I smiled.

"Listen, Joan, where are you going after this?"

"Home," I said.

"You know damn well what I meant."

"You *know* where I'm going," I said warily. I went back to packing up my things.

Rhodes. The argument with my mother, though it had happened the month before, still brewed hot in my thoughts. I could still hear her voice: pleading, defiant. Same as mine.

"They offered you a *full* ride, Joan," she'd said. "You're going."

We were all in the kitchen—me, Mama, My, and Auntie August, who was plating the Friday meatless dinner: pan-fried perch with a side of buttered green beans Mya and I had picked from the back garden after school.

"I know Rhodes's art program like I know myself, Mama. I won't learn anything there."

"You'll learn how to be a goddamn doctor!"

I had never heard my mother curse. She had pounded her fist on the counter as she said it, emphasizing the finality of her argument.

Mya burst out in tears. My, for all her pranks and sass, had a sensitive side. She hated when Mama and I fought, but fight we did. And more and more often, it seemed.

"Y'all stop; look what y'all doing to My," Auntie August said, and stopped dishing fried fillets onto My's plate. She sat down beside her at the kitchen booth and wrapped her arms around her.

Mama let out an exasperated sigh. At the counter, she could not look at any of us when she said, slow and tired, enunciating each syllable, "I just don't want you to be poor, Joanie. You can draw.

Lord knows, you can draw. But if a man up and leaves you . . . or you up and leave him, how will you survive? Selling sketches in the streets? Name me one successful artist with a dark face. With breasts. Name one Black woman famous artist. Go on. I'll wait. Be a doctor, Joan. For Christ's sake. Be a doctor." She'd paused for a few seconds, then she said in a whisper, "However nice they are, don't matter a lick. No daughter of mine going to press food stamps into white hands."

I didn't want that, either—poverty and the shame it brings—but I was willing to risk being chronically poor the rest of my life so that I could draw. Art mattered more to me than anything else. If there was a chance I could make it work, that I might make a living off it, however meager, I had to try.

Professor Mason thrust his cane down hard on the wood floor to get my attention, startling me back to the studio. We'd been painting nude models. He went over to the stool the model had been using and took a seat. The room was empty now. It smelled like pencil shavings and paper. Other than Mama's cobbler baking or Auntie August's chicken and dumplings cooking, I knew of no better smell.

"Go to London," he said.

"What?"

"Go to London," he repeated. "You're bigger than Memphis. Rhodes, I hate to say it, can't teach you any more than I already have. The College is still accepting applications. And I know someone there. I won't hear any objections," he said as I began to protest. "I've already put in a good word. Yes, yes, don't scold me. I'm an old gay man in Memphis. I do what the fuck I want, love. You should, too."

The College. I knew exactly which one he meant. It was laughable. I shook my head. Perhaps Mama was right. I couldn't be a doctor, not with my science skills. Mya did most of my Biology homework. But I could be a lawyer, easy. Writing and history and argument had always come natural to me. Maybe art was something I could do on the side of my life. Become a part-time art teacher. Or teach art in the summers. Maybe even abroad. See the world that way. Hold down a decent job. Make Mama proud. The first attorney in the family . . .

"My family——"

"Will understand," he said, striking his cane hard on the floor again. "For the love of God, don't be stupid, girl. If you stay, at best, you will end up an old art teacher like me shaking his cane at young folk and calling them stupid. Rightfully so. But if you go. If you go . . ." He trailed off.

Auntie August was waiting for me in the red Caddy outside.

"Joanie!" she shouted out the window. "You know I have to set Miss Dawn's hair tonight. Get yourself in this car!"

I sprinted to the car and placed my large knapsack filled with oils and brushes and inks in the trunk. Closed the trunk and opened the passenger seat with a hurried, "I'm sorry, Auntie."

My mind was racing. Professor Mason's words had ignited a fire in me. For better or worse, I was born this way. I was born to be an artist. Placing pencil to page felt like worship each and every time. Of course, I did it. Of course, I was obsessed. Art is air.

How can Mama not see that? I wondered silently. *How can she not see that I may just be great at it? That just maybe a dark-skinned skinny girl from North Memphis can draw something that will silence this world?*

After a few minutes of driving from Rhodes on North Parkway, after a few minutes of listening to Anita Baker on the radio, I couldn't help myself. I had to tell her, someone, my plan.

"Auntie?"

"Child, you better be telling me how sorry you are for making me wait and that's it."

I loved her. I knew where Mya had gotten her sass. It was genetic, apparently. Passed down through the generations.

"Auntie, I don't want to be a doctor."

She kept her eyes on the road, the streetlights flickering on in the darkening November evening, but she also reached out a hand to turn down Anita's voice on the car radio.

I took that as my cue. "Listen, I've been talking to Professor Mason. And he says, he says there's still enough time for me to apply. I've got 'til Christmas; that's when the application is due. And Professor Mason says there's a fellowship—just one—that they dole out once a year to an outstanding *American* application. A fellowship! That means a *full ride*, Auntie. Same as Rhodes. But this way, this way, I get to be an artist. They need a portfolio—that's a series of paintings in all different mediums—sorry, I'm going on and on, but Auntie, will you sit for me? I have an idea for my portfolio. All the women in the neighborhood. Well, not all. But you, Miss Dawn, My, the beauty shop, Mama. Lord, I don't know how I'm going to sketch Mama without her knowing."

"Joan—"

"Maybe I can use old photographs for Mama . . ."

I couldn't stop now that I had started. I could see my plan laid out before me like cobblestones I simply had to tread.

"Joan!" Auntie August shouted.

"Yes, ma'am?" I had forgotten myself, my place. My elder was Auntie August. I knew I was not honoring her by not listening. I held my peace, though it hurt to do so.

"Where?"

"Ma'am?" I asked, deferential in tone.

"Where, child? What school is this? What on earth are you talking about? I'm listening, I am. But I just have no idea what you're saying, niece. Explain yourself."

I did. The entirety of that car ride home.

By the time I finished, we had pulled up to our driveway and Auntie August had turned off the ignition of the Cadillac and reached into the car's console for her pack of Kools. She took her time rolling down the old Caddy's window, took her time lighting one. I knew from the way she exhaled her cigarette smoke that she was serious, deep in her thoughts.

"I can sing," she said, exhaling a plume of cigarette smoke, then taking another puff. "You've heard me before. Don't do it that often. Folk pass out. Honest. Once, years back, at your mama's wedding, man fainted in a back pew. Had to be carried out. Hadn't even noticed. Just went on singing Aretha in a way I do doubt Aretha could do it. But I never *did* anything with it. My voice. Not sure I wanted to, how folk went on and on whenever I let out a note. And well, I knew *Who* gave me this voice. But I did love piano. Wanted to play jazz. Loved Gershwin."

She sat smoking in silence for a few moments before she continued.

"I will help you, niece. And I'll work on your mama. Win her over. Guess I must. Because you have a gift. I think it's high time somebody in this damn family with a gift use it."

Auntie August finished her cigarette and, with a quick flick of her wrist, tossed the butt onto the driveway's asphalt.

I began to gather my things, starting to think over what she'd said, but that's when I felt Auntie August's palm on my head. She began brushing back my stray hairs. My box braids, which she had done the month before, needed a bit of tightening in the front.

"I just may start praying after all. Because, Jesus Christ, who the hell going do your hair all the way over there in London, child?" she asked, as concerned as I'd ever heard her as she smoothed back my edges.

I laughed. "I probably won't get in."

Her hand stopped abruptly. It went to my chin and lifted my head so that our eyes locked. "You best get in. You hear me, niece? Do whatever you have to do. Draw as many hours a day you got to. I'll help you. We'll figure out a place to hide your drawings." She paused, seeming to steel herself for something, then took a deep breath. "Derek's room. Yes, child. We got to stow them somewhere. I'll go in there if you won't. I'll do what I can, but you got to do what you must. And you must go over there and show them all, Joanie."

From that Saturday onward, I stayed after class with Professor Mason and worked on my application to the Royal College of Art. The application consisted of my grades, my ACT score, and finally, my work. The Royal College required a portfolio of ten different works all focusing on a single subject matter. A series, as it's called in the art world. Women. I wanted to showcase the women of Douglass, of North Memphis, of my family. Miss Dawn's lovely hands. Miss Jade's elaborate updos. Mika's red acrylic nails. Ten in total. All in different mediums—oil paintings, charcoal drawings, black ink—and each on its own ten-foot-tall canvas.

I wasn't sure if I would get in, if I was good enough. Every time I finished a piece, I would stand back and study and doubt would nestle into my thoughts. But Professor Mason insisted. Whenever I mentioned how unlikely it would be that I won the fellowship, he'd throw up a hand to shush me.

"No one in London is ready for these, child," he said, examining a new portrait I'd brought in. "But you need more. And try watercolor this time."

Miss Dawn, bless her, still sat for me once a month. I had spent long, lazy summer days on her front porch for years, and now I went over on weekends as the last vestiges of fall faded. I'd sketch her breaking green bean or picking butter lettuce and we'd talk of things that were and things that would be. She told me stories about my grandparents. How everyone in the neighborhood knew my grandfather had been a war hero. The only Negro combat engineer in his battalion. She told me that Myron came home from the war and everyone watched him in that yard picking out stones to lay the foundation of his wedding present to Hazel. As I sketched her, I listened to her tell the story of how Myron had built his Taj Mahal for Hazel.

Miss Dawn's fading pink house was still standing. Amazingly, an ancient willow grew right through the center of it. Marsh

wrens and hummingbirds nested in its maze of branches. One Oc-
tober evening, sitting before Miss Dawn on her crooked porch
steps in the fading light, I filled her in on my plan.

"Hmmm," she said when I had finished, and she patted her
head underneath an elaborately tied headscarf. She was sitting on
her porch swing wearing a long shift dress in a bright batik pattern that looked like fireworks over water. I sat beside her and
after all the years I had sketched her, I still could not take my eyes
off of her hands.

"You know your grandparents would sit here and talk nonsense, steal kisses, eat their ice-cream cones . . ." When she trailed
off, she broke out into unrestrained laughter. "Your Papa could
draw. Sure could. Drew up the plans for y'all's house himself. Isn't
that something? And now, you runnin' off to London—"

"I haven't gotten in, Miss Dawn," I chimed in, but she cut me
off.

"And now you runnin' off to London. I'll help you. Your mama
might burn down my house when she finds out. I know her heart
set on you being a doctor. But that's the path for your sister. You"—
she aimed a bony, ancient finger at me—"you need to go ahead
and dig up that boy's comb. Yeah, I said it. Yeah, I remember, and
I know you do, too."

Derek. He would come into my thoughts every now and again,
and I would push him back out. He was where he belonged: away
from us. His absence had brought relief to my life. No more stom-
achaches at the very sight of him at the kitchen table. No making
sure to avoid him, to leave whatever room he was in. I could wander around in my own home. I even discovered parts of the house
I never knew existed. The back hallway leading to the west wing
had a small enclave built into the wall. And there, surrounded by
brick, was a hand-size Virgin Mary, her face painted a lovely doe
brown. *He's gone,* I'd remind myself, placing my pencil to the
page. *Thank you, God. Thank you so, so, so much, God.* I prayed my
gratitude to the Mother as I drew. Said three Hail Marys.

I dreaded all mention of him. Would switch the radio to Smooth Jams whenever I heard Three 6, his favorite, blaring. My called me old, always listening to old-folk music. But Whitney and Anita and Chaka never made me want to break something.

But my efforts to erase Derek from this earth were limited. There were still pictures of him throughout the house. On the bathroom wall, there were still pencil marks, though faded, showing his height, his age. And Derek phoned the house. I hated when he called collect to speak to Auntie August. She'd always be upset after. I'd hear her side of the conversation from the hallway phone. Always "It's gonna be okay, baby" and "Keep that head of yours up, D." I'd hear the receiver click and her footsteps toward the kitchen shelf, straight for the whiskey. I wasn't sure if my burying that comb was what landed my cousin in prison, but I thanked God—and Miss Dawn—for the magic of it.

Miss Dawn was looking at me hard, and I didn't challenge her—no use pretending to her or myself that I didn't think of Derek, that I didn't remember burying that comb. "Dig it up," she said again. "Or you won't be going anywhere."

"What does that mean?"

"You know damn well what it means. Did I stutter, child? How come no one in your family listens to Miss Dawn? For the life of me, I can't understand it. Y'all some hardheaded women, dear Lord."

But she agreed to increase our monthly sessions to twice weekly.

The next month, I brought Professor Mason two pieces: a canvas of Auntie August painted in broad black ink strokes on a stark white background. She wore her legendary kimono, stood for me smoking her legendary Kools. The other was Miss Dawn. Her hands mostly. They held a bouquet of blackberry bush bramble. Both women were ten feet tall on white canvas.

"You're ready," Professor Mason said, admiring my work.

"What happens now?"

"We submit and we wait," he said.

Later, on Christmas night, stomach full of neck-bone meat and turkey legs and chitlins, I headed out into the backyard, but this time I took a shovel. I dug until I found it. The comb. The teeth shining black in the moonlight. Its wooden handle was covered with dirt. I stood over it, panting slightly from the work. Then I spat on it. Again and again and again.

CHAPTER 22

Miriam

2001

She was snaking a needle into a vein when her patient, an elderly white woman wearing pearls and her hair in a high bun, exclaimed, "Jesus, Mary, and Joseph."

The woman had one of those old Memphis accents. She reminded Miriam of Scarlett O'Hara, the older and much-lived version, but Scarlett nonetheless. Miriam sat back, inspected her work, which looked fine, and frowned. She was known for being gentle with all her patients. Two years more, and she would be a nurse.

"Just bear with me, ma'am, almost there," Miriam said.

She'd found the vein on the first try, no digging around, but she was prepping this woman for surgery, and she reasoned that that was enough to make anyone feel on edge. Miriam released the rubber band around the woman's arm.

"Chile," the woman said. "This world on fire, and you fussing about an old woman's veins."

Miriam followed the woman's gaze to the television in the corner and saw buildings as tall as titans on fire. She fumbled for the remote and turned the volume up. Apparently, planes had flown into them. She saw folk covered in soot and ash and debris, coughing up blood. Miriam put hand to mouth when she realized that in the debris, like confetti falling from some heavenly party, were bodies. She and her patient watched human beings jump from the buildings. Reports were coming in that there'd been another crash in Pennsylvania.

Was this woman right? Was the earth on fire? But what made Miriam break—what made Miriam drop her entire tray of needles and gauze and sterilizer—was the announcement that there had been yet *another* plane crash.

The Pentagon had been hit.

It had been six years since she last saw Jax. After Miriam left, fled in the night with their children, Jax had advanced in the Marines. He had made lieutenant colonel. Miriam knew he had been transferred from Camp Lejeune to the Pentagon because of the forwarding address on the divorce papers.

"You all right, chile?" the patient asked, concerned.

Miriam bent to pick up the upturned tray. She did not know how to answer. She honestly did not know if the North house could bear any more loss.

Four years had passed since Derek's arrest. He had been charged with first-degree murder on two counts. Miriam had sat in the Shelby County Courthouse, her hands tightly intertwined with those of her sister, every day of the trial. They both had worn black.

The courtroom smelled like the hickory benches that lined the small room on two sides. Derek was there in his blue prison jumpsuit, sitting at a long table on the left side of the room, flanked by his public defender.

Three Black boys had entered the courtroom shortly before the call to order and had sat directly across from the North family pew and stared at Derek. They wore sagging jeans and royal-blue

T-shirts. Apparently, Kings Gate Mafia had sent troops to monitor the battle playing out in the courtroom. They were there every day of the trial. So were the Douglass Park Bishops, known for their bloodred bandanas tied around still-growing biceps. The guard had stopped many a brawl in the aisles, separating Black child from Black child clawing at each other.

Derek never confirmed his involvement with the Douglass Park Bishops, but he did not have to. The judge, the Honorable Dorothy White, was from the streets of Memphis, knew that a seventeen-year-old boy does not own an AK-47; that weapon had been gifted. She, and the jury, also knew that a boy from North Memphis had no valid, reasonable reason to even be in Orange Mound, much less with an automatic weapon used in warfare, all to kill two people he had never met. The jury took all of thirty minutes to issue a guilty verdict; didn't even need to break for lunch.

Miriam remembered only letting go of her sister's hand when she took the stand at Derek's sentencing. The prosecution was pushing for the death penalty; Derek's best shot was life without parole. August wore a black cape dress that flared out at her arms so that she looked like some medieval sorceress. A black funeral hat with a lace veil covered most of her shell-shocked face. Her kitten heels clicked on the marble floor as she swung open the saddle doors separating public from judge and took the stand.

"Raise your right hand," the security guard had bellowed.

August obeyed.

"Do you solemnly swear that you will tell the truth, the whole truth, and nothing but the truth, under penalty of perjury, so help you God?" he asked.

"Yes," August said.

"Ma'am, we need you to state your full name for the record," Derek's defense attorney began. He was a stout, bearded, middle-aged man, and he wore a well-tailored suit, a red carnation at the lapel.

"August Della North."

"And state your relation to the defendant."

"He's my son."

"Ma'am, what is your occupation?"

"I'm a hair stylist. I have a little shop I run out the back of my home."

Derek's attorney paced, nodded his head, and stroked his beard. He spoke slow, pronouncing each syllable so that the courtroom understood the gravity of the situation. "Ma'am, why don't you begin by telling us a little about your son?"

Miriam remembered seeing her sister take a deep breath, exhale. She had never seen August so utterly spent. She looked like she had been to the underworld and back and could speak the language of the dead and the lost.

At first, it didn't seem as if August would be able to speak. She sat on the witness stand and Miriam saw her shoulders rise and fall in deep, concentrated breaths. The silence got to the crowd. There were snickers from the Kings Gate Mafia pew.

It seemed as if August took no note. She lifted her veil so that her eyes were exposed. Even from her seat, Miriam could see them: They were two dark holes. Looked like they contained the suffering of the entire world.

August began: "That boy's father was Lucifer. I mean that. Kind of man make you believe in evil in this world. Know it in your bones. Feeling you get when you stare at an abyss and know in your heart that there, below, dragons roam."

The courtroom fell silent. There were no more snickers.

"We met on Beale Street," she said, her voice steadier now. "He was walking down Beale, cigarette in hand, and offered me one. I had never tried one before, and it tasted so good, like a freedom I didn't know I needed. He had on this black leather jacket. Sideburns. He was the color of fall—golden brown. Stole my heart. Took it, beating, right out of me. Felt like I didn't even have a say in the matter.

"He never hit me. Didn't have to. I knew what a demon was, what it wanted, what angered it. Miss Dawn—she an old family friend—she once told me, 'Djinnis are real.' But I didn't believe her until Derek was born.

"Derek was born in the middle of a thunderstorm in March. The power out. Six hours into labor, an elm had fallen on a power line. People drowned that night. Derek came out silent as a lamb through all of it. His father held him first. Can you imagine? Wouldn't even let me be the first to hold my boy. He said, 'He'll be a Spartan.' God, that man lived up to his promise. Brutally. Ruthlessly. Once, I found D—we call him D at home—in a closet, shivering. He had held a bucket of water in his hands. For hours. You hear me? Hours. He was ten years old. I was at home, but I had ten washes and sets that day—" She broke off, reached for a tissue from a box on the witness stand.

All the hairs on Miriam's body were raised. She'd known Derek's father was no good, but she'd never heard most of what August was telling this room. August had a secret side no one in the family had ever been able to penetrate. As a child, she'd always be pounding away at the piano keys, her face unreadable, lost in some reverie that Miriam, even Hazel, couldn't understand. Or she was hiding up in some tree, listening in to the fireside political debates at the house, her thoughts her own. Yes, August had always been the mysterious one. So, when she got pregnant, far too early, no one had even asked who the father was. Miriam knew her sister would never tell.

"Sometimes, I'd come back from Stanley's—Stanley's is a deli by the house—and I'd find the house dark, the lights all turned off. D would be shaking, just shaking. Wouldn't let me touch him. Wouldn't say nothing. He'd hide in the cupboards sometimes. The closets. Like some scared, hurt animal. And his father. I don't think I should even name the nigga. I'd find him sitting at the kitchen table. Drinking black, cold coffee. Asking me, 'How long 'til dinner?' "

A strange knocking thud had sounded in the courtroom. Miriam saw Derek was pounding his head against the defense table in slow, methodical thumps. His attorney went to him. He placed a hand on Derek's back and, stroking it, nodded for August to continue.

But Miriam wasn't sure she wanted August to. What she'd heard, and Derek's reaction—it all terrified her. For the first time, and however unwanted, Miriam felt a connection to her nephew. She, too, knew fear. The anticipation of pain. Bruised and beaten on her Camp Lejeune kitchen floor, reaching for the phone to call her sister, Miriam had always reckoned moving back home to Memphis would be safer than staying in North Carolina. Jax was a large man. And trained by the greatest, the most elite branch of the armed services to kill, expertly, with his bare hands. Lying on that floor, in the haze and chaos of being punched in the face, Miriam calculated that Jax might one day kill her. Maybe not intentionally. But just the right blow to her head . . . She'd had to leave. And where else did she have to go but home? Her mother's words on the evening before her wedding came to her on that floor: *My lovely, beautiful daughters, both of you can always, always come home.*

August cleared her throat. "He left one day. Without reason. Went out for a pack of Kools and never came back. The nigga died likely just how he came into this world: killing somebody. And then, I thought we were safe. He was gone. But even after his father left, D would hardly let me touch him."

My God, Miriam thought. She realized that both she and August had been battling terrors too difficult to face alone. And yet, they had.

Miriam felt shame, like it was Jax swinging at her.

She should have left that son of a bitch sooner. Should have come home the moment, the very first time, he hit her. Miriam could hardly remember when. But it was after the Gulf, after she had forgotten something trifling—an ingredient in that night's dinner, Joan's math homework, to post the *Jet* subscription bill. And he had hit her. Miriam stood holding her burning cheek in open-mouthed shock. He had *hit* her. Jax. From the record store Jax. She was dumbfounded in her grief. It took time for her to process what had happened. Felt like she had stood at the counter, open-mouthed and silent, for nearly a month, frozen in fear. Why on earth did she stay when Joan was raped and Mya was still inside her? Jax had lifted her off the ground with one hand at the hospital. Lifted her by the neck and squeezed.

Miriam put a hand to her neck and shuddered. Jesus Christ, why didn't she leave then?

The things women do for the sake of their daughters. The things women don't. The shame of it all. The shame of her daughter's rape, the shame of her husband's violence, her nephew's psychopathy.

If I ever, ever, ever fail my sister, my daughters, again, Miriam told herself, *let demons take me.* She made the sign of the cross.

August reached for another tissue. Blew into it. "All of this to say, don't kill my son. I'm begging you, Judge," she said, turning to appeal to her directly. "Don't send my boy to death row. I did the best I could. Motherhood is an anchor. It has devoured me entire. I did the best I could. If love was enough . . ." August trailed off.

Miriam didn't know what to think. She had always feared Derek, did not want him anywhere near her daughters—which in turn subtly meant she didn't want him in the house. But it was his as much as her daughters'. It was the only home he had ever known. Miriam shifted between pity and loathing, but she steadied herself.

Perhaps it was her faith, but it couldn't have been solely that, because Jax she could not forgive. Maybe it was blood, having the same line as Hazel coursing through both Derek's and Miriam's veins. Perhaps it was her mother's memory, urging forgiveness from the grave, but for whatever reason, Miriam thought, *Pity the boy, Miriam. Pity the poor thing. He ain't never known a kindness. He ain't never known. Lord, why?*

Miriam heard the ache in her sister's voice when August said, "Killing my son won't bring back nobody from the dead. You know this. And y'all going to kill him? That's the question we came down here for today? How? How, after this, how y'all going to sleep at night?" She turned now to the room at large, her arms outstretched, challenging, beseeching them all.

Her chest was heaving, but her eyes were dry. Hands shaking badly, she reached into a pocket of her black dress and pulled out a pack of Kools and a small, pink lighter. She could barely light the cigarette. Finally, fumbling slightly, she brought the cigarette up to meet her full, peach-colored lips.

The security guard made a motion toward the stand, but the judge held up a palm to halt him. She shook her head in a tender, slight no.

August exhaled a thin stream of smoke. She shook her head back and forth and said, "Men and death. Men and death. How on earth y'all run the world when all y'all have ever done is kill each other?"

"I said, you all right, chile?" Miriam realized she was on her hands and knees next to her now-soiled medical instruments. She hadn't yet picked up a single one—she was just kneeling there, still. Miriam hadn't answered her elderly patient's question.

"My hus—, my *ex*-hus—" Miriam stumbled. "My girls' father works in the Pentagon."

The white woman snorted. Miriam looked up, startled, to see the woman let out a small chuckle.

"Now, is that such a bad thing? Might be a blessing—a dead ex-husband," the woman said.

Miriam rose. The tray shook slightly in her hands. "Growing up without a father . . ." She paused, considering. "It's a lonely life, ma'am."

CHAPTER 23

Joan

2003

Thunder sounded again, rattling both the house and Wolf. She whined as I petted her, scratched her ears.

Used to the raging weather all that month, my family slept through the storm. No one but me was awake when the rotary phone in the hallway rang. Or maybe they simply couldn't hear it over the rage of the storm. I yawned and hurled pounds of quilts off me. Wolf whimpered in the blankets, nestled herself farther into them.

"I don't blame you, girl," I whispered.

The phone rang again. I shuffled into my pink slippers, wrapped myself in my matching pink terrycloth robe. "I'm coming, I'm coming."

The grandfather clock in the hallway read five-fifteen. *Who on earth?*

A thought blossomed in me, overtook my mind like the large

leaf of a moonflower. What time was it in London? I wasn't supposed to hear back until early May, but that was only a few weeks away. I picked up my pace, forgetting in my excitement that colleges don't call; they write. I grabbed the receiver, and it shook in my hand on the third ring. I held the pearl-handled receiver up to my ear, and before I could say, "North residence," I heard a loud voice recording at the other end of the line.

"You have a collect call from"—there was a pause, a click, then a man's gruff voice—"Derek North." The automated voice recording continued: "An inmate at Riverbend Maximum Security Institution. To accept, press or say 'one.'"

In all the years since he'd been arrested, I had never once answered a call from Derek. Never had to—he timed his calls for when My and I were at school.

Instinct told me to hang up. But I didn't. I hesitated. And I swore I heard Miss Dawn's voice: *Hardheaded women.*

Maybe she was right. She'd been right that year we first moved to Memphis. I remembered waking Mya at midnight, shaking her gently, a forefinger pressed against my hushed lips. We tiptoed in our matching pink slippers to the shared bathroom, lifted Derek's comb—I'll never forget the weight of it, the wooden handle—and went through the kitchen, crept through Auntie August's shop and out the back door. We knelt underneath the magnolia in the back. The moon was a sliver of silver crescent above us. Mya held a flashlight. What we didn't plan for was the digging. I scanned the yard for something, anything, to dig with, and saw nothing. I dug with my hands. My nails were filled with grass and fertile Memphis soil. Mya was above me with the flashlight, and when she tried to pull me from the earth, I pushed her away and kept digging. I was crazed. A nail broke off. I winced, continued. Ignored Mya's exclamations. She kept asking what had the boy done to me. I ignored her. Ignored the worms I found in the warm soil. Ignored the blood from my broken nail pouring forth, mixing with the ground. I used my elbow when my right hand grew numb.

When the hole was deep enough, I whispered hastily for the comb. Snatched it from Mya when she wouldn't give it, threw it in the dark earth, and smeared dirt atop it. I told Mya to angle the light so I could inspect my work, and inspect I did, wiping my hands down the front of my nightgown.

Hardheaded women. Miss Dawn's words came to me then.

Fine, Miss Dawn, fine. This North woman will listen to you.

Now I said, "One." I curled my finger in the coils of the phone cord and bit my lip in expectation. The phone's pearl-handled receiver was cold as stone against my cheek. Despite the years, despite the distance between Derek and me, the prison bars that separated us, my stomach dropped out of its bottom as I waited for the click that would announce our call had been connected.

"Mama?"

I froze. The voice—so male, so obtrusive—took me back to the moment we moved to Memphis and that massive corn yellow door swung open. The voice had lost its edge of adolescence. Derek sounded full grown now, and his voice was deep, almost a baritone.

"Hello?"

"Hi," I said, after a long pause. "It's Joan." I heard static. Derek was silent. After a time, I said, "Listen, I'll tell Auntie August you—"

"No," Derek interrupted. "I've been here awhile now. Had time to think. I have something I want to say to you. I think it's time."

I knew what he meant. After all, I had dug up that comb. And now this phone call. Part of me wanted to listen to him. To see if Miss Dawn's magic was real. To see if I could stomach Derek. It would be a lie to say I hadn't thought about the perfect string of curse words to hurl at him. I'd fantasized about what I could say to him to hurt him as badly as he'd hurt me. Felt like I'd been building toward this moment since I was three years old. I was all of eighteen now. Had just turned the month before.

"I reckon so," I said, slow.

Derek gave an unexpected small laugh, cutting some of the tension. "You sound like Auntie Meer," he said.

"Well."

"How she doin'?"

Mama had shocked us all—she had graduated nursing school a year early. It was unheard of. Her years of throwing herself into her studies, years of falling asleep on top of her books, in mid-conversation with me or Mya—they had paid off. August, Mya, and I had all attended her graduation ceremony. She had asked us to wear white. This, this was her wedding day, she had proclaimed. We had all helped her with her valedictorian's speech. Auntie August chain-smoked, and pointed to the page, saying it's got to wow them. Mya, of course, wrote the jokes.

Mama. In the months since Christmas—since I turned in my application to the Royal College—Mama had grown quiet. She still let out a defiant *hmph* whenever she saw me with my pocket sketchbook, but she held her tongue. I trusted that Auntie August was doing as she promised: was working on Mama for me. I kept quiet and prayed and prayed and prayed every night on rug-burnt knees that I would get in.

Derek kept quiet on the other end of the line, waiting for me to respond.

The anger came then. And it came swift. "I should go," I managed. I wanted to scream at him, to make him feel some of the fear and shame and disgust I'd felt for years, but the words seemed to be gone from me now.

I was so engulfed in the call, so enraged at the mere fact that I was on it, that I did not see Mya. She must have been standing there for a minute. A socked foot reached behind her other leg and scratched the back of her calf. She wore her nightgown, a long African-print housedress, and she was eating a peach as she stared at me.

She was only fifteen, but Mya planned to follow in the steps of both our mother and grandmother: She wanted to be a doctor. The child was good with numbers and science and all the things that confused me, like dark mass and periodic tables and inertia. And she loved saving things. She'd sit on our front porch steps and tend to creatures—bathe and treat small wounds on the calicos and the tabbies, help birds with broken wings. Mya was equally talented at the guitar. Her genius with numbers transferred so easily to reading sheet music, remembering chords. My wasn't just technical; she could really play that thing. Her musical talent must have come from Auntie August, who still played at the piano in the parlor every so often. Mya played her guitar for the shop. Had the women in there howling. And every day, she looked more and more like Mama. She took after her—petite and bright, with burgeoning hips.

I'm not sure how her tiny self did it, but in a sudden and nimble move, Mya snatched the receiver out of my hand.

"The fuck—" My anger spun toward my sister. I reached for the receiver, but Mya had it tight in her grasp, held it pressed firm against her ear.

"Mm-hmm." Mya's tone was serious.

"My," I said. I was exhausted. My anger and adrenaline suddenly went to my knees. I felt I needed to sit, have a cup of tea.

"Mm-hmm." Mya nodded. She bit into the ripe meat of the peach as she listened, the nectar spilling onto her chin. "Hmmm." Her tone shifted to consideration. The phone's cord twisted around her body as she kept dodging my attempts to take back the receiver.

"All right then, Negro. We on our way," she finally said.

"What?"

She unraveled herself with a spin. Mya, as swiftly as she had taken the receiver, abruptly dropped it down on its hook.

We stood there in the foyer glaring at each other.

Mya took another big bite of her peach. "Well," she said between chews, "guess we should put some clothes on."

"Mya, that prison sits right outside of Nashville." The distance wasn't really the issue, but I grasped at the logistics like they were some sort of lifejacket that could save me from this plan.

"Mm-hmm," Mya said, chewing.

"That's three hours from here," I said.

"Mmmm."

"And it's Tuesday," I said, slow.

"Right you are. Go on." Mya motioned with her peach.

"Right, and on Tuesdays we have school."

"Reckon so."

I desperately wanted to sit. My chest expanded and contracted with the long breath that left my body. "I'm going to see Derek, aren't I?"

"You're going to see Derek," Mya said.

"I'm taking the Shelby," I said.

"You're taking the Shelby," Mya repeated.

"And I'm skipping school."

"We."

"Huh?"

"*We* skipping school. I'm coming with you." Mya bit into her peach and, between bites, said, "And on the drive, you can tell me what the fuck that boy did to you all them years ago."

CHAPTER 24

August

2001

Three days. It had been three days since the sky fell. Three days since she had run out into the yard and met Joan and Mya. Joan's history teacher carried Mya like she was a sack of potatoes in his arms. She was wailing. Neighbors came out to inspect. Heads over hedges, craning to see the daughters of that military Yankee man stumble up the drive.

Joan said nothing. Walked alongside her teacher with her sister in his arms, resigned, quiet. August stopped her at the front door. Put both hands on her niece's shoulders, stared deep in her dark eyes, and said, "You better be a fortress for that girl in there."

August turned off the television in the parlor. She held a cigarette in one hand, the rotary phone receiver in the other, and declared that the phone lines were likely down. They'd hear from him. She was sure.

All of August's and Joan's pestering could not convince Mya

that she should eat something. She lay on the daybed in the quilting room and refused to do anything more than that. August expected this: The girl just likely lost her father. What August hadn't expected were the gifts of food at her front door every night. Left by nameless angels. The doorbell would ring, and August would open it to find spiral honey ham or chicken broccoli casserole or a plate of beef ribs.

August closed her shop that week. No one in the mood to get their hair done anyway. Get dolled up to sit in front of the TV and cry? August closed the shop, and she and Joan sat in silence most of the day until Miriam came home from the hospital and rushed to Mya's bedside. The girl would not move from her bed. August walked past the quilting room and caught sight of Miriam, still in her scrubs, stroking Mya's hair and whispering things to her. Mya moved not.

On the third night, August heard the doorbell again. Everyone was home that night: unusual. Miriam had to work most nights, but she'd pulled back on her shifts that week. It was far past everyone's bedtime. Midnight had come and gone. But no one could sleep, so no one told anyone else to go to bed. August, Miriam, and Joan sat around the kitchen table, forks in hand, eating directly from Miss Jade's pan of chicken noodle casserole, which she had pushed into August's hands earlier, shaking her head and exclaiming what a shame it all was, somehow every lady up in this house loses a daddy.

Wolf raised her head from Joan's feet and growled.

August turned to her sister. Perhaps it was instinct. The basic, intrinsic knowledge of danger can overwhelm a body. Or perhaps August, born on a Wednesday, had been accustomed to woe. But she knew that knock on the door was no neighbor.

"Fetch Mama's gun," she whispered to Miriam.

August saw her sister nudge herself out of the booth and walk, very calmly, into the quilting room. When Miriam came back, walking in those same slow strides, she tossed the Remington to August, who caught it midair, nodded for Miriam to follow her.

The door pounded again. The bell rang.

Wolf uncurled herself with some effort from Joan's feet. The years were getting to Wolf. She moved a bit slower, but her protective instincts had kicked in. She got into a stalking position, crouched low to the ground. She had stopped growling; now she crept, inching toward the door, whimpering slightly.

"Mama?" Joan asked. "Auntie?"

August led, and Miriam was her shadow. The sisters walked as calm and graceful as some ancient African queens: out of the kitchen, down the hall, through the parlor, and up to the door. The bright yellow of the door dulled in the dark of the September night; the door now resembled tall maize in a night field. The door became something August had to wade through, a field of yellow poppies that August had to cut back, regardless of their Siren's power. But she made it to the door, and just as August leaned to peer through the peephole, the door's golden hinges shook with more pounding.

Her head jerked, and she jumped back. She didn't get a chance to take a good look, but she'd seen enough to know that two unknown men stood on their porch steps at nearly two in the morning.

"Mama?"

August heard her niece. Heard the worry in her voice. Joan must have followed them to the parlor.

Gently, Miriam pushed August out of the way and took her place at the door. She held the door handle. August could tell Miriam sought her approval.

August gave it with a quick nod. In one swift motion, she aimed the rifle, and Miriam swung the door open.

"No!" Joan cried.

As the September wind rushed in and August tried to make out who was standing there in the dark, the first thing she became aware of was Wolf. She stood up straight and made an unexpected sound—not a threatening bark or a growl, but a submissive, almost curious whine.

August kept the Remington aimed. Her eyes adjusted, making out the figures on the porch, and involuntarily, her shoulders contracted, then relaxed, then contracted again. For a second, she thought about pulling the trigger anyway.

"Well, damn, Jax. We survived all hell just to get killed by some crazy Negresses in North Memphis." The voice was male, foreign, and yet familiar.

August felt herself grow nostalgic. She lowered the weapon so it hung loose at her waist, and then, after a few deep breaths, rested the handle on the hardwood floor, barrel toward the ceiling. August had opened that same door for this same man many, many years before.

"Joan," August said, breathless, panting the adrenaline out of her system. "Your daddy and 'em here."

CHAPTER 25

Miriam

1968

In the early evening, Miriam paused on the way home from her piano lesson to regard her figure reflected in the sheet of ice coating a house window. There was no denying it. She was the exact image of her mother. She had the same doe eyes, the same shade of brown skin; she even bit her lip the same way when she was deep in concentration. She was beginning to grow hips that she expected would eventually turn into the curved vase of her mother's figure.

Miriam sighed, disappointed.

She had wanted to look like her father: tall and dark. It was her way of being close to the man she had never, and could never, meet. *Let me have his face, please God*, Miriam prayed. Instead, she thought she looked like one of the calico kittens that came to her porch in the evenings: bright and petite, the spitting image of Hazel. She couldn't hate her looks, though, not after August was born five years before and Miriam saw both her and her mother's eyes staring up at her from her baby sister's face. And maybe God had been listening, just a little late, because even though she knew August's daddy wasn't Myron, her sister had that darkness, that long body, that Miriam had always wanted.

The blizzard of two weeks before had added an extra minute to Miriam's routine walk from Douglass Middle to her home on Locust Street. It was still freezing outside. Patches of ice and dirty snow lined the curbs. When the snow began, Miriam's mother had gone into a dark lacquered chest with Japanese geishas painted across the top and pulled out Miriam's winter coat. Her mother shook her head, muttering that she had just put the coat away for the season.

Although it was March, a freak blizzard had dropped ten inches of snow and ice on the city. No one knew what to make of it. Miriam and her friends played in it: built ice forts and hurled snowballs at the kids who went to Trezevant, Douglass's archrivals. Miriam was delighted to have a few snow days off school, a small miracle for southern children, and August was equally delighted to have her sister home on what felt like a holiday.

Miriam was still wearing the wool coat as she admired her reflection. It was tied at the waist and was the color of moonstone. She thought back to the last time she'd worn it before the blizzard. It was early February. She had opened the door to find her mother home. Rare. She was sitting on the chaise sofa in the parlor. No quilt at hand. No radical pamphlet clutched in her grip. Even more unusual: Her mother was sitting in the dark, not looking at anything in particular.

"I saw the bodies," Hazel had said, after some minutes of silence.

Miriam knew exactly which bodies her mother meant. Everyone in Memphis knew. In the hospital, her mother had seen the two sanitation workers who had been crushed to death by the very trash compactor they serviced, the two men's cries and screams falling upon the deaf ears of their white counterparts.

"They were all crunched like, like folded-up paper," her mother had said, staring at an indistinct point on the wall. "Just like paper," she had muttered again.

That very night, after August had gone to bed, Miriam had helped her mother paint big, bold, black letters onto a large white placard. The sign, so simple, stated, I AM A MAN.

The two North women had regarded their work and smiled, pleased.

The deaths of the sanitation workers had provoked an already tense Memphis. Ignited the place with a fury. Miriam could feel the anger well up in her city. Folk spoke different. Had an altered, higher pitch to their voices, the end of their questions rising in a way that made Miriam wary.

Memphis had raised Miriam. After her father's death benefits had run out, a mere year after Miriam's birth, her mother had had to go to work. That or sell the house Myron had built for the both of them. And as her mother often told her, it was the talk of the town that Southwestern, over on Parkway, had a nursing program. One of the first in the country to offer admission to Black women.

Miriam had grown up with her mother's passion tied around her like yarn: revolution. Ever since Miriam could remember, their house had been filled with leaflets proclaiming the power of Black women, detailing the humanity of Black men. The built-in bookshelves in the parlor were filled with faded spines that still sparkled with gold lettering. Books written by Frederick Douglass, Claude McKay, and Nella Larsen. On Friday nights, the porch and the front parlor would be filled with other young, chain-smoking, and cursing-like-sailors revolutionaries. Women in dark leather jackets wore sunglasses with lenses the size of mason-jar lids, even when they were inside the house. Even with half their faces obscured, Miriam could tell they sneered at every woman who walked by with permed hair. They rolled their eyes outright most of the time any man said anything.

As a baby, Miriam had been passed between the hands of Miss

Dawn and Miss Jade. A revolving carousel of established, notable Southern women in the neighborhood came together to fetch Miriam when Hazel needed to study or work or sleep. They left pies at the doorstep. The men left deep coolers of fresh-caught crawfish.

The priest, Father Hunter—a big, round, jovial man who had baptized her mother—came over once a month, religiously, for dinner. Always brought over a case of wine and a pound of red meat, waving away Hazel's objections, calling out in his homily voice that this is what Fathers were for. Over the years, Father Hunter had taught little Miriam how to fish. How to hook a bouncing cricket without flinching. How to cast perfectly, as if steered by the hand of God.

When Miriam turned six, Stanley insisted in his thick German accent that she must learn to ride a bicycle. He stood outside the house, one hand attached to a lipstick-red Schwinn with a bow on its handlebars the size of a bird, his other hand honking its tiny horn.

And it was Miss Jade who took Miriam to get her ears pierced when she was eight years old, just after August was born. Which simply meant she marched a shaking Miriam down to Miss Dawn's leaning pink house, where the wise woman sat on her porch, fire-hot sewing needle in one hand, cigarette in the other.

Although the neighborhood had raised her and raised her with love, Miriam missed the father she'd never known. Was curious as to how the mere mention of him would send her mother to another room. Always, her mother would reemerge, red-eyed, but ready to answer any and all questions Miriam might have about Myron.

Would he recognize me, Miriam pondered. Miriam looked for another long moment at her figure in the iced-over window. She placed her mittens against the small of her back, poked out her chest, and thought, *Maybe, one day, I will be tall.*

She continued the short walk home, turned right onto Chelsea, and passed Stanley's. For a moment, she thought about entering.

But it was too cold for butter pecan ice cream, and Miriam had never taken to other cold-weather sweets—peppermint, licorice, gingerbread.

A woman exited the shop. She was older. Miriam could tell by the way she clutched at the door handle and took careful, deliberate steps toward Brookins Street. She was wrapped in a beautiful pale-pink coat with a high collar. The pink reminded Miriam of Miss Dawn's house. *Odd,* Miriam thought. The woman was crying. Sobbing openly. Not even bothering to wipe her face.

Miriam furrowed her brow and continued on her cold walk along the icy streets of North Memphis. She turned left onto Locust Street and was taken aback by all the cars parked along their street. As she climbed the porch steps, she could hear the soft voices of adults inside.

The door opened for Miriam just as she reached to turn the knob. Miss Dawn stood before her, resplendent in a long batik housedress the color of a thousand rubies. Her head was wrapped in a matching scarf.

"Don't you worry your mama with a thousand questions today, you hear?" she said, ushering Miriam into the warm house. "Your sister's down for a nap now, too, and today is not the day to go waking her up."

Inside the wallpapered parlor, Miriam saw many of the neighborhood women she knew and others she did not. Most were weeping. Miriam could tell by the smoke coming from the back of the house, and by the sound of deeper voices there, that men were chain-smoking in the kitchen. Unlike most of the political meetings that occurred at the house, this one seemed muted, melancholy.

"What kind of questions?" Miriam asked.

"You already doing it," Miss Dawn whispered.

"Why won't you tell me what's going on?" Miriam persisted. "Why isn't the record player on? Who are all these people? Why is everyone so upset?"

"She don't know?"

Miriam heard her mother's voice. She sounded weak, like a

hurt bird. "Mama?" She scanned the parlor until she found her mother, perched on the piano stool. She had been obscured by a crowd of women holding handkerchiefs to their faces.

"You don't know?" Hazel said.

"Know what? You know I stay late on Thursdays for piano."

"Ah yes," her mother said. "I forgot."

There were whispers among the women in the front room. Miss Jade, wearing a houndstooth coat and a tall beehive, cried out, "Lord, what we going to do now?"

"It's the end of the world," said another woman in response.

Another groaned.

"Mama?" Miriam's voice was pleading.

Miriam saw a flash of ruby. Miss Dawn was by her side again, the hem of her housedress sweeping the room's Persian rug. She looked like a beating heart there in the dim room. She went to the large bay window.

"I should have known," she said, her back to the room.

"Should have known what?" Miriam asked.

"There be stories of a cold settling in when an old king dies," Miss Dawn declared, staring out the window. "Dr. King was shot." Miss Dawn didn't take her eyes from the window as she added, "And killed."

"Shot down like a goddamned dog," Miss Jade said.

Miriam's mother did something foreign, especially in front of all the guests. She hung her head and cried.

Miriam stood frozen, her coat still on, feeling like the only person not moving in the entire room of women weeping, wailing, blowing their noses, and rubbing each other's backs. Unwittingly, she found herself catapulted into a memory from five years before, when she was eight and August was just a newborn.

That morning, while August slept, her mother had awoken Miriam with her favorite meal: breakfast. Miriam found fried green tomatoes, shrimp and grits, fried salt pork, spicy scrambled eggs over rice, and buttery cornbread muffins to soak it up all laid out on the kitchen table.

Her mother had stood by the stove, watching Miriam eat. Her face, a stone wall.

Miriam, distracted by the smorgasbord in front of her, had not noticed her mother fill up the water jug. Suddenly, she'd felt cold water splash over her face and soak into her shirt.

She'd gasped, choking on the water, when a second unexpected thing happened: Her mother pushed her. Not too hard, but with enough force that Miriam rebounded against the green velvet cushions of the curved kitchen booth.

Miriam had propped herself back up and steadied herself for another blow.

Instead, her mother nodded. "You ready," she had said.

Hazel took Miriam to her first sit-in that afternoon.

Four little girls had been blown up in a church that week, down in Birmingham. Hazel had pounded the kitchen counter as she told her daughter the news. Had to wear her hand in a bandage for a week.

Soaking wet and silent, her breakfast ruined, Miriam had understood.

Just as now, at twelve, Miriam saw, through the sea of bodies, the same wrath in her mother's face as she had seen when those four girls were bombed and when Medgar died or whenever her father's name was brought up.

In a rush, Miriam went to her mother, maneuvering between the other women's stockinged legs like they were branches of a magnolia. She knelt at her mother's feet. Reached up and cupped her mother's face in her hands.

"Look at me, Mama. Go ahead. Look at me," Miriam said, brushing away the foreign flowing tears. Her mother looked up and then into her daughter's eyes.

"I got you," Miriam said. It was both a declaration and an invitation.

Her mother's face broke into a smile. She kissed Miriam's forehead. Then she rested her head on top of Miriam's. Closed her eyes.

"I got you," Hazel repeated back.

CHAPTER 26

Joan

2001

When Daddy and my uncle Bird stepped fully into the parlor, Wolf cried. She lay on her back and showed Daddy her belly. He knelt to her then. I'd known it was him as soon as I heard Wolf whimper at the door. She made that soft cry for one person and one person only.

Uncle Bird's voice was unmistakable. He had a sharp Chicago slant to his vowels. *Ma. Pa.* I had spent years listening to him and my dad talk on the phone long into the night, the both of them howling like hyenas. My father's Chicago accent blossoming on those calls: *mane* instead of *man.*

Daddy wore his tan Marine Corps uniform, his cap in his hands. My uncle Bird, Daddy's clone except a head shorter, wore a black leather jacket and balanced a toothpick between his pursed lips. Even though they stood before me, it was hard for me to register what I was seeing.

Six years. It had been six years since I had seen Daddy. Every time I thought of him, more often than I wanted to admit, I had pushed the memory away from me. Picked up a pencil. Lost myself on the page. But here he was, in front of me. And he looked so heartbreakingly familiar, down on one knee, rubbing our dog's belly.

"Hey, girl," he cooed. He glanced up at me.

It hurt to look at his smile.

We stared at each other for a long time. No words came; I didn't smile back.

He shifted his focus to my mom, who stood in the parlor with her arms folded over each other. "So, you're alive," she said. Mama was cold rage. She glared at him. I suspect that if her eyes could have turned into bullets, she would have let them.

Uncle Bird walked over and kissed Mama, sheepishly, lightly, on the cheek. He took off his leather cap and held it in his hands, shuffled his feet. "It was hell getting here, Meer," he said.

"I bet," said my Auntie August. I could see that she still kept an eye on the Remington she'd left by the door.

Uncle Bird pointed his cap at Daddy, who was still stroking Wolf, but his eyes were trained on me and Mama. "And it was all because this nigga didn't kill enough Hajis in the first damn war."

"Don't say that," I snapped.

History had awakened me to the fact that racism is the only food Americans crave. Mornings in class with Mr. Harrison had taught me that Americans had reduced the world's most elite soldiers to a single word: *Jap.* I had grown up hearing my father's Marine friends, even Uncle Mazz, use *Haji.* I wasn't having any of it in this house. I was prepared to deal with the fallout, the blowback of sassing an elder and kin, but—*To hell with it,* I thought. I wasn't having any of that low ignorance up in my house. Especially not from him.

"Niece!" My uncle crossed the room in a few wide strides, lifted me off the floor, and spun me before setting me down. Felt like something my daddy would have done, should have done, except that neither of us seemed able to bridge the six years of near-silence that lay heavy between us. My anger subsided in my uncle's embrace. He smelled like him, his brother. I took a deep whiff of sandalwood, cigarettes, and shoe polish.

"Looking just like your daddy. Look at them long spider legs. And you dark as night, girl," he said.

I blushed.

"And what the hell is wrong with that?" Auntie August rested the shotgun against the front door.

Uncle Bird raised his hands in capitulation. "Not a damn thing. The girl is beautiful. It is well known that North women can stop traffic. Speaking of, you wouldn't believe the traffic out of Virginia. Nothing I ever seen before. Standstill. Hell, our drive took us all day, all night.

"Now, Meer." My uncle turned to face Mama. "I know you and my brother got, um, words need saying. That's fine. But a cup of coffee? Slice of one of your pies? What you say?"

Mama refused to brew Daddy any coffee, so Auntie August put on a pot. Mama's silent rage was understandable. She had raised us for six years without any help from him. Three Christmases back, she had opened an envelope filled with five one-hundred-dollar bills and sent it right back to him with a note that read, "Our sorrow is priceless."

I, too, was stalwart in my contempt. All of us now seated at the kitchen booth, I held my mug and sipped my coffee, never taking a raised eyebrow off Daddy, seated across from me. As a girl, I had loved him more than I loved drawing. At fifteen, I realized he had brought us nothing but pain. And recently he had scared Mya near to death so that the girl wouldn't move for three days. In my brewing antipathy, I had figured that if the planes fell, it was somehow his fault.

Mama's arms never left their crossed position. Her eyes were daggers. She sat next to me at our round table and glared at Daddy. Uncle Bird and Auntie August were busy brewing coffee and chain-smoking by the stove.

Silence grew around us, heavy with my mother's and my un-spoken accusations. It was a wonder how Mya stayed asleep with all the earlier commotion in the parlor. It was the first the girl had slept in some days, so Mama had decided not to wake her.

Mya had been near comatose those three days. Days before, when she had refused to move, I took the television that usually sat on top of the microwave, unplugged it, brought it into the quilting room, and put on her favorite show. Mya was just a small brown face in a cocoon of blankets. She did not rouse when I ma-neuvered the television set so it rested in her eyesight. Even *Sailor Moon*'s opening theme song did not rouse her.

Uncle Bird was the only person who seemed at ease. He played house. Cigarette in his mouth, he served Mama a cup of hot coffee, asked if she wanted any cream.

"She takes hers black, lot of sugar," Daddy said quickly, sound-ing grateful to have something to say. The intimacy of his voice unsettled me.

Then Mama did something so heroic. She reached across the Formica kitchen table, took a long cigarette from August's pack, lit it, and exhaled a plume of smoke in Daddy's face.

Daddy showed a hint of surprise, but not shock. I believe he could remember the power my mama had over him. He opened his hands in forgiveness, but said nothing.

In that long moment, I truly believed that my parents, in some past time, would have crossed the Sahara for each other. Arms out-stretched, seeking each other out before water.

"You"—Daddy pointed to Mama, then to me—"you were the first thing I came for. When I saw that wall of fire . . ." His voice caught. He looked away from us. Gathering himself, he cleared his throat.

He started to tell his story haltingly. Said how the burning bod-ies were what would stay with him. That and the initial sound of the plane's engine careening toward the building. He said that he and Bird and Mazz had run to one wall, their fatigues and service shirts bandaged over their hands and mouths, so the fire wouldn't burn them and the smoke wouldn't choke them as they pulled people out of the burning rubble. Folk were covered in soot. Head to foot. Others, simply on fire. Screaming into melting concrete.

We were quiet, listening. Mama's arms were no longer folded—she was taking sips of her coffee—but she seemed determined to look unaffected by the hell Daddy was describing. I tried to mirror her.

In a rush, Daddy explained that he had tried calling us, but my aunt had been right: The phone lines were down. For three days the phones did not work. He couldn't catch a flight. Every airport in America was closed. So, he hopped into that black Mustang of his and drove.

Daddy took a deep breath then and began again, speaking more slowly this time. We were all looking at him, but he was looking only at Mama. That and the desperation in his voice, the way it sounded almost like a plea, gave me the impression he was offering up this story to her as both explanation and apology for something else altogether.

He told us he'd been smoking a Kool with Uncle Bird and Uncle Mazz outside the southwestern corner of the Pentagon. Uncle Bird had flown down from Chicago to see his big brother make lieutenant colonel. The ceremony was scheduled for the morning of the eleventh.

Daddy said he'd been looking at the yellow underbellies of the leaves on an oak in the Pentagon's entrance when they heard a low roar. Approaching. Mechanical. Growing louder. The three of them had scanned the parking lot for a truck, but they only saw a handful of latecomers and a wide sea of parked cars.

Then, out of the corner of his eye, Daddy described seeing the cigarette drop from his brother's mouth. He'd followed Uncle Bird's eyes, and that's when he'd seen it.

The Boeing 757 barreled straight toward them. Low. Lower than he'd ever seen a plane except at an airport. Bird or Mazz had shouted, but the sound of the engine was so loud now, it drowned out whatever they'd said.

Daddy said that though it was irrational, he'd been certain the plane would stop. That it would turn at the last moment, or pull up, fly past the building where he and Mazz and Bird and twenty-five thousand other military personnel and civilians worked alongside one another.

But the plane did not stop. It angled itself farther toward the innards of the building and flew straight into the western side of the Pentagon.

The kitchen was quiet except for the sound of Daddy's voice, low and steady. Eyes still on Mama. She put her cigarette out on the ashtray and took a sip of coffee. But I could see the muscles in her neck were tensed.

The anger I had felt for years at my father was what I had had instead of him. It was all I had of him. So, I carried it with me always, like a rose quartz in my palm. And it was slowly disappearing, my quartz. Growing tiny. I was hardly feeling the rough edges of it anymore. I realized, as time passed in the kitchen, the grandfather clock in the parlor having sung its swan song three times now, that love was wearing me down. Love, like a tide, just washing over and over that piece of rock. And I believed that only God—and maybe Miss Dawn—could change a tide.

Daddy went on. He said the three of them had been knocked off their feet by the impact, but that the first thing they did was to grope around in the smoke and dust to find each other. Mazz and Daddy found each other at nearly the same time—their Marine training making them uniquely suited for the aftermath of the world exploding—then searched frantically for Bird, who had been thrown farther but was okay.

Almost as soon as they found Uncle Bird, they started hearing faint, urgent sounds through the ringing in their ears. The screech of metal; stone breaking. Screams of people trapped inside the building. The fierce roar of fire engulfing both plane and building, peppered with the noise of metal snapping, stone falling.

That's when they realized that people were running out of the building and that those people were burning. Daddy said he could smell it—charred hair and seared flesh.

I saw Daddy wipe his eyes with the back of his hand, whereas I had just let mine flow, the taste of my tears turning my coffee salty. We had started weeping at the same time some hours before. How similar we were . . . I was his daughter whether I wanted to be or not.

He took a sip of his coffee, and I realized his hands were shaking slightly. He looked more exhausted now than he had when he first walked in.

Early dawn light made the kitchen glow a pale blue. It had taken the length of the night to tell his story. I heard birds outside start to sing.

I looked at Mama. Her arms were crossed tightly in front of her again.

Uncle Bird passed a lit cigarette to Auntie August, who accepted. They had stood like that the entire time, their shoulders touching lightly.

Daddy cleared his throat. "I said 'oo-rah' and ran toward the broken wall, the one people were running out from. We all did. But there was nothing we could do. The heat alone. The heat from it. I. I can't. There aren't words. It was so hot. And the people. The people were on *fire*, Meer." He pounded a fist on the kitchen table, and it made me jump.

"It was just like that night in that barbershop." I didn't know what he was talking about; my mother's face remained impassive. "Meer, the nights we fought. That one Easter night. Or the night of the Marine Corps Ball. The hospital . . ." he said when my mother stayed silent, turning to me for the first time since he'd begun his story.

I started and pushed back in my seat without meaning to.

"I had to come here. Had to see you. I was sick of all the death, don't you see? Everywhere I go, there's a war."

No one said anything. I heard Wolf whimper to be petted. She had sat and slept underneath my father's feet the whole of the night.

Daddy reached down to stroke one of her ears.

"I need to get ready for school," I said, my voice croaking slightly. I had stopped crying but was still emotional, overcome with the new feeling of love I had for my father.

Daddy jerked his head up from his coffee. He gave me a puzzled look. "It's Saturday, isn't it?" he said.

Mama threw her chin up. "Joanie takes *college* art classes now," she said, dragging out the word *college*.

"We been fighting our own battles here," Auntie August added.

"And we been winning," Mama said.

Silence fell again, Daddy looking down at his coffee mug to avoid their fierce glares, Uncle Bird's eyes trained on the ceiling.

"Yeah, you have," he said, resignation in his voice. "You've done one hell of a job, Meer."

Mama scoffed, swiveled her upturned chin away from Daddy.

After a minute, I heard the sound of soft feet padding across the floor.

Mya always had perfect timing. She appeared in the kitchen. She had on a long calico nightgown and was rubbing the sleep out of her eyes and yawning. She walked right past us at the table. If she saw Uncle Bird standing next to Auntie August, her body gave no sign of acknowledgment—unlike her, especially in the mornings. She usually had more energy than Wolf at the crack of dawn. But now, Mya was still awash in her sorrow, her despair at having no news from Daddy. She went to the fridge, opened it, pulled out a pint of orange juice, turned from us, and set it on the counter.

I heard Daddy laugh. "Meer, didn't we raise our girls to say 'good morning' to family?"

I saw Mya's shoulders flex and pause. Her back suddenly stiffened. I saw that she had let the orange juice overflow. She had been pouring herself a glass, and now the juice was running from the counter and dripping onto the floor.

"Here, niece, let me." My uncle Bird gracefully, gently, took the orange juice from Mya's hands.

"Am I dreaming?" Mya whispered. She turned her head sharply to Uncle Bird, and he shook his in response.

I saw a sigh leave her body. Saw my sister steady herself, turn from the counter, walk to the kitchen table, and take the crystal box in its center. Her face was glowing, her smile wide and beaming. Mya's face made the blue morning light coming through the kitchen windows look pale in comparison.

She opened the crystal box and read aloud the scripture printed there. "See, God has come to save me. I will trust in Him and not be afraid. Isaiah twelve-two," she said. Then she walked straight to our father and collapsed into his arms, leaning the side of her head into his chest.

I never knew a smile could be another, better thing until I saw Mya's face. Never knew it could be the sun itself, stretching on and on, warming us all.

CHAPTER 27

August

2001

She woke to "Clair de Lune." Under the piles of quilts stacked on top of her, August heard the unmistakable knell of the old piano in the parlor. Disoriented, she remembered—Jax and Bird had arrived three nights before. August had given up her bed to Jax and slept with her sister when he refused to take Derek's room. It was the first time in years the house had been full of men.

Fall morning light illuminated her room. It had been her mother's. Wood-paneled, the ceiling mounted to a high point, octagonal witch's hat in the center. The walls of the room were covered in collages: Papa Myron had collected contemporary Black art that her mother had loved. Prints of Allen Stringfellows and Romare Beardens made the room come alive in a wash of vibrant colors. The paintings were all of Black folk going to church, sitting at the hair salon, simply living. August caught Joan in her room often, staring up at the prints. She tried not to scold. They were something to behold.

Since Derek's trial, getting out of bed had become a daily battle. Sadness would not overtake her so much as cynicism. It would come in waves. At first, a small, malicious thought would creep into her head as she swept cut hair from her shop floor: *You going to die alone.* She'd shake her head to try and push the thought away, but then she'd hear: *Just like Mama. Alone in your garden.* She'd stop sweeping. Let the broom fall to the floor with a small thud. It was as if her appetite for everything—for doing hair, for cooking, for singing in her shop—had left her, and all seemed so tasteless. What was the point of anything? What did it matter if she got out of bed? If she ate that day? If she sang? Fried up green tomatoes? She had been up the morning D gunned down two human beings. Her being up or staying in bed couldn't stop the chaos inside or outside her house.

August propped herself up on her elbows and yawned wide. She reached for her kimono—the only damn thing her baby daddy ever gave her—and she was off to investigate who was playing her mother's piano, the piano that hadn't been touched in years.

The melody was hypnotizing. August walked through the house and wondered how everyone else could sleep through this. Each individual note sounded so light and yet carried so much weight. The song seemed to envelop the house within its melody because August's footsteps on the hardwood creaked in time and in tune with the music coming from the parlor.

When she reached the parlor, she was momentarily blinded by all the light streaking in. The morning light hit the stained-glass windows, creating a million refractions of the ivy leaves unto the floor. Dust bunnies danced and floated through the air, somehow in sync with the music.

Bird sat at the piano. August saw his back sway gently with the classical tune. A trickle of smoke rose from a cigarette caught in his mouth. August saw his fingers move deftly over the keys. Then, with a slight awe, she noticed that his head was not bent forward.

He wasn't even looking at the keys. He knew the melody perfectly by heart.

Part of August didn't want the song ever to end. She wanted to stand in that parlor illuminated by morning light and listen to this Black man beat away at a classical French ode on an old, untuned piano.

August waited until the song was over before she spoke. It broke her heart to ruin such a moment. "You looking rough," she said.

Bird sat on a small stool and he spun it around quick to face August. He smiled.

To August, Bird was the damn-near clone of Jax. But there was something that she had always liked about Bird, ever since she saw him stride into her sister's wedding reception, pistol-whipping white men and dancing with her all night. August looked him up and down and tried to figure how this small, dark man who badly needed an edge up and a shave ran most of Chicago's South Side.

"Yeah? I could do with a cut." Bird ran a hand down the back of his neck. "I heard your shop was famous."

"That all you Yanks do? Lie?"

Bird's smile never faded. "Don't be like that, sis." He drew from his cigarette.

"Ah, I forgot," August said, crossing her arms, "y'all hit women, too."

Bird had risen to discard his ashes in August's white teacup turned ashtray, perched atop the mantel, but he stopped midstride.

"I've never——"

"Come on, then. Follow me. Can't have no half kin of mine walking 'round looking like Kunta Kente. Let's at least get you looking like the Ike Turner you is."

He trailed her into the kitchen. "Hey now, didn't your son *kill* some women?"

August froze. How did he——? She answered her own question mid-thought: Mya, the only one who talked to Jax anymore. She wondered briefly what Jax had thought when he heard, but she pushed the ugly thought out of her head and rounded on Bird, ready to attack, when it suddenly struck her what he *hadn't* said. He was trying to give as good as he got, but he wasn't aiming to kill—just to spar.

"Again, you lucky we kin," she said.

Bird held up his hands as if August had aimed an actual gun at him instead of her eyes.

She let him wait for a minute, keeping up their play fight, letting him sit with the possibility that she might kill him right there in her kitchen. Then she opened the door to her shop and led Bird inside.

"Wow." He whistled, then pointed to a framed *All 'n All* LP cover hanging on one wall. A large pyramid and a series of Egyptian pharaohs chiseled in gold were set against a pale blue sky. "I saw them niggas in Chicago, and when this had just come out. Whew, they could spit fire." He began humming.

"Mm-hmm. Sit." August pointed to a plush red barber's chair.

Bird hesitated. "Déjà vu," he said, slowly taking a seat.

"What's that now?"

"This chair." Bird settled himself into it. "It takes me back."

"Back where?"

"Midnight on the corner of King Drive and Sixty-third."

"That's awfully specific like." August laughed.

"Jax killed his first man that night."

August's laughter died quick. With a seasoned stylist's flare, she threw a vinyl cape around Bird.

"Lost a man, too, goddamnit. Lost a good one."

August reached into a drawer and pulled out her clippers. Bird's hair was a nest of thick, coiled curls. She eyed it, placed her hands in it, selected a number five.

She wasn't sure what it was about her chair, but it could bring out the innermost secrets of the most hardened individual God ever made. The Black women of Memphis confessed to her everything: their infidelities, the children they loved and the children they did not, their hallucinations in the morning, their prayers at night. August knew the favorite psalm and favorite sexual position of every woman worth a damn within a ten-mile radius. Stylists in the South were priests. And this was the only religion August felt she ever needed.

"Your hands in my hair feel damn good." Bird's back was to the large mirror, August facing him, so she knew he could see her eyebrows rise to an extreme point.

"Again, Bird. We *kin*," August said stressing the last syllable.

"*Half* kin. My brother and your sister no more . . ."

August felt something that she had to steady herself to compute: Bird's hand was sliding up the front slit of her kimono. She waited a bit too long to move back from it, and she knew it.

"Don't mean we can't be friendly," Bird continued. He winked and withdrew his hand, leaving room for August to let it be a tease, nothing more—if she wanted.

August swiveled the barber's chair around so that Bird faced the mirror. She stood behind him and turned the clippers on. She felt his eyes on her in the mirror. She pretended to be busy with the clippers.

"Remember the last time I was here? The wedding? You killed in that yellow."

"Who'd *y'all* kill?" August, ever the expert conversationalist, knew how to steer him toward safer ground. She could tell there was something he wanted, needed, to get off his chest, and though she wasn't sure if she cared to hear what he had to say or, more important, if he deserved to be witnessed by her, it felt less like a choice and more like the inertia of ritual. If he hadn't been in her chair, it might have been different. But he was. And she, too, was in position, attendant.

Bird relaxed in the barber chair and he confessed all.

"It was 1976," he said, regarding himself in the mirror while August got to work, "and not yet spring. I remember the look of the dirty brown snow smeared on the dead grass along the curbs. Chicago's South Side stretched around us, like a patchwork of intersections. Brick row houses lining both sides of King Drive. The barbershop wasn't anywhere near as nice as yours—just a one-story lean-to directly underneath the Line station that shook every time a train passed overhead, every three minutes.

"At the time we killed that nigga, Jax and me was only twenty-one years old. He was going through this phase where he wore a mustache that desperately wanted to be thicker. My black leather bomber jacket was lined with thick shearling, but I was still freezing. Had forgotten my gloves. Jax was wearing a wool caramel coat he'd just gotten for Christmas—I'd forgotten about that coat. Went with his whole mustache look.

"It would wind up being the second time me and Jax would steal that day. Earlier, we were rummaging through shelves at the local library, Jax had slid a faded and beaten, spine-long-gone, second edition of Fitzgerald's *The Great Gatsby* in the long front pocket of his coat. He'd checked it out enough times, told me he figured he pretty much owned it by then, anyway.

"Holmes was waiting for us outside—he was this guy Jax had been running with for a time. He had this real sharp goatee that made him look like an exact replica of Malcolm X. We all stood outside the barbershop for a minute, shivering, cupping our hands and breathing into them for warmth. Holmes nodded to Jax. 'You ready?'

" 'We really doing this?' Jax asked.

"Holmes nodded. 'Let's roll,' he said and opened the swinging door to the barbershop.

"Right there in his barber's chair, with a shotgun laid across his lap, was a massive bear of a man. That was Red.

"Red had two enormous front teeth with a gap between them the Hoover Dam couldn't fill, and two prostitutes he pimped out, and five children he saw on Christmas, sometimes Easter, and a bright red shirt he always, always wore, and a ruby the size of a chicken heart on a chunky pinky finger. He was as big as a barn. You can see why the name 'Red' stuck.

" 'What in the entire fuck are you doing with that?' Holmes said, nodding his head at the rifle.

" 'For y'all, nigga,' Red said back. 'I made an appointment with you, Negro. You. I don't know these other dusty niggas'—and he makes this sweeping motion with his right hand—'from Cain.'

"Jax spoke up: 'I look like a cop to you?'

" 'Nigga, was I speaking to you? I swear to God I wasn't.'

" 'God would be right, as He tends to be. You weren't. But I'm speaking to you now, aren't I, you fat motherfuckin—'

"That's when I stepped into the center of the room and threw open my leather jacket. Red was stupid, but the nigga wasn't blind. Any man could've seen the black gleam of my nine-millimeter.

"Holmes spoke: 'Gentlemen, gentlemen. In the city of Chicago tonight . . . no, in cities across this country, can we not concede that there are a significant number of Black men killing other Black men? Let us not add to that number recklessly.'

"Holmes had a way of speaking like some old Confederate general. Elegant. Slow. He took a seat in an identical, but smaller, barber's chair across the room. Crossed his long legs, pulled a pack of Kools from his right pocket, a lighter in his left. He held the lighter like a baby mouse in his hands, cupped around the shaft of the cigarette, and lit it. He looked like a daddy longlegs in that chair. Waiting. Smoking. Patient. Then the floor began to shake with the arrival and departure of another L train.

" 'Here's how I figure'—Holmes took another drag off his cigarette, blew the smoke above him in a halo—'You can take my money right here.' He tapped his breast pocket. 'And we can continue our mutually beneficial agent-procurer relationship, or I can release them'—he pointed his finger at me and Jax—'this storm of men, upon your Black ass and your Black establishment. Trust me when I tell you it would be wise to choose the former.'

"Red spit on the floor. 'I don't do business with niggas I don't know.'

"That's when Holmes went in. Said, 'The Wanika tribe of East Africa eat their king when the old man dies. Take his bones and boil them in a broth they all sip for days, lamenting with hands

and cries and drums. Red, which one of us niggas here you think
will suck on your bones, old man, before this night is through?'

"Let me tell you something. That nigga had it coming. While
Holmes was making his speech about niggas eating each other, Jax
signaled 'quiet' at me. Red was creeping his fingers up the trigger
of that rifle. He may have seen my nine-mil in my holster, but he
didn't see Jax's thirty-six come out the inside lining of his new
winter coat. Before Red could do anything, Jax shot that nigga
twice in the heart. Pop. Pop.

"We rolled out after. Cut the Shelby's engine in front of an
abandoned cathedral on the corner of Dobson and Seventy-eighth.
We partied all night. It was something. The nave of the cathedral
was all mahogany and elm and pine that extended one hundred
and fifty feet above and mounted to an invisible point somewhere
in the darkness. The ceiling shone with gold. Every buttress and
arch and stained-glass setting was painted in gold fleck. The gold
paint within reach had all been chipped away: Addicts had stood
on pews and altars excavating the gold, had left bits of fingernail
lodged in the wood. There were fires in the holy water. The urns
that had once held the promise of redemption were now make-
shift hearths filled with red fire. And moving in the halo of the
burning red glow, bodies huddled for warmth. There were bodies
everywhere, August. Bodies strewn across pews with still faces of
half orgasm, the settled look of the high. Humans huddled around
the holy water fires warming brown, bandaged hands. It was the
Sistine Chapel in reverse: skinny Black bodies crawling, clamber-
ing on the ground, searching this hard earth for a savior and coming up short. It stank of piss.

"Sugar ran it. Big redbone who Holmes was sweet on. Had
been for years. Sugar was a big woman. Built like Cleopatra must
have looked sitting atop her gilded chariot crossing the Nile; she
was six feet tall and the color of a saddle. She let us in muttering
to herself that it was always her curse to trust Black men, that
they'd be the death of her, that Holmes was her favorite Achilles'

heel. She took Holmes's hand and led him behind a heavy crimson curtain that half-hid a long line of confessional boxes.

"I don't remember much after that. Must have fell asleep in a pew. High out of my mind. But I do remember waking up to screaming. Jax was just hollering. Calling out, 'Holmes! Holmes!' over and over.

"Holmes was sitting upright in a pew, but something about the angle of his body didn't look right. His head was hanging all the way back on the top of the pew, as if he had thrown eyes to heaven and asked God directly what it was that He wanted. A trail of white spit dribbled from his open mouth to his cheek, then farther to his ear. His glasses—just like Malcolm X's, too—lay crooked in his lap.

"Jax loosened the leather belt that was still tied and twisted around Holmes's left bicep, all the while talking to him in lovely, choked, cooing whispers in the same tone of encouragement kind adults bestow on children lost in a store: *It's gonna be okay. It's gonna be just fine.* His hands were shaking.

"I had to drag my brother out of that hell screaming and crying, snot everywhere, kicking at the air itself and cursing God. A week later, I held the gas can as Jax shot his pistol into the dome of the cathedral, exclaiming that if these niggas wanted to see another day, they would all file out, and they did—filed out into the snow tweaking and scratching their faces.

"We set the damn thing on fire. You say what you want about the South. But I've never seen anything more beautiful in my life—that wretched church first in flames and then, later, crusted over in frost and icicles from the fire station hoses. That house of God morphing into an igloo of death. Damn.

"That same week, Jax enlisted. Figured he couldn't take it. Riding around Chi in that Shelby without Holmes. He pulled that car into the nearest Marine Corps depot he could find, and I was the one drove him to the bus station early one morning."

August put the finishing touches on Bird's fade. She sprayed his hair with leave-in conditioner and wiped away the stray hairs with a large, soft kabuki brush. A less seasoned stylist might have thought Bird's story was over, but she knew by the way his eyes were unfocused, by the way he seemed not to notice she was done, that if she stayed quiet, he'd say more. And she was right, of course.

"The first person Jax loved more than me on this earth was Miriam," Bird said. "Then when Joanie came, then My—he'd call to tell me about their eyelashes, their little fat bellies, the way it sounded when they giggled. How he was pushing himself hard in the Corps, so those little girls would never see the stuff we did growing up. He called me crying once, when he'd gotten home late and found the girls sleeping together nose to nose, looking like two wolf cubs nestled together." Bird blinked and stole a quick glance at August. "I've never heard him more in love," he said. It sounded like a plea.

August stood back and observed her art. She had made him look handsome. His hair now faded into the soft milk chocolate of him. She was proud of herself, thankful she'd gotten out of bed and followed that sound of music.

Bird beheld himself in the mirror. "Your reputation precedes you, ma'am." He threw out a hand from underneath his cape, but August slapped it away.

"Ain't done yet," she said, and she laid a hot towel across Bird's face.

He groaned underneath it. "I needed this." He sighed.

Maybe that's what did it. Something about hearing the moan of a man under her made August hurry to her shop door and lock it from the inside. Made her undo the beet-purple man's necktie that held her cream kimono together. Made her climb on top of Bird in that chair, cup his hands around her dark, waiting breasts, and ask him what else exactly he needed.

CHAPTER 28

Hazel

1968

Hazel loved that throughout the many years, Stanley's had remained the same. Small changes were acceptable to keep up with
the times. The Victrola was replaced by a coin-operated jukebox. A
television—a luxury—was mounted above the door. And in 1964,
Stanley, finally, was able to pry off the COLORED signs. But other
things were imprinted in memory. The fresh cuts of prime meats,
the Southern delicacies found in jars—pickled beets, hot chow
chow, hot pepper sauce—still lined the cedar shelves. And every
Friday afternoon, Hazel would stop in and order three butter
pecan ice creams and hand one each to Miriam and August. Then
the three'd walk to the home Myron had built.

Hazel pulled her blond mink coat tighter around her as she
made the short walk to Stanley's. It was freezing for April. But she
needed a few groceries in preparation for the fish fry she was set to
host on Friday. It would be partly to honor Dr. King, who had been

killed a week ago now, and partly a planning session for what steps to take next.

Since Myron's death, Hazel's house had become a mecca for young anti-segregationists. Preachers and college students stayed in the quilting room en route to register voters farther south in Mississippi or Alabama or Georgia. The house was packed whenever there was a wave of sit-in protests. April was always a busy month—protestors came to the house intent on supporting the first Black students enrolled at various institutions throughout the South. Hazel opened her home to the hopeful, to the idealists of the world. She loved it all and hoped, prayed every night on worn knees, that Myron would be proud of her.

Myron. Hazel grew to know grief as well as a sister. The first year after Myron died, she had refused to speak to God. Whenever she passed by the spot near the large sleigh bed where she had usually bent knee and spoken to her Father, she would spit at it instead. The second year after Myron's death, when Miriam caught whooping cough, Hazel finally broke down and spoke to God. Demanded He save her child. Said she would come there herself, come to those pearly gates and shake them down with her own two hands, if He dared, dared, take another human being from her. She vowed she'd haunt God. Stalk the Son of a Bitch throughout the decades, if He dared take her daughter. When Miriam pulled through, after nights of Miss Dawn chanting over the toddler and burning frankincense, Hazel dropped to her knees and recited her favorite psalm: "I will tell the world of all thy marvelous works."

No matter how many years had passed since Myron's murder, Hazel's conversations with her dead husband never ceased. She spoke to him often. As if he were still alive, just hovering over her shoulder as she made dinner.

But she was still a woman. And from time to time, amid the students, there'd be a man. A professor maybe, or one of the preachers. They'd pass through her parlor, and the fire in their eyes would match the burning in her heart. Their righteous anger could become, temporarily, a safe harbor for her. She'd never love someone the way she loved Myron, but she didn't mind taking someone to bed once in a while. Then, five years ago, she'd had August. Hazel hadn't told August's father. He'd been one of the more charismatic leaders she'd met in the movement, but he had started going 'round the country by the time she realized she was pregnant, and she didn't feel any need for him to be anything more than he was for now: a conduit for this new little girl, for Miriam to have a sister. When August asked who her daddy was, Hazel would tell her the truth, that he was off doing God's work and that all her family was already here: she and Miriam. Miss Dawn, Miss Jade, and all the women in their neighborhood. Hazel wasn't opposed to revealing August's father someday, but she wouldn't force it before then. It would happen in God's time.

Hazel's gloved hand held her list: cornmeal, two pounds of perch, two pounds of whiting, two pounds of catfish, green onions for the spaghetti. She scanned the shelves for the cornmeal.

"Hand me your list, and I'll get it for you, Mrs. North."

Stanley had come from the back meat freezer. His long white fingers brushed off a bit of something slaughtered from the front of his apron.

"How's that clone of yours?"

"All A's and one B last six weeks." Hazel smiled and handed over the grocery list.

Stanley frowned. "What was the B in?"

"Geometry."

Stanley's face grew severe. His German accent became dominant. "That won't do. I'll talk to her."

Hazel laughed. "You harder on her than I am. You and Miss Dawn. Miss Jade. All y'all."

Stanley shrugged in fake outrage. "Miss Miriam's our jewel," he said.

Hazel shook her head. "That jewel got you wrapped around her finger."

"And how is little August? She still following Miriam around like a shadow?"

"Sometimes even closer than that, Mr. Koplo. They'll both be running Memphis before long," Hazel said.

Stanley threw up his hands as if swiping at a fly. "This is a fact, I know," and then, coy smile on his face, he said, "And I've got something for them."

Hazel saw delight in Stanley's face, a sparkle in his eye. "Oh God, now, Mr. Koplo. What did you get the children now?"

"Just some plum preserves. Throwing in a jar." Stanley held up a finger. "Just one. Don't look at me like that; I know Miss Miriam likes them. For all her A's. But not that B. Tell her not that B. That won't do." He added the small jar covered with a red cloth to Hazel's basket.

Hazel put her gloved hands on her hips and continued to shake her head. "I'll send you back a plate of this fish," she offered.

Stanley shook his head, went back to collecting her groceries. After a moment he said, "But I'll take one of your lemon meringues."

Hazel cut her eye. "Go ahead and throw in some lemons into my order, you crafty old man."

The television above the door, which had been showing an orchestra rehearsing Bach, cut suddenly to a rainbow of colors, made a screech, went black, then cut to a white newscaster.

Both Hazel and Stanley turned their heads toward the TV.

It was Hazel's turn to frown. "I could've sworn he comes on later?" She posed this as a question.

"Good evening. Less than a week after Dr. Martin Luther King Jr.'s assassination, another leading civil rights activist has been shot to death in Memphis, Tennessee."

Hazel froze. A coldness she hadn't felt since Myron's murder seemed to ice her veins, paralyzing her. She heard a name she'd only whispered at midnight in her prayers.

The newscaster was still speaking, somehow. Hadn't the world stopped? Hadn't an Arctic abyss claimed them all? She shivered and felt her teeth rattle. "He was a stalwart in the march for equality and civil rights in this country, an apostle of nonviolence in the civil rights movement. Police have issued an all-points bulletin for a well-dressed young white man seen running from the scene. Officers also reportedly chased and fired on a radio-equipped car containing two white men."

Stanley dropped the bag of lemons, and they scattered like tennis balls across the store's floor. Hazel, for the life of her, could not move an inch to pick them up. She was still so cold; she didn't figure how gravity existed anymore, how the lemons themselves hadn't frozen midair. Her face was glued to the television.

She would not look away. How could she?

The screen was showing the face of her now-dead lover.

"The Negro leader had recently returned to Memphis to assist in the Sanitation Workers' Strike. He was at a gas station this afternoon, filling his car up, when, according to a companion, a shot was fired from across the street. In the friend's words, the bullet could only have come from an expert marksman. The gas station was crowded. It was three o'clock in the afternoon.

"Police responded to the scene within minutes. Medical personnel soon thereafter, but nothing could be done. The wound was fatal.

"Police said they found a high-powered hunting rifle about a block from the station, but it was not immediately identified as the murder weapon."

Hazel cursed God then. As much as she loved the Lord, He just didn't seem to stop taking from her. All He did, it seemed, was take and take and take from Hazel.

While the journalist spoke, Stanley placed Hazel's basket on the counter, turned his back to the television, and spat on the floor in disgust. He let the lemons be.

No one spoke in the deli. Stanley bent down and began to retrieve the lost lemons, placed them in Hazel's basket. But Hazel didn't take it. She was a stone. She did not scream and curse. She did not cry. She held a gloved hand to her open mouth. She stood for some moments staring at the television. Then she exhaled one long breath. "Myron died for no reason. Not a single, goddamned reason," she said.

Stanley was the one to wipe away tears. Used the crook of his arm. Through sobs, he was able to articulate that he'd carry these groceries all the way home for Hazel. Wouldn't hear of anything less. "No trouble at all."

Later, after everyone had left Hazel's front room and kitchen, Hazel gestured for a cigarette, and Miss Dawn, raising an eyebrow, obliged her one. They stood at the entryway of Miriam and August's bedroom and watched them sleep. Quilts covered the walls of the room. Hazel had placed Della's Singer in one corner. The adjoining anteroom, now stacked with dolls, had once been her babies' nursery.

Hazel took a quick intake of cigarette smoke. Fought back coughs. They came regardless. She cupped a hand to her mouth to stifle them.

Miriam stirred in her sleep. Turned over in her bed.

"Get in the kitchen before you wake the girls," Miss Dawn whispered.

Hazel acquiesced and led the way down the hallway, still coughing slightly.

Miss Dawn took a seat on the emerald cushion of the kitchen bench. "You got any whiskey?" she asked.

It was Hazel's turn to oblige. On tiptoe, she reached for the bourbon hidden away in a cabinet over the stove. It took Hazel some reaching, but bottle retrieved, she pulled out the stopper and poured Miss Dawn two fingers' full. Hazel handed Miss Dawn the whiskey, saying, "To the fallen."

When Miss Dawn raised the crystal glass in a toast, Hazel thought her long fingers were a marvel to behold. Miss Dawn sipped her whiskey. Hazel thought she looked like Circe considering Odysseus's ship stranded offshore.

Hazel stood smoking her cigarette, one arm braced against the other. "I never told him," she said shakily, though she knew Miss Dawn already knew. "How am I—what on earth—what the hell am I going to tell August when she's older? What am I going to tell folk when they ask all her life where her daddy is?"

"Tell folk the truth," Miss Dawn said after some time, shrugging her shoulders, the red of her dress iridescent even in the dark of the unlit kitchen. She took a shot of whiskey, and the wide arms of her dress resembled newly struck fire. "Tell 'em that nigga dead."

CHAPTER 29

Miriam

2001

Miriam's hips swayed as she walked in the September light up to Jax washing his Shelby in the driveway. Remembering countless late afternoons when she would blend a pitcher of margaritas and sashay it out to Jax, tinkering with his car in the drive. He hadn't aged much in the past six years. The only difference was there were more medals and stripes fixed to the lapel of his Marine Corps uniform.

Miriam eyed him for a time. The day before, she and August had stood on the porch and watched Joan, Mya, Bird, and Jax climb into the low black Shelby.

August had shaken her head, reached into the deep folds of her kimono, and withdrawn a cigarette.

Miriam arched an eyebrow. "Let me have one of those," she said, hand extended. August eyed her sister. "Oh, shut up and give me one." Miriam snatched the Kool from August. "I been through it."

"And I haven't?" August asked.

Miriam turned, and her face spoke a thousand apologies. "We all have," she said. She nudged August, gave her a playful jab. "Plus, it's only one cigarette."

August clicked her tongue against her teeth. "You had one last night, too," she said.

"Okay, Mama," Miriam said. She saw then, to both her horror and pride, that Joan, not Jax, was backing the Shelby out of the drive. "That girl."

"She'll be fine," August said.

Miriam coughed on her first inhale of the Kool.

August rolled her eyes. "Put that damn thing out. You ain't proving nothing."

"Why you always think I'm going to turn to drink or become addicted to something?" Miriam had choked out her question.

" 'Cause you light-skinned, your husband a damn Yankee." August exhaled. "And your kids crazy."

And now, in the morning light, Jax wore only a wifebeater as he threw a soapy rag into a bucket and then onto the hood of the Mustang. He and Bird had been in Memphis for two days.

"Remember when I tried to sell the damn thing for free? The sign in the yard?" Miriam figured Jax wouldn't flinch at the sound of her voice, even though his back was to her. He was a Marine, after all. In all their many, many fights, Miriam could never get the upper hand, could never conquer the element of surprise.

"I remember," he said, as he ran the wet rag along the Mustang's spine. "Was in the Officers' Club when Mazz burst in hollering that I better come and see what you had done."

Miriam laughed. It was a bitter one. "Why you here, Jaxson?" She was tired of having him in the house. The scent of him was overpowering. It brought back too many memories, that sandalwood, that musk, that shoe polish, the cigarettes. It was hard for Miriam to stomach.

He paused in his cleaning. "To see my girls."

"Our," she corrected.

"Our," he repeated.

"No, *mine*." Miriam pointed an angry finger to her heart. "I'm the one raised them these last six years. Me. Without any help from you. Not a dime. You think it'd be any different had you died? That inferno on the TV, that hell you escaped, is nothing, nothing compared to what we've lived through here. And you didn't see *us* jump into a car and come find *you*."

"No, *you* jumped into a car and left." Jax stood, his voice rising.

"I saved myself," Miriam shouted back. "You were hell, Jax. Nothing but."

Jax kicked over the bucket of soapy water. It hit a stone and flipped itself over. Water splashed around their feet. Miriam watched in silence as the bucket slowly rolled down the drive and rested at the mailbox.

Jax hung his head. His shoulders went up and down as a heavy sigh escaped him. "I know I wasn't the best husband—"

Miriam crossed her arms, scoffed.

Jax raised an eyebrow, threateningly. He began again. "I know I wasn't the best. But Meerkat . . ." He cleared his throat, shuffled his feet.

Miriam's stomach turned at the sound of her pet name. She hadn't heard Jax say it in years. The sound of it brought her back to when she was first pregnant with Joan. At month eight, she had worried and fretted over every burp; every pass of gas became an instant alarm of labor.

"The Gulf got the better of me," Jax said, pleadingly now. "It got the better of me, Meer."

Miriam took in the full picture of him. He looked pitiful. A tall, dark man ravaged by ghosts and war standing in her drive-way, holding a soapy rag, apologizing to her in the best way he could. Years ago, hearing regret in his voice would have meant everything to her. Now she found it meant almost nothing. She had raised their daughters the best she could without his help. Raised them to ensure that they always provided for themselves, never relied on the whim of a man, because how far would a Black woman get with that? In that moment, Miriam remembered what Jax had spat out at her one day:

Say, you can't leave me. Where the hell you think you going go, how far you think you going get, with two babies, no degree, and a Black face?

Miriam watched Jax wash his prized pony and realized that his entire life had been and would be dominated by war. "Just don't break Mya's heart" was all she could think to say. She turned to go back in the house.

"What about Joan?"

Miriam herself was surprised by the harshness of her own laugh. "You broke that girl's heart long ago," she said. She climbed the steps made of stones her father had selected and wondered if she meant her own heart. She wondered why her marriage couldn't have been like her parents'. Her mother had told her stories of her and Myron sharing secrets over their ice cream, being in such love on Miss Dawn's porch swing. Miriam had wanted that for herself all her life. Simple, Black love. For the life of her, she couldn't place a finger on what exactly went wrong or why. It was as if she held a broken teacup in her hands but couldn't remember breaking it and had no idea how to mend it.

The next day, Jax was gone. But the black Shelby Mustang remained. There was a note next to the keys, which he'd left on the kitchen table: "Joan, Treat her better than I ever treated your mountain of a mother . . . Oo-rah."

CHAPTER 30

Hazel

1985

The sun was bright that morning in Hazel's garden, and the purple morning glories that lined the back fence were open and fragrant.

Hazel wore her gardening uniform: overalls, a straw hat, her yellow gardening gloves dotted with small sunflowers. It was the planting time of year—late April, when she was sure the last frost of the season was behind them. She carried a wicker basket full of seeds: sweet peas, haricots verts, hot peppers, lettuce.

Hazel knelt among the sprouting collard greens, the sweet corn stalks beginning to emerge, the sunflowers grown toddler-tall in her garden, and began to hum a Nina Simone song. *Memphis in June, sweet oleander.*

She thought of her daughters. August, inside with Derek, who'd turned five a few weeks back. And Miriam, pregnant with her first. She was thirty now, just four years younger than Hazel had been when she'd had her.

Hazel hadn't liked Derek's father, though at least he was out of the picture now, and she didn't care for Jax, either. He and Miriam had married in a rush, and Jax had taken her daughter away just as quick. Hazel and Miriam's interactions were now limited to Christmases, Easters, and phone calls between Camp Lejeune and Memphis.

"Well, you come on home to have the baby," Hazel had told Miriam when she'd called to announce she was pregnant. "I want my grandchild born in Memphis." They were set to arrive later that month, in time for the baby's due date.

She knelt on her hands and knees in her raised garden bed and made neat rows spaced two hands apart for the planting. A hummingbird appeared in the hedges. Emerald green and dazzling. Hazel heard the quick beat of its wings and caught sight of it. It was so dark that, in the light, it was almost a dark purple, the color of indigo.

She wondered then if Myron could see her squatting in the garden he had built for her, planting her vegetables for the coming summer. She wondered whether he would even recognize her now, hair gray at the roots, thighs thickened from years of work and motherhood and suffering and laughter. What she never stopped to wonder, even after all the years, was whether Myron still loved her. That was fact. Always had been. She still spoke to him, albeit less often.

"God, I miss you," she said aloud, pulling at a stubborn dandelion weed near the base of the bed.

A pain exploded in her outstretched arm. A second later, her entire chest felt like it was burning. She clutched at her heart. It was beating with the ferocity of a symphony's final overture. She rested on her haunches and tried to catch her breath. She reached for the basket to steady herself, but it toppled over on its side, seeds spilling out into the dirt in haphazard abandon.

Awareness crept over the old nurse as the pain spread and spread. Hazel almost laughed. She was unafraid then. She no longer clutched at her chest. She lay down. Let her head hit the ground with a soft thud.

She let her mind wander.

I wonder what they'll name her, she thought.

Strangely, the pain had subsided now. But she felt her breaths grow shorter and shorter as she lay there in the red dirt.

Hazel's love of the Lord had always been a battle. She had shunned God when Myron died, and the silence was deafening again after August's father's assassination. But now, Hazel smiled. She almost damn-near called God a salty bitch—because, in that moment, Hazel's mouth was filled with the taste of butter pecan ice cream.

"Myron," she said softly. "Myron." She smiled at the morning sun and was gone.

There was still a smile etched on Hazel's face when August found her an hour later. August ran down Locust Street in pink pajamas screaming for help, for someone to call a doctor, turn back time, murder God.

But what could be done? Hazel had died. And August, feeling that not only her mother but a queen had died, thought of Churchill's words on the death of a king, and tried to calm herself: Her mother had passed away as any Southern woman brought up to fear and love the Lord can ever hope to do—she died, very much loved, in her warm garden.

When Miriam got the call from August screaming into the phone, she sank to the floor with her first child inside her. She knelt there for a long time in silence. She lifted her head to Jax and said, "Why even bring a child into this world if she won't ever know my mother?"

"You think it's a girl?" Jax asked.

Miriam opened her hand wide. "Hand them over," she said.

"What?"

"Your keys," Miriam said with a determination that would brook no argument. "I'll drive the damn Shelby myself if I have to, but my *daughter*"—Miriam, still on the floor, rubbed her eight-month-swollen belly affectionately—"will be born in Memphis."

CHAPTER 31

Miriam

2003

The front door of the house was illuminated by a porch light, and the yellow, the warmness of it all, was just the balm Miriam needed after a fourteen-hour shift shadowing the RNs in the maternity ward.

She had spent the day soothing worried mothers, wiping their brows, telling them to breathe, to push, to stop. And the children, how they came. Came into this world screaming and gangly and bursting with life. The nurses told her that the joy, the miracle of it all, would fade with time, but Miriam wasn't so certain. She took to nursing. Loved it nearly as much as her daughters.

But she was not sure if she had ever been this tired before. Perhaps, after Mya was born. Her birth had been difficult. Came a month early. Miriam couldn't diagnose this medically, even with her growing expertise, but she knew in her bones that Jax had caused it. And Derek, too, somehow, though she tried to focus her hatred on Jax, not the boy. He was only a boy, after all. A child. Jax was a full-grown man and had abused her all the same. Derek wasting away in prison, and Jax out free, medals on his chest.

Yes, Miriam was tired, needed to see her home's hearth. She wanted her bath more than anything.

She placed her key into the lock and entered.

"You need to see something."

"Dear God in Heaven!"

The lights of the parlor were off. Miriam had only the faint glow from the kitchen's light to see. She hadn't noticed August sitting at the piano stool, draped in her kimono, smoking a Kool, of course.

Miriam dropped her purse in the scare of it all. She bent and reached for its strap. "You scared the Christ out of me, Aug." Miriam shook her head. "Nearly killed me."

"You need to see something," August repeated. She took a drag from her Kool, uncrossed her legs, and rose.

Miriam rolled her eyes. She was exhausted. She wanted to put down her bag, get in the shower, and not think in there for fifteen minutes. Her nightly ritual. She'd let the too-hot water pour over her, and she would not think: Not about the girls. Not about money or the lack thereof. Not about the seemingly never-ending rounds of exams. She wouldn't even pray. She'd let her mind simply rest. She'd allow herself that respite. For fifteen minutes, she was free.

"I am so dirty. Let me shower first."

August came close to her sister. Miriam hated that she was the oldest and August always mistaken for it; she was just so tall. Miriam felt August hover over her. Not threatening, but persistent. Like a mosquito. Or a sister.

August exhaled her smoke so that it did not wash Miriam in a plume. Blew out the corner of her mouth and said, for the third time, "You need to see something." She grabbed Miriam's wrist lightly, an olive branch.

Miriam agreed. She had no other choice. August's eyes were dark pools in the room, but Miriam knew she would not let her be. Her shoulders fell. "Lead the way," she said.

She followed August from the parlor through the dining room and into the back hallway that divided the house into its two wings, east and west. August turned left toward her wing, the wing that still held Derek's room. August stopped in front of Derek's door. She had her hand on the handle.

"August, I don't want to go in there," Miriam said, and she did not. Derek was such an unpleasant memory for Miriam, to say the very least. She thought about her shower, the warm water, the forgetting. She craved her fifteen-minute oasis and nothing else.

August turned and faced Miriam. "You open it," she said, stepping aside.

"I don't want to go in there."

August put a hand on a hip and, this time, blew her smoke where it went, directly into Miriam's face.

Miriam swatted away the smoke.

"Then I guess we stand here looking at each other all night into morn."

"Fine!" Miriam exclaimed, her frustration mounting. "Hardheaded as I don't know what."

Miriam twisted the handle and threw her right shoulder against the door, and it swung open.

Unlike the rest of the house, Derek's room was brightly lit. At first, the light dilated Miriam's pupils, blinded her a bit. It took a few moments for her eyes to adjust, longer for them to process what she was seeing.

For the second time that night, Miriam nearly had a heart attack. She could have fallen to her knees, dropped down onto the hardwood floor and prostrated herself in front of all the beauty.

She had never really looked at Joan's drawings, her sketches. All these years of telling Joan to put her sketch pad away, asking her bluntly if she had finished her calculus homework, Miriam had never really seen anything Joan had done. At least, not since she was a child. And now Miriam was certain her daughter had grown up into such a fine thing.

For all around that room was Joan's art. Ten pieces, as tall as the ceiling, lined the room. And they were all of folk she knew: Miss Jade. Mika. Other women from the shop. It would've been almost sacrilege, near blasphemous, not to have recognized Miss Dawn's hands. Joan had used ink on white canvas, and like in some ancient Japanese print, Miss Dawn's dark hands held a branch thick with blackberries.

And August. Miriam saw her sister awash in vivid colors that belonged only in heaven. The cream of August's kimono looked like the buttermilk she soaked her chicken in. Joan had even got the plume of August's cigarette smoke just so; it looked like lace. The pale green of the Kool box was the color of a hummingbird in her sister's hand.

Miriam turned her head to the right and froze. She saw herself. In soft pastel watercolors. In it, she lay asleep atop a thick medical book. She must have fallen asleep right at the kitchen table after a long shift. And Joanie—bless the child—must have draped that quilt over her. Must have painted away.

August moved to stand in front of her own portrait, and it was shocking to Miriam how lifelike the painting was, how Joan had captured August so perfectly.

"You asked that girl once to name you a famous artist who was a woman, who was Black." August's cigarette was out, but her face was set in stone. She hadn't minded the fact that the cigarette singed her fingers. "Joan Della North. That's who. If she has to be the first, then so be it. Because she gon' go to that fancy school overseas, Meer. You hear me? I don't mean no disrespect. I love you"—she lifted her arms in the air, so elegantly, like a Bolshoi ballerina reaching for something—"like the stars. And I know I shouldn't be telling no mother how to raise her kids. But I am a mother, *too*. And Joan. My. They mine, *too*."

August's voice never wavered from this stoic, determined tone. But she stumbled here, just a bit, when she said, "Joan been touched by . . ." She couldn't finish. Miriam knew her sister well enough to know she would not, could not mention God.

"She gon' go to that school, Meer. If she get in, she gon' go, and she will paint this world. Our Joanie will paint it all."

Miriam forgot her shower. She stayed in that room, kneeling, until the sun came up. Then, she made the girls grits. Kissing them more than usual but unable even to say "good morning." Not for lack of trying. She was still so tired. And there was laundry to do, the light bill to pay.

CHAPTER 32

Joan

2003

The storm cleared up thirty miles east of Memphis, near Mason. We'd driven east through Tennessee in heavy hail. We left our neighborhood of pecan trees and Stanley's deli and saw cotton farms and fields of ripening crop lining I-40. When the hail raining down became the size of biscuits, I pulled the Mustang over, and we waited it out beneath an underpass.

"This tornado weather," Mya said.

Mya did not like storms. I was amazed she had forced herself along on the trip. She behaved more like Wolf on them, growing quiet and huddling in a corner. But there she was, sitting in the passenger seat of our father's car, tuning the radio station to K97 and waiting for the storm to end so we could go visit a cousin who'd done nothing but rape me and murder other women.

After a half hour, the blackness of the storm lifted. The hail turned to sheets of rain that turned to drizzle. A dark cloud stretched the entire horizon behind us, and in front of us was brilliant sunlight. Hardly a cloud in the sky. Soft rain misted the windshield of the Mustang, and I told Mya to look in my purse for my sunglasses.

"Andiamo," Mya said and handed me the pair of dark glasses.

Mya had abandoned her British accent long ago. Now she spoke Italian at random intervals. Where she learned Italian, no one knew, and Mya would not say except in Italian, which no one understood. But she spoke it with such passion, shaking her hands at us in the kitchen, that Mama—tired from overnight shifts—said, "Just let the child be herself."

I pulled out of the underpass, and the engine roared as I shifted from first all the way to fifth. "You see? You can pop the clutch once you get up to fourth. You don't have to ease into it as much with first."

"No, non lo so."

I laughed. "You're so fucking weird," I said.

"And you're not? You've been walking around in some daze like you're fucking da Vinci. Me and Auntie August been taking bets for when you going to chop off your ear."

"That was Van Gogh."

"What?" Mya snapped.

"Van Gogh cut off his ear and gave it to his lover."

"The fact you even know who!"

"I can't believe we skipped school."

"Why? We make all A's."

"That's because you do all my math and science homework, and I do all your English and history," I said, checking the rearview mirror so I could pass a slow-moving eighteen-wheeler.

"Ugh, when you go off to London, you still got to help me. Mr. Cook's fascination with iambic pentameter is . . . disturbing, frankly. I'm not doing that shit on my own."

"Shut up. I don't know if I got in. Don't jinx it."

Anger rose in me again. I should have been in school. School was close to the house, and the house was close to the mailbox, and the mailbox would hold the decision that would change the rest of my life.

Mya raised an eyebrow. "You worried about getting in? Why? Figured you and Miss Dawn made some midnight blood oath. Sacrificed a goat. A virgin. Small, innocent child." She shrugged.

Just when I felt an argument was about to brew with Mya, she'd say something so funny, so ridiculous, I couldn't help but laugh.

"No, but Joanie, you'll get in," she said more seriously, patting my arm.

It had taken all day for Daddy to teach me how to drive stick. He showed me the inner workings of the car, too. Lifted its hood and showed me where to put oil in and how much, where the battery was located, how to jump-start the car if ever the battery ran down. It had taken me the entire day to figure it all out. I had missed my art class that Saturday—something I had never done before.

I drove us around Memphis instead. Mya and Uncle Bird were in the backseat, and he was showing her his gun. He had triple-checked that it was unloaded before giving it to Jax for a second look; Jax had then handed it, begrudgingly, to his daughter.

"Okay, see that bend in the road?" Daddy had his eyes on the gearshift. "I usually take long turns in second."

"Why not just shift to neutral and coast it?"

"More dangerous that way. You always want to be in a shift when you're in motion." He saw my blank, uncomprehending stare and continued. "Okay. Say a kid runs out in the street. If you're driving along—say, in third—fine. You brake. Hard. Right then. Stall out the car. Whatever you got to do to get it to stop, right? But say that kid came out when we were turning this corner and we were in neutral. To stop in neutral, you'd have to throw the clutch and hit the brake. Too many movements to make in that split second. So, always, always, drive stick in a certain gear—first, second, doesn't matter. Use neutral only when you're parking."

I felt the power of the car underneath me as I shifted into third after the turn and we roared down Poplar. As I drove, the demands of my art class dwindled away. I lost track of time. I began to fall in love with driving, with the power it gave me.

When I took a right at the corner of Poplar and McLean, by the Memphis Zoo, I made sure I shifted down to second, instead of riding it out in neutral. I kept my eyes on the road, but I could still see Daddy smile wide as I made the turn.

I had not forgiven him for abandoning us. That was too big a thing to forgive. But driving in the Shelby through the streets of North Memphis with my daddy, I couldn't deny how lovely it felt to have one.

He left in the early hours on the third day. I heard the door of the quilting room creak open. Wolf's head immediately left the comfort of my lap, but then I heard her whine in that way she did only for him.

I'd felt the edge of my bed sink from the weight of him and pretended to sleep on as he perched there. But it was all I could do not to sob outright when he planted a kiss on my forehead, rustled Wolf's mane, and closed the door, quiet, behind him.

Mya twisted the radio station dial. The Mustang went from blaring Three 6 Mafia to 101.1, Memphis's Smooth Jams.

"God, that woman can sing. Mama damn near wore out her *Fairy Tales* album," Mya said. She began humming along.

"She gets it," I said, thinking of how I'd never really said goodbye to my daddy either time.

"Gets what?" Mya asked.

"Heartbreak," I said.

"That your kid?" That was our welcome to Riverbend three hours later.

"No," I said.

"That *his* kid?"

"No!"

"Well, then, no minors without a parent or guardian."

The prison guard who ran the visitors' office had a Southern accent that was slightly different, a tad more tonal, telling me we were far from home. He had a dark, full mustache, in direct contrast to the growing bald spot at his crown. He sat at a desk behind bulletproof glass and barely looked up from his paperwork as he spoke.

"My, you may have to sit this one out."

The Riverbend Maximum Security Institution was a massive compound made up of tan slabs for buildings, cut against the green, sloping Nashville acres surrounding it, giving it the impression of a pyramid rising up out of the earth. The colossal fortress could be seen from I-40 a mile out. Giant oaks lined both sides of a narrow access road that led to the prison's gates. The visitors' center was a heavily guarded separate building to the immediate left of the prison's main complex. To enter, Mya and I had passed through two sets of metal detectors before reaching a windowed box that contained the gruff prison guard refusing Mya entry.

It was hard to argue with or deceive the man. Mya looked her fifteen years. We both wore our school uniforms. It would have given us away to Mama had we left the house in ripped jeans and Converse. I could envision Auntie August's raised eyebrow, the tone of her question: *Y'all ready for school today?* No, we had to wear our uniforms. Mya wore a maroon polo tucked into a pleated plaid skirt, looking the part of a too-young child. Her thick socks came up knee-high. I, too, wore a polo shirt with Douglass's crest embroidered over my left breast. But seniors were allowed to wear dark jeans instead of the pleated skirts and pants sets, so my polo was tucked into a pair of black, less conspicuous cropped jeans.

Mya stared hard at the prison guard. He ignored her, circling something in his stack of papers.

"Fine," she said after it was clear he wouldn't be intimidated by a fifteen-year-old's glare.

I pressed the Mustang's keys into her palm. "You wait in the car," I said. I didn't want her in that prison without me, although, truthfully, the interior didn't look so much like a prison. The visitors' area was a long, rectangular room with cafeteria tables in the middle and a children's play area at one end. A TV was mounted high in the middle of the room, and it played CNN on silent, subtitles shooting across the screen. It was mundane enough.

The men were what worried me. The inmates sat at the tables in the center of the room. I saw men as big as barns wearing navy-blue prison jumpsuits. When I heard the repeated clang of their handcuffs against the hard surface of the tables, I realized, in horror, that they were shackled to them.

"Wait in the car," I repeated.

"Ugh, you sound like Mama," Mya said.

"Don't go nowhere."

"I don't know how to work that car even if I wanted to. Don't worry about me. What about you? You got this?" Mya bit her lip and scanned the room. I could tell she didn't want to leave me in that place alone, either.

"I'll be okay."

She stood on tiptoe, planted a goodbye kiss on my cheek. "*In bocca al lupo.*"

"What does that mean?"

"Means 'good luck,'" Mya said.

Later, I looked it up. Translates to "into the mouth of the wolf." Mya always had perfect timing.

Derek had aged in the six years since his arrest. His peach fuzz had grown into a long, knotty, and unkempt beard. Tattoos now covered his arms. Made it seem like he wore extra sleeves beneath his prison clothes. And though he wasn't more than twenty-three, the heavy lines underneath his doe eyes—so similar to my mother's—made him seem much, much older.

A metal ring was mounted to the middle of the table, and a short chain led from the ring to Derek's handcuffs. His handcuffs clanged against the table when he moved. He noticed that the sound startled me and gave an apologetic shrug.

"Not the best of digs, I admit," he said. He spread his hands as far as the chains allowed. "But what can you do?"

"Not murder folk," I said coolly.

He sat back in his chair. "You've got a point, cuz," he said. There was just enough slack in his chains for him to reach down into the deep front pocket of his prison jumpsuit and explore there for a time. I saw the outline of his fingers work against his breast as he searched. Relaxation settled across his frame as he deftly, slowly, retrieved a single cigarette from his pocket: a Kool.

He must have heard my sharp intake of breath.

"You mind?" He lifted the cigarette.

"No, it's just that—you look just like Auntie August," I said.

"Really?"

"Just like."

Guards were stationed at all four corners of the room, and one roamed the center. Other prisoners sat with their families, their wives. I saw a tall, thin Latino kid not much older than me with tattoos up to his neck pat the hand of a woman who had to be his mother. She sat sobbing, a rosary intertwined in her fingers. I heard a child shout "Daddy!" and run up to a man as large as a billboard, with locs that almost swept the floor. A skinny, pock-marked white man hugged his identical twin tight until the roaming guard, baton in hand, separated the brothers.

I shifted uncomfortably in my seat. I did not want to be there. I wanted to go home. "What do you want, Derek? My told me you wanted to speak to me."

"You still draw?"

My stomach was beginning to hurt. Talking to Derek had always disgusted me. Time had not altered that. "Yes," I said. "I still draw." It was like asking if I still breathed.

"That's good." Derek nodded. He bent his head to light his cigarette, cupped his cuffed hands around his lighter, and, after a moment, sent the first exhalation of smoke far above his head. "Important to have a passion."

"I'm leaving," I said. I grabbed my backpack.

"No, Joan. Stay. Please."

"For what? For you? You ain't shit. Such a waste of my time." I threw my bag's strap over my shoulder, instinctively feeling in my pocket for my keys, before remembering I had given them to Mya. "Fuck this. Fuck you, Derek," I said.

As I stood to leave, I felt a dark presence over the room. Another inmate had entered. He was massive. If the other men were barns, he was a building. Looked like he could have easily eaten the guard that led him through the room. I was tall both for my age and for a woman, but this man made most other human beings seem Lilliputian. His skin was the color of dark ash, and he pulled at his short beard as he strutted among the tables. He seemed to observe the other inmates and their families with a sort of derisive amusement, sneering at them as he walked. His gait suggested a stroll through a park rather than a walk through a roomful of prisoners. Like he hadn't a care in the world. Like this was his natural habitat.

I'd come close to crossing his path if I left now. As I hesitated, he scanned the room, and his eyes rested on me. He smiled, and a chill went down my spine. Instead of teeth, a gold front grill flashed.

I sank slow back to my seat.

Derek had his back to the huge man, hadn't seen him. His eyes widened a bit, surprised I had taken my seat again.

"Listen—" he began, but I shushed him.

"He's coming over here," I whispered, frantic.

Derek frowned. "Who?" he asked. He glanced over his shoulder to see where I was looking. He froze.

The massive man was being steered toward our table. When he got within a few feet of us, he slowed his walk even further. His smirk deepened into true malevolence.

I saw light flickering in the coal black of his eyes as he scanned me, my body. I clutched my backpack tighter to my body to block it from his gaze. But his grin only grew when he saw me retract.

Derek had turned rigid.

The man was upon us now. He stopped, hovering over Derek. The guard frowned, tugged at his chains.

Derek shifted so that his head angled away from the man. But I could tell that this slight retreat would do no good. This man wanted his presence to be known, and known it would be.

I knew instantly, glancing from Derek's downcast eyes back to the man's shining black ones, that they knew each other.

The man peeled his gaze from mine, focused on Derek.

Derek's body was braced as if for some terrible impact.

The man reached up—his chains clanging—and stroked his beard, waiting for Derek to acknowledge him. He made a sound— a combination of the clearing of a throat and a laugh.

I saw Derek, slowly, unwillingly, lift his head to meet the man's unyielding glare.

The man's lips drew in from his perpetual snicker to a tight point in the middle of his mouth. There was a sharp intake of air as—in both contempt and domination, in both incitement and provocation—he blew Derek a kiss.

The guard yanked harder at the man's chains. "Move it!" he yelled.

The giant kept his eyes on Derek for one moment longer, then allowed himself to be steered away, his laughter fading with each step he took away from our table.

Derek said nothing for a time. The chains allowed enough slack for him to rub a long, furrowed line over his brow. He closed his eyes and did not say what was so apparent: that Derek knew— as did I—just what it is like to live among demons. To be played with, unwillingly, like a child holding a magnifying glass over an ant. Or one burying a comb deep in a backyard, underneath a magnolia.

If I had the power to break a man, break him I had. Not a soul, not even Derek, deserved that kind of damnation. And from my hand. I felt utterly ashamed.

After what felt like a lifetime, Derek said, his eyes still closed, "It's just real nice you came, cuz. Real nice."

The drive back with Mya took longer than we'd planned.

First, when I left the visitors' center, I found that Mya had killed the Shelby's battery listening to K97. When the ignition would not catch, no matter how hard I threw the clutch, I clenched my fist and pounded the car horn in utter frustration.

That goddamned comb. What the fuck had I done? I had gotten the revenge I had waited my entire life for, and yet, I was disgusted with myself. Had I done this? Created this evil? Lord only knew. And I prayed He would forgive me. Because no matter what Derek had done to me, to others, to Memphis, that nigga's trauma could never heal mine.

I cursed under my breath, then crossed myself. And then, I did what I had to do, what I knew I could do. I kicked open the door, climbed out, popped the trunk, then the hood, and thrust my arms deep into the entrails of that ancient car and fixed it myself.

Once we got back on the road, scattered thunderstorms forced me to steer the Shelby to an underpass and wait it out. We sat for fifteen minutes as hail and sheets of thick rain barreled down around us. The storm got so bad, the radio went out. Sinatra's voice dissolved to static. I shut the radio off.

The roar of the storm was overwhelming in the silence of the car.

Mya cast sidelong glances at me. She bit her lip the way Mama did when she was deep in thought.

"You weren't even alive," I said, finally. "When it happened.

Mama was pregnant with you. Daddy was training somewhere, so Mama and I came down to Memphis so she could have you."

Mya brought her knees up to her chest, rested her head there, and her eyes never left mine as I told her what I could remember. Looking up at the quilts from the floor of the room. How carpet can hurt like hell when a body twists against it with the sharpness of the pain. How I had felt it everywhere. Everywhere. Like electricity going through my body. Like I had been struck by lightning. How I didn't know if I would die from what Derek was doing to me or from choking on the pain of it. How he had held me down. How he had held his palm over my mouth to muffle my screams.

When I finished, despite all my efforts, I was crying.

"I'm glad I wasn't allowed in," Mya said, wiping a stray tear that slid down her face. "I would've gone for that nigga's throat."

"You don't understand," I said.

When I told her all that I had seen in that prison, she unbuckled both our seatbelts and she held me like Mama would have. She stroked my hair and cooed into my ear that I was not evil. Forehead as big as the moon, but not evil. Combs just combs, after all. That I wasn't in no kind of wrong. That it was a right fine thing I did, agreeing to send Derek drawings while he wasted away in that hell. A right fine thing.

We made it back to Memphis in the early evening hours. I parked the Shelby in the drive. Seeing the house in the pale-blue dusk light, the yellow door set in the evening glow, the calicos on the steps, knowing that inside were my kin, buckled my knees a bit. Seeing that yellow door, I was never so happy to be home. Mya and I, weary warriors, gently nudged away stray kittens with the tips of our Converses as we slowly climbed the wide porch steps.

Always faithful, Wolf greeted me and Mya at the door, her tail thumping against the hardwood. In the kitchen, we found Mama by the stove, Auntie August at the counter, both wearing aprons and fussing over something that smelled delicious and familiar: blackberry cobbler. A delicacy. A godsend. Where they found ripe blackberries that early in the spring, I hadn't a clue nor the energy to ask. But silently, I thanked God for small miracles.

I settled into the booth. Leaned my head back against a thick cushion and exhaled.

Mya was brilliant. Invented some story about helping Mr. Cook after school. Somehow, she made it seem plausible—our late arrival, our wet and disheveled clothes, our hair loose. The storm, you see. Mya spat it all out with convincing nonchalance. Like we had never been to the bowels of Hades and back.

We never told anyone what we had done, where we had gone, what we had learned. Some things are best kept between sisters.

Mya and I didn't seem to be the only ones in that kitchen hiding something. Mama and Auntie August threw each other furtive glances like it was the bottom of the eighth and Miller was signaling to Zambrano. Quick, sly.

"Now?" Mama said, once Mya had wrapped up her tale.

"Give it to her. Lord knows, you can't hold water," Auntie August said from her place at the stove.

"Give what?" I asked.

I saw Mama reach into the front pocket of her apron and pull out an envelope the color of butter pecan. She took a few steps toward me, then faltered, stumbled slightly. Caught herself on the counter, and covered her face with the envelope, sobbing into it.

"Mama?" I started to rise from my seat, but Mama held up a warning finger. She shook her curls.

"No, no. I can do this," she said and composed herself. She wiped her tears on the back of her hand quickly and stood tall. As tall as her petite frame allowed her. But Mama seemed like a giant to me in that moment. A goddess. She straightened out the wrinkles in her apron and took two slow steps toward me. She placed the envelope on the Formica kitchen table I knew so well, slid it to me.

I caught it with my fingertips and felt the heaviness of the envelope before I saw the neat typewriter font on the front, before there appeared the pale face of Queen Elizabeth minted on British stamps that covered the thing.

Touching its corners, I thought then about all that had passed in the eight years since we arrived in Memphis. The eighteen-hour drive in a busted-out van. The screaming matches with Mama every time I opened my sketchbook. Derek. Seeing him again and being so stricken with fear that the piss just came. I remembered the night Derek was arrested. Auntie August, beside herself, muttering that a Black woman would never know the meaning of freedom. And I realized then that even my auntie could be wrong. Because I knew it now. Freedom. As God as my witness, it tasted just like one of Mama's warm blackberry cobblers.

I didn't need to open the envelope to see the victory within. Glory was so plainly etched on Mama's and Mya's and Auntie August's faces. And then, I just knew.

Perhaps I should have known all along. Perhaps this was always in us: this gift. Maybe each of us had always carried it around, unknowingly, like a lost coin in a deep pocket. My hands likely knew what to do, the rubric inside me somehow, placed there eons ago.

I should have known. My namesake, Joan of Arc, was a prophet. I should have known ... Hadn't I slept underneath them for years?

I laughed so hard at the reveal of it all that I cried.

Because I heard Mama declare, her voice stumbling and faltering with emotion, but beating, bearing on, "August, now you go ahead and open all the chests. My, every armoire. Open them all. Joanie not running off to that London cold without us making her a proper quilt."

Acknowledgments

Daddy. You remember all them years back, back when we were stationed in Okinawa? That night you decided to reach for that thick, ancient black book on the shelf and read me and Kristen a poem instead of a story? You remember me gripping your wrist, asking you what on God's earth was this? It couldn't be a poem; that was a line from Brothers Grimm. *Yes,* you said. *But poets can tell stories, too.* You remember me asking, demanding you start over, repeat what you had just read? And you did. In a clear, ringing voice. *Once upon a midnight dreary* . . . So thank you, Pops. Because when I was all of four, you gave me a gift that would shape the rest of my life—that poets can tell stories, too. *Oo-rah.*

Mama. Whenever I would despair, about ready to give up, take a desk job, live out the rest of my days without poetry, it was you who would tell me to shush. "I don't want to hear it," you'd say. "You have a gift from God. Thank Him, then get to work." And

248 ACKNOWLEDGMENTS

haven't we both worked for this, Mama? Wasn't it you who thrust our family's second edition of *The Great Gatsby* into my fourteen-year-old hands? Wasn't it you who sat me and Kristen down to watch *The Color Purple, Waiting to Exhale*? Wasn't it you who played Anita Baker on Saturday mornings and Mahalia on Sundays? And wasn't it you who always made sure, no matter how poor we were, no matter how meager the meal on the table, that I always had a fresh writing journal? What a mother you are. What a woman you are.

Kristen and Adam and Breonna and Andre and Turquoise and Winston and Jerell. How blessed am I to have spent my entire life as your sister. Every word of affection in this novel was inspired by all the moments of my life with y'all. I will say it again: Every human being on this earth needs a sibling like a sailor needs a compass. How y'all have been my North Stars. How I'd wander without y'all.

Aunties and Uncles and Cousins and 'em. Auntie Winnie (in her kimono), Auntie Rita, Auntie Joyce (in heaven), Auntie Carlis, Auntie Gayle, Auntie Betty Ann, Auntie Charlene, Auntie Rosie (in heaven), and Cousins Tia, Larniece, Lamar, Alexis, Erica, Nicole, Xavier, Quinton, Malcolm, Lauryn, Dahlia, Sean, Vincent, Terumah, TJ, Nia, and Uncles Sput, Effrem, Errick, Thomas, and Flamingo. Y'all have showed me what it means to be a graceful, gallant Stringfellow woman. Next time we meet, let's pour one out for Papa & Grandma.

Soumeya. My stalwart protector, my fiercest champion. Few folk have ever believed in me as much as my literary agent, Soumeya Bendimerad Roberts with HG Literary. Soumeya, you took a chance on me when I had twenty pages of this novel, a negative bank balance, and another year yet to go of my master's thesis. I signed with you on the same day I signed my divorce papers. We soldiered through this with nothing but the belief in each other. And the beautiful, unrelenting Marine in you never wavered. You charged that hill, carried me wounded on your back up it, staked that flag. I have no idea how or why. But I'm Catholic.

So, I reckon a large part of me believes wholeheartedly in miracles, and thus, in angels. *Grazie mille*, Soumeya.

Katy, in short, you dazzle me. I have been blessed with the most brilliant of editors, Katy Nishimoto, who took such care of both me and my words. I am in awe of you and your steadfastness with this labor of love. And though your work was tantamount, the poet in me believes fate had a hand in this. Both of our grandfathers served in World War II. Hers, in the majority Japanese 442nd Infantry Regiment, the most decorated unit of its size in military history. Mine, lynched upon his return. When I had finished the novel, I wrote Katy a note: *I believe we did our grandfathers, our ancestors real proud, Katy. We did a right fine thing here. A right fine thing.*

To my entire Dial family—Donna Cheng, Sabrena Khadija, Jenna Dolan, Robert Siek, Matthew Martin, Debbie Glasserman, Debbie Aroff, Avideh Bashirrad, Michelle Jasmine, Ayelet Durantt, Corina Diez, Maya Millett, and Andy Ward—thank you for taking such good care of both me and my words. Y'all have made this entire book process into an actual fairy tale for me; every edit was a step through an enchanted forest. Whitney Frick, the care, the attentiveness, the affection you have as the leader of this powerful family has always been so evident to me. You have done me, my kin, and the city of Memphis a great honor by publishing these words. So I thank you. With everything that's in me, I thank you.

Professors—Dr. Reginald Gibbons, Dr. Juan Martinez, Dr. Julia Stern, Dr. Barnor Hesse, Dr. Darlene Clark Hine, Dr. Christine Sneed, Dr. Rachel J. Webster, Dr. Simone Muench, Dr. Chris Abani, Emeritus Poet Ed Roberson, Dr. Bartram S. Brown, and Dr. Haki Madhubuti—you are not professors, nor mentors, but family. I am forever beholden to Professor Ragy H Ibrahim Mikhaeel and Charlene S. Mitchell for their last-minute Arabic translation. I must also put in a special note of thanks to Dr. Tracy Vaughn-Manley, who taught me many things at Northwestern University, but I believe the most lasting of all was how to quilt.

Wildcats, this wolf would be lost without her pack. Michael D. Collins Jr., Naliaka M. Wakhisi, Uchenna T. Moka-Solana and Wole D. Solana, Ama M. Appenteng-Milam and Jonathan D. Milam, Dr. Jason A. Okonofua, Mónica Guevara Del Bosque, Camille E. Trummer and Daniel Yeguezou, C. Russel Price, Pauline R. Eckholt, Lisa E. Weiss, Christopher J. Williams, Pascale J. Bishop, Caroline E. Fourmy, and Dr. Kiran Kilaru—we made fire in that Chicago cold, didn't we? With nothing but the love of each other, we made a spark up in that darkness. Watched it explode over Lake Michigan.

Law school mates Johanna Ojo Tran, Mary K. Volk, Jennifer Rexroat Lavin, and Laura B. Homan. Y'all have taught me that sisterhood comes in many colors, in the most unexpected of places.

Brooke A. Fearnley and Elizabeth M. Sampson. Oh ladies, y'all have lit a fire in a hearth in my heart that I'm certain will never die out. Simply put, we are sisters. Stay out of the woods. Love that man of yours. Stay sexy and don't get murdered. Call me always.

Hair is as much a part of this novel as music is. So I must acknowledge my lifelong hair stylists for simply making me feel beautiful. All my life. Ms. Vivian Hunt of Harvey, Illinois, and Ms. Adrienne Hughes and Ms. Angela Caster of Memphis, Tennessee, I thank and love y'all.

All the flowers to the following female artists who kept my spirits high, who reminded me of the pride that comes with Blackness, who kept me writing: CHIKA, Ashian, Latto, Nicki Minaj, Megan Thee Stallion, Cardi B, Ella Mai, Corinne Bailey Rae, SZA, Lizzo, Noname, Mara Hruby, Chloe x Halle, Mary J. Blige, Marlena Shaw, Roberta Flack, Monica, Lady Leshurr, Rico Nasty, Alice Smith, Big Bottle Wyanna, Beyoncé, and, of course, Ms. Anita Baker.

I'd also like to thank a few actors. Cinema, more than anything, inspired me during the writing of this novel. A few performances over the past years have simply floored me. And I drew upon the pathos of these dazzling performances in order to bring my own characters to life. I have never met these women, but I feel as if I am beholden. I could write a million poems to Niecy Nash, Janet Hubert, Dominique Fishback, Viola Davis, Aunjanue Ellis, Karen Aldridge, Taraji P. Henson, Lupita Nyong'o, Radha Blank, Shakira Ja'nai Paye, Bria Samoné Henderson, Wunmi Mosaku, Cynthia Erivo, Regina King, Whoopi Goldberg, Jada Harris, Angela Bassett, Natasha Rothwell, Kayla Nicole Jones, and, once again, Mary J. Blige.

It is difficult for me to pen how extraordinary it can be for a Black woman to sit alone with her thoughts in public without being accosted or heckled or told to go back to Africa, or to pay the bill upfront, or that she looks exotic, or to smile more, or to keep it down, or to hurry up and eat, or to remove herself as quickly as possible so that the white man at the bar can sit. So. I'd like to thank the following restaurants, all over this world, that treated me with some dignity while I wrote this book. I wish more American establishments were on this list, but alas, my country has a very long way to go in learning how to treat Black women little better than dogs. *Grazie mille ai questi ristoranti:*

Chef Bahía	Matanzas, Cuba
Ranchón El Valle	Monserrate, Cuba
Calypso Relax	Bocale, Italy
Casa del Popolo	Fiesole, Italy
Terrazza 45	Fiesole, Italy
Vinandro (Vino e Desco Molle)	Fiesole, Italy
The Bourgeois Pig	Chicago, IL
Schwa	Chicago, IL
Steadfast (at the Gray Hotel)	Chicago, IL
La Canasta	Alhaurín de la Torre, Spain
Restaurante Casa Sardina	Alhaurín el Grande, Spain

La Bodeguita	Alhaurín el Grande, Spain
El Tapeo del Soho	Malaga, Spain
Billy's Seafood	Kill Devil Hills, NC
The SaltBox Café	Kill Devil Hills, NC
The LINE Hotel	Los Angeles and Washington, DC
Bidwell Restaurant	Washington, DC
Cozy Corner	Memphis, TN
Local on the Square	Memphis, TN
Porch and Parlor	Memphis, TN

Lastly, I'm quite certain that I wrote every single word of this, that I placed every single punctuation mark on the page, for my kids, for my tenth-grade English students at White Station High School in Memphis, Tennessee, and KIPP DC College Preparatory in Washington, DC. Read, my loves. Read. Read. Read.

And write.

—THE AUTHOR

About the Type

This book was set in Walbaum, a typeface designed in 1810 by German punch cutter J. E. (Justus Erich) Walbaum (1768–1839). Walbaum's type is more French than German in appearance. Like Bodoni, it is a classical typeface, yet its openness and slight irregularities give it a human, romantic quality.